WE DON'T HAVE TIME FOR THIS

BRIANNA CRAFT

HYPERION

LOS ANGELES   NEW YORK

First Edition, July 2024
10 9 8 7 6 5 4 3 2 1
FAC-004510-24108
Printed in the United States of America

This book is set in Adobe Caslon Pro
Designed by Phil Buchanan

Library of Congress Cataloging-in-Publication Number: 2023952678
ISBN 978-1-368-09233-3
Reinforced binding

Visit www.HyperionTeens.com

SUSTAINABLE FORESTRY INITIATIVE

Certified Sourcing

www.forests.org
SFI-01681

Logo Applies to Text Stock Only

To everyone working to protect those
we love in this time of crisis. Thank you. Join us.
Love is climate action.

CHAPTER ONE
TINDER FIRE

Isa

ASH FLAKES COLLECT ON THE WINDOWSILL OUTSIDE MY bedroom on the first day of junior year. I rub the sleep out of my eyes with a sigh. Will these wildfires ever end? We've had so many this summer, and, of course, they're still burning for the first week of school. The smell of smoke wafts in with the breeze through my window, open just a crack.

I roll onto my back, reaching for one of the vibrant turquoise streaks in my hair. Mom, Kat, and I worked so hard on them, and the color is amazing. The brilliance of the blue-green mix makes me grin even in the dull light. But with the window open last night . . . I bring the curl to my nose and sniff tentatively.

Crap. I smell like a campfire.

"Isa? You up, Bo?" Grandma's voice carries from downstairs. "What do you want for breakfast? We've got pears in."

I sit upright, my skin sticky with sweat. The antiquated fan in the corner does another useless swivel. For most of the last few weeks, we've been advised to keep the windows closed, but it's impossible to sleep without airflow. I pull the window frame down as quietly as possible. It squeals in protest. Outside, the sky is gray—smoky gray, not the gray I've come to think of as normal-Pacific-Northwest-overcast gray.

Barefoot, I pad from the beige carpet of my bedroom out onto the hardwood of the upstairs hall. The door to Mom and Tama's bedroom is open. No signs of life. Down the stairs, I find Grandma's short figure walking through the open-plan living space toward the kitchen. She's still got her head wrap on.

"Smoky again today," she observes when I lean in to kiss the rich color of her cheek. She's put peanut butter puffs and soy milk out on the low counter that separates the kitchen from the dining area. "Will you show me the maps?"

I look around for my Chromebook, spotting it on the sofa closest to the TV. It's a good thing Lakewood High School lends laptops to students; it's the only computer in the house. Dad had an iPad once, but no one's seen that in ages. Lost at sea and presumed dead.

Armed with a bowl of cereal, I settle in at the coffee table to assess today's situation. The NWCC interactive wildfire and Washington smoke information maps are already open. Mom must have checked them before she and Tama left.

"How close are the fires?"

"Biggest one is fifty miles away," I slurp. Even though the peanut butter puffs stick to the roof of my mouth, I crunch them down hungrily. Grandma's still in the kitchen, so I speak up. "Only 13 percent contained. Snoqualmie's under evacuation orders, and I-90 is still closed."

"Lord have mercy."

I click and scroll, concentrating. "Nothing else close. The one along the Oregon border is more contained. The fires out east are massive." I swivel the laptop and point, but Grandma doesn't look up. She doesn't have her glasses on, anyway. I turn back to the laptop. "Want to watch the wildfire briefing? There's a link."

"No." Her voice is nearer. "Not if it's not close."

A bowl of pears materializes in front of me. I admire the mix of red and green slices, crunchy and sweet. The fans set up down here shift, and I look over to see Grandma's housedress shiver in the artificial breeze. Her shuffling steps round the recliner, pass the table, and take her back to the kitchen.

"Thanks." I click over to the smoke map, where the dots near Lakewood still glow dangerously red. The air quality index nearest our house points unrelentingly toward HAZARDOUS. "The air's still bad today. All advised to stay indoors." I pick up pear slices as I scroll down to the forecast. "The wind's supposed to shift and blow the smoke east, but looks like that won't be until tomorrow."

"Warm one again today, too?"

I laugh. "It's been more than warm, Grandma. High nineties again. The heat dome's supposed to last until the weekend, and there's still no rain in the forecast." I'm going to have campfire head forever. "Climate change is the worst," I gripe, gathering up my now-empty bowls.

"Heat dome." Grandma chuckles. "Who comes up with these names?"

"When did Mom leave?"

"She and your dad left early, before I was up."

"He's not working today?" It's both statement and question. I cross the room to the kitchen in hurried steps so I can rinse my dishes and stack them in the washer.

"No, but rumor has it a shipment of air conditioners came in. They went to check it out. You know you can't get those for love nor money these days."

"Maybe I can cycle down and meet them."

"It's a school day, Bo. You've got your own things to do." Her tone is stern. She glances out the window, then resumes filling a lunchbox with way too much food. Out front, I can just about make out the street. It's so hazy, though, that I have to squint to see the numbers on the town houses across it. "And no biking in the smoke," she adds. "You'll get hit by a car."

My phone buzzes from the kitchen counter. It's a text from Kat, who lives in a town house nearly identical to ours a few streets over. Kat and I are so close that Grandma and I don't need to read it to know what she's asking.

"You can go ahead and tell Katherine that you'll see her on the bus."

Kat is going to *love* that.

"Fine." I pout, texting back in a whirlwind of thumbs. Grandma's slow but constant movements stop. When I look up, she's wearing the glasses that were hanging from a chain around her neck. She studies my face.

"I've packed you some Pani Popo. Made them this morning."

I can't help smiling. "Really?" Grandma's baking is legend. She usually fuses my favorite Samoan coconut rolls with a southern touch. That's why it doesn't smell like smoke down here. It smells delicious. Like bread yeast, coconut—and did she add nutmeg? She's been through so much since we moved, and she still makes so much time for me.

I shuffle close and wind my arms gently around the soft middle she always complains about. Grandma says her curves have taken over, but even though she's constantly trying to lose weight, she never pulls away when I do this. "Thank you." I beam at her.

She kisses the top of my head.

4

"Will everyone be in tonight? Did Mom and Dad say whether they're taking shifts?"

"No. I'm sure someone will be around, though. Shouldn't you be the one who's out?" Her eyes glint behind her round glasses. "A wild sixteen-year-old hitchhiking across the country? Running off to Vegas? Boarding a ship to take you around the world?"

"Nope, not me. I'm *never* leaving." I wrap my arms a tiny bit tighter.

Grandma straightens me up, the side of her mouth pulling into a grin. We have the same beauty mark, a mole, tucked behind our right nostril. Hers is harder to see because her skin is darker than mine, but from this close I can see it move slightly.

"Trust your winds to fate and that God will bring you back one day."

"Sure." I shrug. Grandma's full of philosophical tropes like this these days. I don't want to think about why. All I want is for us to be together. I don't want anything to change.

Next door, baby Devon wails awake. Okay, maybe sharing a wall with a toddler could change. The newly built town houses in our neighborhood look nice, but the walls between apartments are thin. Outside is a mix of carefully harmonized roof slopes and wood siding painted in neutral hues of green, blue, and brown. Identical one-car garages, white-trimmed windows, and stamp-size squares of grass stretch down the line of town-house apartments on both sides of the street. Just like on most of the streets running this side of the freeway.

Grandma sighs. "You'd better get a move on."

She's right. The oven clock over her shoulder says the bus will be here in twenty minutes.

I dash upstairs to the bathroom I share with Mom and Tama to get the shower running. When I catch my reflection in the mirror, the state of my hair makes me laugh out loud: It's huge. Long, dark waves fall past my shoulders. I've got volume, too. When I pick it out, I can get it higher than Mom's. It's so much—with the turquoise accents, it's absolutely fabulous.

I gather it beneath a shower cap so I can at least scrub the sticky night off my skin. There's no time to attempt to wash the campfire smell out of my hair. After the shower, I rub my joints with coco butter and brush my dark eyebrows into place. I scramble to dress and grab my stuff, and by the time the bus stops on the corner, I'm standing with a handful of other kids, T-shirts pulled up over our noses to keep some of the wildfire smoke out of our lungs.

At the back of the bus, Kat's petulant face waits to greet me. A bridge of summer freckles sits glumly across her cheeks. She flicks her blond bangs in a futile attempt to keep them from falling to the left.

"The bus?" she grumbles before I've even sat down next to her. "We were *supposed* to make a statement this year. We might not have our own cars, but we were gonna rock retro and bike."

"Come on, would your mom have let you cycle in this?" I wave a hand toward the front window, where the bus's windshield wipers are on to keep it ash-free. "It's literally raining fire." The wildfires that have plagued Washington this summer are the largest in the state's history. Growing up at the end of the world blows.

"*I* wouldn't have asked. Your family's the only one that has to talk about everything. You don't see my brothers on here, do you? They boarded."

"What?" I sit up to search for Liam, a senior who would definitely object to taking the bus, and Isaac, a freshman. I'm shocked to come up zero for two. "Isaac's got asthma!"

"He also has self-respect," Kat sniffs. She's worked through her petulance now and slumps over to rest her head on my shoulder. Then she twists a strand of my turquoise around her finger. "Your hair still looks amazing, by the way."

"I can't bring myself to wash it and risk dulling the color. I'll crack soon, though. I smell like a campfire."

"A cool campfire." She lets the strand go and settles her slim frame against mine. At five foot four, Kat's shorter and thinner than me. Even so, she's not someone who's easily pushed around. I look down and suppress a laugh at the contrast of our intertwined arms. Her skin looks so white, even though this is the tannest she'll be all year. Her green eyes close.

I smile, still slightly unbelieving. This is my third consecutive year at Lakewood High School. Before Lakewood, we moved around a lot because of Dad's jobs. There was only one other place I'd stayed for three years, and it wasn't somewhere I had a best friend. Kat, who's spent the last several weeks complaining about going back to school, doesn't know what it's like. Getting to go back to the same place feels incredible.

Outside, I try to watch Lakewood come into focus. There's no hope of seeing Mount Rainier today. When the weather's clear, the mountain towers, beautiful and snowcapped, behind us as we drive west away from Interstate 5, the Pacific Northwest's largest highway. I-5 carries eight lanes of cars north to Seattle and extends all the way south to San Diego. The lakes and fir-shaded suburbs of town occupy the strip of land between the interstate and Puget Sound. School's close to the town center, which isn't all that far from our neighborhood. It only takes us fifteen minutes to bike there, when we can see (and breathe).

When the bus rounds the last corner, we pull slowly through the haze into the school's front parking lot. Lakewood High stands obscured in smoke. I can't make out the buildings at all—not even the aquatic center, which is the closest. It's even hard to read the WELCOME OTTERS! flashing across the digital sign. Ottey, our mascot, is painted on the front of the building. He's a waving otter, floating on his back in a tranquil blue lake surrounded by green fir trees. *If only.*

Kat stretches, squeaking the pleather of our bus seat. "Here we go. Only three more days till Friday."

"You can't be counting down already? It's day one. Of the first week!"

"Yup. That means only a hundred seventy-nine school days until summer break and three fifty-nine until graduation, when I'll never have to see Mr. Hoffman or an algebra book ever again," Kat says as the bus stops.

Everyone runs through the smoke toward the school's double doors. When we cross over the air-conditioned threshold, a few of the boys ahead of us let out audible sighs of relief. They aren't the only ones.

"Thank God!" Kat says, breathing in the cool, unsmoky air. "I'm so sick of being sweaty *all* the time." She smiles at me, waiting for a response. Then she remembers. "You're not still stressing about greenhouse gases, are you?"

We've entered the big central atrium that opens straight through to the cafeteria. Four halls of classrooms branch out from this space. I take in the expanse, wondering just how much energy it takes to cool such a large building. Goose bumps are already forming on my arms. "It's so many emissions, Kat!"

She rolls her eyes. "Live a little," she says. "Anyway, weren't you going on the other day about how the state is powered by renewable energy? 'Member?"

"I knew you were up!" Kat is often on the receiving end of my late-night internet wormhole research.

"Yeah. And the next time you text me at one in the morning, the reason better be more exciting than dams. 'Did you know that Washington State generates over half of its electricity from hydropower?'" Kat says, perfectly mimicking my accent. Then, in a dramatic sweep, she flips her hair over to one side like I do when I'm thinking.

I'm crying with laughter.

"Kill me!" She's laughing now, too.

"Isa!" I hear over the noise of students hurrying through the door. It's Susie—we were paired up for a couple of assignments last year, which neither of us did very well on. Still, it was nice having someone new to talk to about how terrible math is.

Her head of red curls is just as brilliant as usual. It's not every day that I get to meet someone with hair as striking as mine. As she bobs toward us, I realize that something about her looks different.

"I'm so glad we all have history together this year." She smiles at Kat and me.

"Me too," I say distractedly, trying to place what's new. "Oh! Your teeth look great!"

She beams. "Thanks! I was soooo happy when my braces came off this summer. I can't stop doing this." She runs her tongue over the outside of her teeth and laughs. "Trust me, if you hadn't done that in years, you'd understand. It feels amazing! You're so lucky that you didn't have to have them."

"I know. They seem pretty awful." I leave out how we could never afford them and feel suddenly self-conscious about the gap between my front teeth.

We push forward as more students come in. Still unsure of our

WE DON'T HAVE TIME FOR THIS

new schedules and where we're meant to go, we walk straight through toward the cafeteria. The wall of double doors at the back of the school would normally stand open—letting kids lounge on the grass or take the outdoor paths across campus. They're closed today. "Do you think the smoke will ever get better?" I ask.

Kat shakes her head. "Doesn't feel like it."

Susie folds her binder against her chest. "It's so scary, isn't it? My cousins live in Snoqualmie. They had to evacuate last night."

"Oh no," I gasp. "I'm so sorry. Are they okay?"

"Yeah, they're fine—well, they're physically fine. They're staying with my uncle in Seattle. But how crazy would it be to not know whether your house will be there when you get back?"

Kat shudders. "That's awful."

We've stopped walking and have tucked ourselves into a corner of the cafeteria, out of the way. "I'm so sorry," I say again. I can't help adding, "Shouldn't we be doing something?"

Susie looks perplexed. "The firefighters are doing as much as they can. . . ."

"Oh, no. I mean, do something about climate change. Do something about what's *causing* the fires."

"Right," Susie says, her face full of all the uncertainty I feel.

"I don't know." I struggle to explain. "It's like they tell us what climate change is, but then what? Like, what are we supposed to do about it? And the world's on fire! How is that not what we're learning?"

Susie shrugs, defeated. "I just want my family to be safe." The bell rings its loud, shrill call. "Oops! We'd better hurry."

"Where's first period again?" Kat asks.

I pull out my schedule, which is nearly identical to hers, and we navigate through the building along with everyone else.

🔥

Before I know it, the last bell rings, setting us free for the day. I load books into my bag as I hustle out of last period, eager to exit the building. I forgot about the smoke, though. I pull my T-shirt up over my nose and gather myself before pushing through the exit.

The parking lot is mayhem, which I usually think is fun, but everything's taken on a menacing quality in the heat dome's firescape. The air outside is now a hazy brown, and the light that filters through the smoke is a strange orange color. Kids skateboard past. Buses honk final warnings. Lines of cars are forming, waiting to exit the parking lot. It's going to be hard to find the car in this chaos.

My phone buzzes with a text from Mom.

I'm here! Got a spot on the street by the fire hydrant.

I head toward the streetside parking. Squinting to see, I make out Mom's waving form and register, again, how similar we look. As of this summer, I'm as tall as she is. We have the same curvy build and similar medium-brown skin tones. The same round faces—though my cheeks are more "pinchable" than hers, and the left one dimples when I smile—and the same full lips. The same dark brown eyes. Today, she's even wearing one of my T-shirts.

Our most noticeable difference is our hair. Her dark curls are tighter than my waves, and their volume sits up above her shoulders, though most days she pulls them back into a high bun. And she doesn't add colors to her hair. We jokingly argue sometimes about how the other is prettiest.

I jog toward where she's waiting on the sidewalk so we can dive into the safety of Grandma's old Honda Civic.

"Let's get the AC going," she says. I can't believe it still works. Grandma drove this car over from Alabama decades ago and refuses to give it up.

Mom swivels to identify a gap to pull out into, and someone slows to let her in.

"You found a good spot," I say, complimenting her.

"I know! I'll try to nab the same one on Thursday." She turns right at the second light, taking us away from the ring of traffic. "How was school? Your first week of junior year! I can't believe it."

"It was fine, Mom." I laugh at her overenthusiasm, then sort through the highlights. "Kat and I have four classes together. There are more Samoans at Lakewood High now, too—some of the girls from dance are in my language arts class, and their sisters are freshmen. I know so many people here. It's like a reunion!"

"That's great, Bo. But I mean, how's it going? How are your classes?"

"Oh." I shrug. "Uh, fine. Nothing too difficult. Actually, I think algebra is going to be hard this year. Kat is dreading it. She thinks Mr. Hoffman hates her 'cause last year he caught her drawing caricatures of him." I laugh at the memory of his face, and Kat's. I'm surprised that Mom's not laughing with me.

"We should probably start thinking about colleges, huh?" she asks instead. "You could go up to UW, or maybe somewhere in California?"

I laugh again. "The University of Washington? I don't have those kinds of grades." In subjects I like, I'm a solid B student. In ones I don't, I just aim to pass. "And we can't afford Seattle. I don't want to waste money."

Mom raises her chin. "We'd make it work." I still find the defiance in her tone comforting, even though I'm old enough now to know it's more aspirational than practical. Neither Mom nor Tama finished college. "Besides, your dad and I want you to be able to build the life that you want."

We've had this conversation before. "What I *want* is to work in *your* restaurant and to live *here*, where we're all together." I remind her, smiling at the image in my mind. I also want to stop talking about a future where I'm being sent away for a degree I have no practical use for, which would cost everyone I love a fortune that we don't have and can't pay back.

I stare out into the haze until Mom's blinker clicks, then I grin.

We've arrived at what looks, on first glance, like an old house with white wood shingles and a mossy roof. Everything seems perfectly residential except the slide letter sign that reads DANCE, LANGUAGE, MARTIAL ARTS CLASSES, SPACE RENTAL. As we pull into the parking lot, though, the halls, ramps, and rooms extended out the back make it clear there's a lot going on at the Asia Pacific Cultural Center.

I love this place.

Everything about it. From the moment Mom took me here for my first dance class and bought us mango sticky rice from a Thai market. I still remember the hustle and bustle in the parking lot that sunny summer day. Now, Tuesday and Thursday afternoons— and Saturday mornings—are some of my favorite times of the week because I spend them here. I smile at her as we park in our usual fir-shaded spot close to the entrance.

As soon as the engine's off, I sit up, rigid in my seat. Mom takes the same posture and locks eyes with me.

"Contestants ready?" Her hand moves left to her seat handle. My hand's already on mine.

I count, "One, two, three."

"Go!" she yells. And with one jerky movement, I race to recline my seat all the way down before her. We scream with laughter. It fills the car, bouncing off the windows. The noise drowns out all other thought. Suddenly, all we can see is each other.

This is our world, our own private kingdom. Mom's and mine. Built over a childhood spent bumming along the Pacific coastline in beater cars with crappy seats, giggling under car roofs. Waiting for Dad to come back and rejoin our life as it moved from port to port. "I win!"

"No, I do!" She laughs, wiping her eyes.

My cheeks ache from grinning so wide. And it doesn't matter. The race isn't about winning. It's about me and Mom, and this: the one thing that's stayed the same, no matter where we moved.

Once I've got ahold of myself, I look over the crown of my head toward the back seats. I can smell the bags of produce. "How was the market? What did you get?"

"I feel bad for the vendors—what a terrible run of late season farmers markets. The port, too. It's been too hot. I wasn't the only one complaining. But . . ."

She reaches back and pulls out various bags. "The last of the peaches; they're at the end of the season. They had huckleberries, too, but the prices are insane—they want eighty-five dollars a gallon, and I could only haggle them down to seventy. Good mushroom haul, though. And I got to the lady who makes glass noodles first. I'll make sapasui tomorrow when I'm off."

"Did they have cherries?"

"You'll never learn." Mom laughs. "The season for Rainiers ended months ago. No cherries, Bo. Red or white."

I frown. White Rainier cherries are magic. Since we moved here, I've eaten myself sick on them for weeks of the summer. And I still won't stop.

The center console between us becomes a buffet of food. All color and scent. Feast and fusion. Markets have always been where our money went, fresh food the only thing worth splurging on.

Mom smells something and passes it to me. "Look, the purple green beans are back! And a woman had mustard greens and edible flowers."

"They're pretty," I say, nibbling. I prop myself up on one elbow. "You should use them when you cook for Jay. Good presentation."

Mom's forehead bumps with concerned ridges. "I don't know. I still couldn't get the right fish."

Our beat-up cooler rests on the floor in the back. I raise my seat so I can peak in, careful not to let too much cold out. "Oysters?"

"Yup. They were all that were worth buying. They're stressed out, but they should be alright."

"But couldn't you cook these for Jay?"

"I think I'll just wait. There's bound to be a better catch when things cool down. And it'll be Chuseok next month. It'd be fun to use different flavors. Those rice cakes, and the cabbage kimchi!"

I'm momentarily distracted. The center's home to so many, there are like forty countries on the welcome board. I love all the different events it hosts, and we won't miss Chuseok, the Korean mid-autumn harvest festival. The celebrations fill the hall with a dozen languages and smells. And so much food. Mom loves it, too. There's a APCC calendar with handwritten notes on the dashboard so she won't forget anything. It looks like the recipes that cover the fridge door at home.

My teeth break through the fuzz of a peach, and I lie back down.

"Suck some mint." She hands me a leaf. "It's good, right?"

"So good." Mom's the best cook I know, but we've always moved around too much for her to spend any real time in the kitchens of the restaurants she's waited tables in. I know cooking's what she wants; it just never seems to happen.

"Come on, Mom." I sigh. "You've worked at Jay's over two years now, and you know he's willing to give you a shot. You're so ready for this. You don't have to do the oysters. You could make something else."

"Don't worry, there's no rush." She shrugs. "Especially now your dad's a big union man. You should have seen him at the port today."

I won't be waylaid this time. "But what about you?" I insist.

"We're good, Bo. We're all good." She holds my gaze for a moment, then props herself up and looks over my shoulder. "Oh God, there she is! Go, or she'll yell at me again."

I don't need to turn around to know that girl time is over and Mrs. Surh O'Connell, the center's founder, is standing, arms folded, at the door. She's a bit of a character. The center is her baby, and she's not to be crossed.

I pull my seat upright and reach for one of the plastic flowers on the dash while Mom rummages for a lavalava in the back.

"Take the yellow one, it'll look cool with your hair." She hands me a pink patterned wrap. "Go, go! I'm working a shift tonight, so call Dad when you're done. Love you."

"Love you, too!" I'm out of the car and waving to Mrs. Surh O'Connell, who holds open the door for me.

"Don't want to be late," she tsks. "Class starts in a few minutes."

Her insistence on punctuality is a stark contrast to the attitude I know is waiting for me down the hall, in the dance studio on the right. I don't argue, though. Instead, I hustle past the sculptures and carvings at reception. The walls are covered with hundreds of framed certificates, plaques, and pictures. Lanterns hang from the ceiling. Fans and masks adorn the pillars. And decorations cover every inch of the hallway leading past the community spaces, classrooms, and offices to the dance studios. When I make it to the familiar door, I leave my shoes among the pile and enter with the greeting, "Talofa."

"Talofa lava," everyone inside says back.

At the mirror wall, I wind my hair up into a bun and tuck the flower behind my right ear. The room's full of the chatter of girls and a collection of parents, mostly moms who will probably stay for the class. I wrap the lavalava around my waist, tying the corners in a knot so it looks like I'm wearing a long straight skirt over my shorts.

After several minutes, Mrs. Leota announces from the center of the room, "We start in a circle and finish in a circle." She waves everyone forward, drawing people around her commanding form. A bunch of yellow flowers are tucked into the braid of her dark hair, and her wrap is covered in a large leaf print. Mrs. Leota also wears her signature red lipstick and dramatic blush that runs to her hairline, diva style.

I shuffle over the woven mats, enjoying the texture against my bare feet, and fold myself down into the circle. While the others are settling, I smile to the girls I've seen in class before.

"Afio mai. Afio mai," Mrs. Leota tells us. "Welcome to our first dance of the school year! Let's get to know each other some, especially those who are new. My name is Maria Leota, and I'm from Pago Pago in American Samoa. I've been teaching dance at the APCC for, oh, too many years now."

She stops to beckon in the mom and three girls standing in the doorway. "Afio mai. Don't be shy." I wave to them, too. The girls have grown several inches during summer break.

"Isa, why don't you go next?"

Oh, okay. "Talofa, everyone," I start. "I'm Isa Brown. My dad's from Tafuna in American Samoa. I'm a junior at Lakewood High, and I've been dancing with Mrs. Leota since we moved here." In truth, I've taken Samoan dance for as long as I can remember. It's the only thing I've managed to stick with because wherever we went, I'd demand lessons—even as a little kid.

"Thanks, Isa. Let's go around from there," Mrs. Leota instructs.

She gets everyone introduced, then we rise and stand in a loose formation facing the mirrors. Mrs. Leota taps the phone plugged into the sound system, and a chorus of female voices sings through the speakers. Their peaceful rhythm relaxes my shoulders and softens my knees.

"Alright, ladies." Mrs. Leota smiles. "We dance to tell a story." She bends one knee and gracefully draws her arms up, wrists raised. I'm captured immediately and attempt to perfectly copy the motion. Everyone else starts moving, too.

"We feel our story with conviction," Mrs. Leota continues, "from our facial expressions to each subtle gesture of our fingers." She holds the hands she's rippling in hypnotic waves high so that we can see. "Slowly run your thumbs to the tips of your tall fingers. Then move your wrists in time. Good!

"Now, we move our feet." Her body glides forward. "One, two, three—tap your foot behind you. Then again. One, two, three—step back and turn your chin to face your foot." I copy her, smoothly moving toe to heel across the matted floor. I tune in to the music, let the sound fill my mind.

I wish I could understand what the women sing. Wish I could know more than just the beat. Understand the words Tama does, what they say about his home across the sea. I listen, moving gracefully. There's nothing like the feeling of being connected in rhythm to Mrs. Leota and the girls around me. The women of the music. The lapping ocean far away.

The music changes, and Ms. Tilo, another instructor, gives a loud, vocal cry, the signal for us to clap in time. The other dancers in the room join in. "Wave your right arm, then your left. Now CLAP!" Mrs. Leota slaps her knee. "Clap your hands forward in front of you. Now behind your back. Step. Step, step."

Together, we change formation, moving as one. Somehow, time both freezes and passes too quickly. In every place I've been, Samoan dance is what home feels like. I could keep dancing like this for hours. I'm surprised when the music stops and Mrs. Leota says, "Beautiful dancing today, ladies."

"You're really good," a girl who introduced herself as Sina says to me. "We just moved here this summer. Is your mom Samoan, too? E te iloa fa'aSamoa?"

"No." I shake my head. "My mom's from Texas, and I've only been to American Samoa once when I was a baby. I don't speak Samoan; I wish I did."

"Let's come back to the circle, please," Mrs. Leota says. Sina and I move to form part of the ring. More parents have joined us, reminding me that I need to call Dad.

"We'll be working on a few dances for the holiday show, which we'll hold just before Christmas. Starting next month, we'll have some joint practices with the men to work on the choreography of the group dances." A few of the younger girls giggle.

Mrs. Leota carries on. "For our newer dancers, if you'd like some more practice time, Ms. Tilo, who helped us today, will be running sessions on Saturday mornings. But we'll all dance here on Tuesdays and Thursdays. Fa'afetai. Thank you, everyone."

We all clap our thanks, and the circle breaks apart. I retrieve my phone from my bag, stashed in a cubby along the wall, and call Dad.

"Hi, Tama," I say when I hear his voice. "Dance is finished. We're just talking now. Are you close?"

"I'm almost there. I picked up dinner. Got us some Mexican food."

I laugh. Tama's tastes are questionable sometimes. He only gets dinner when Mom's going to be out. "Is it from a food truck?"

He laughs, too, a booming chuckle that always makes me smile. "No, it's from that place your grandma likes, and I got her extra guacamole. Pulling off the freeway now, Bo. See you in a second."

I slowly unwrap my lavalava and take the flower out of my hair before wandering back toward the others. They're all talking about the same thing.

"Hopefully the smoke will shift tomorrow so we can open the windows. Every wildfire season gets worse!"

"Season?" Ms. Tilo brings her hands to her hips. "California had wildfires in *January* this year. There is no wildfire season anymore."

"I just want it to start raining."

A familiar voice calls, "Talofa." And Dad walks in to several voices responding, "Talofa lava." I smile as the feeling of home increases, now Tama's here to complete the picture. These days, he spends more time at the cultural center than I do.

"Any luck?" Mrs. Leota asks expectantly.

"Nope, afraid not. I went down to the port twice today and still couldn't get my hands on any AC units. Sorry, folks." He shrugs his massive shoulders. Like most of the Samoan men I know, Tama's a big guy with a wide, expressive face. His eyes are black, the iris the same color as the pupil, and Mom says they're full of mischief. The kind she could never resist.

"I've tried everywhere." Even though it's cool in here, the woman speaking fans herself. "We've been staying with cousins in Olympia and commuting. Can't get an AC installed, even if you do have the money. Nobody has them."

"Of course no one has them—it never used to get this hot. And now when it does, everyone realizes at the same time."

"The center has rooms set up upstairs," Mrs. Leota says. "If anyone needs a place to stay." She turns to Dad. "Do you think there'll be more in anytime soon?"

"Hard to say," he tells her. "Everything's slow at the port right now. The smoke's not good to be working in. And there's talk that they'll be starting construction soon, which will reduce capacity. I'll keep my ears open, though. You'll be the first to know."

More people head for the door, and we follow. I'm happy Dad parked his pickup right on the curb. One look at the smoke and I realize how exhausted I am. I'm not used to doing full, post-summer-break days yet. Inside, the cab smells so good that it makes my stomach growl. Dad hands me a bag of chips and guacamole, which I start on while he pulls into the street.

"It was nice to see everyone. I'll probably come with you on Thursday. Mom's going to take Grandma to her appointment."

"You're not working?" I crunch.

"Nope. Fewer shifts on right now, so I said I'd stay off for the rest of the week to give some of the newbies a chance."

I stop to pass him a loaded chip, thinking. "Fewer shifts 'cause of the smoke?"

"Mostly because of the construction they'll be starting. They want to retrofit one of the docks for a new pipeline." He holds out his hand for another chip.

"What kind of pipeline?"

"LNG—liquified natural gas—I think." Dad swings the wheel around to get onto the freeway. Then returns his outstretched hand, waiting.

I'm frozen. "They're building a new natural gas pipeline?" My voice gets all high with stress, the calm from dancing instantly gone. "We can't even go outside, and they're building a natural gas pipeline?!"

Dad nods. "That's the plan."

"And this means you can't work? *Will you have to go away again?*" My voice is almost unrecognizable by the end.

The hand reaches over and takes my wrist, holding it in a comforting way. "Breathe, afa'fine." I'm still clutching the same guac-less chip. "Breathe, Bo. It's alright."

Dad waits for me to exhale a few times. Then he says, "We don't really know what things will look like 'cause the plans are still coming together. The longshoremen are meeting about it soon. Whatever happens, it shouldn't mean that I'll go away. I'm a card-carrying member of the union now."

I stare at his face, the one we had to live so long without. Then out the windshield at the smoke-filled haze. The strange, ominous, orangey light that means our headlights are on even though it's only six.

When my family rides together, Mom sits up front and holds Tama's hand—kind of like this. Suddenly, everything in me wants to hold both Dad's hand and hers, and never let go.

CHAPTER 2
RUN, GIRL

Isa

"COME ON, MRS. VETHANAYAGAM!" I HEAR AS THE DOOR pushes open.

An exhale of wonder escapes me as I walk through. Mrs. Vethanayagam's art studio remains an amazing palette of color and shape. I gawk at the high walls draped in colorful Sri Lankan tapestries. They're interspersed with canvases and student artwork. This is definitely my favorite room in Lakewood High. Kat's, too.

"It's my senior year. I'll never get another chance. Please, I'm begging you!" Brian's pleading interrupts my reverie, as does the final bell of Friday afternoon. The first week of school is officially over.

I stop gawking to look for Kat. In exchange for extended studio privileges, Kat and a handful of Mrs. Vethanayagam's other favorite art students are sticking around to fulfill their side of the bargain: providing art for school events.

"No, Brian. No gooey-ducks," Mrs. Vethanayagam says. "And I'm not explaining why again."

As I walk toward Kat, who's standing by a large whiteboard, I can't help admiring Mrs. Vethanayagam's outfit. She's wearing a teal, floor-length wrap dress with peacock feathers printed all over it. The feathers are trimmed in gold, which accents her delicate nose ring. She is so cool.

Kat smiles when she sees me. "You just missed Brian's annual bid to have us paint phalluses for the first assembly of the year," she whispers.

I laugh. "Perfect timing, then."

Though the pep squad gets the credit, it's this group that creates most of the art displayed at school functions. I followed Kat (who insisted that she couldn't do her best work without me) and joined last year. I think Mrs. Vethanayagam lets me attend mostly to keep Kat interested.

"Thinking caps on, please," Mrs. Vethanayagam continues over the muffled laughter. "We need *appropriate* ideas for marine life for Lakewood High's welcome assembly."

While Brian sulks dramatically, the others start brainstorming.

"Go for the classic and stick with otters?"

"What about sharks?"

"How's a shark supposed to hold a sign?"

"What? Like otters hold signs introducing LHS clubs in real life. We're not going for realism here."

On the whiteboard, someone's writing up the list of sports teams, clubs, and other things students can join. I gather the animals' signs are meant to remind people of the options the assembly will introduce.

"What if we just do a giant sun star?" Kat offers. "That way we can have as many legs as we need to hold the signs. Then we won't have to create several sea creatures, just one big one."

"Oh, I like that. Let's sketch it up," Mrs. Vethanayagam says.

"Brian, given your enthusiasm, why don't you start? On a *sun star*," she emphasizes, handing him a marker.

He starts drawing and the others move in closer, offering feedback almost instantly.

"No, more drama in the legs. They need to be long enough to wrap around a sign on a stick."

"Less scary. We're supposed to be welcoming people."

"Do sun stars have faces? Should we give it big round eyes?"

"Maybe it's wearing sunglasses or something?"

A couple of people pick up markers to do their suggestions justice. The rest of us hang back, watching Kat's idea come to life.

"Sorry I didn't meet you earlier," I tell Kat. "I was talking to Susie. She thinks her cousins lost their house last night."

This turns her attention away from the whiteboard. "What? No!"

"Yeah. Most of Snoqualmie is gone. It's so awful. She's devastated for them. I was wondering if there was something we could do, you know? Raise money? Or send something to the high school? Susie says they think it's still there."

"That's a nice thought," Mrs. Vethanayagam says.

I didn't realize she was listening to us and not the babble at the board. The cup of tea she's holding smells amazing—I'm getting cloves and cinnamon. She's drinking it out of a wonky mug a student must have made for her. She stirs contemplatively with a tiny silver spoon.

"Is Susie in the Environmental Justice Club?" Mrs. Vethanayagam asks, looking up at me.

"Um, the what?" I mumble.

"The Environmental Justice Club? It's on the list of things to promote this year." Mrs. Vethanayagam points to the now-complete list written on the whiteboard.

I've never heard of it. "Ah, no. I don't think so?"

"Hmmm. They aren't very well-known. But that would be a great thing for them to do, and I'm sure Susie's not the only one upset about the wildfires. Their first meeting is today. Mr. Mendoza's the advisor."

I've never heard of him, either.

"Why don't you go check it out?"

I stare blankly at Mrs. Vethanayagam. "Ah . . . okay," I stammer, unsure. "Where's Mr. Mendoza's?"

"Come on, I'll show you." She smiles. Kat shrugs at me apologetically as I follow Mrs. Vethanayagam out the door.

This is unexpected.

School's essentially empty now. We only pass two people: junior girls from my history class, who are decorating their lockers. They stare at me quizzically. I probably look like I've scored detention, trailing Mrs. Vethanayagam toward C Hall on a Friday afternoon.

"Keep up, Isa." I quicken my pace to match her strides. "It's down this hall—all the way at the end."

After she finally pushes open a door, we walk toward the front of a science lab, where students have grouped their high stools into a loose circle.

"Sorry to interrupt, Mr. Mendoza, but I've got a prospective club member for you," Mrs. Vethanayagam says, gesturing toward me.

I wave awkwardly.

"No problem," a man with a full mustache answers. He must be Mr. Mendoza. His dark hair is combed back, and his shirt is tucked into his khakis. "Please join us. We're just starting."

I smile and pull over a stool. Mrs. Vethanayagam's gone before I put my bag down.

"It's great to see so many new faces," Mr. Mendoza says. I look around, a bit surprised. There were more people in the art studio. "We've got an agenda up on the board. Before we jump in, does anyone want to share why they're here? Particularly those new to the club?"

A girl to my right puts up her hand.

"I'm scared, that's why I'm here," she says. "Mostly because of the fires, but generally 'cause it feels like the world's ending and unless we get greenhouse gas pollution to zero, it's going to get worse. I'm scared that *this* is going to get *worse*." She waves toward a window. The smoke outside isn't as thick as it was earlier in the week, but it's still hazy.

"Yeah, I'm pretty petrified," another girl chimes in. "But I don't know what to do about it. I mean, I'm happy to strike and post on Fridays, but I guess I just want to know how we can protect ourselves? And you know, do something that will actually stop the climate crisis."

I blink. It's so nice to hear other people talk like this. To hear the things I've been thinking spoken aloud.

"Me too," a girl with pink hair nods. "And I was really upset about Tahlequah this summer." She gauges our reactions and then quickly explains. "The orca whose calf died, and she carried it around for weeks 'cause she couldn't let it go. It was so heartbreaking to watch."

"My dad works at the salmon hatchery," the guy beside her says while the news footage of Tahlequah, one of Puget Sound's resident killer whales, desperately trying to get her calf to breathe, replays in my mind. I'd forgotten about that. "I know they're having a lot of problems with the heat, too."

I lean forward, enthralled. Just as I open my mouth to speak, the girl next to me passes me a clipboard, and, distracted, I pause to add my name and email address to the sign-in sheet.

"Thanks everyone for sharing," Mr. Mendoza says. "I'm glad you've voiced those concerns. I know many of us feel the same way.

"I'm Mr. Mendoza, and I've been advising the Environmental Justice Club—as it's come to be called—for over ten years. I seem to be the teacher students most often come to to ask about environmental issues. I'm happy to create a space where we can increase our understanding together. I'm not happy about how much there is for you to worry about.

"This club and what it tackles has always been up to the students. We've looked into lead poisoning and pollution. We've done habitat restoration. We've gone up to the university and talked about microplastics. The world's your oyster. I'm just here to be the credit card–wielding, Spanish-speaking adult—and honorary treasurer." He laughs warmly.

I'm starting to wish I had Mr. Mendoza as a teacher.

"I'll stop there and hand things over to the club's current president and secretary, Jake and Sophia."

"Thanks Mr. Mendoza," a guy who I assume is Jake says. He flicks up the LHS baseball cap he's wearing, and I notice that his eyes are a startling shade of blue.

"Sophia and I thought we'd start by giving everyone a recap of what the club was up to this summer and the ideas we didn't manage to do last year. Want to talk about the summer, Sophia?"

"Sure." Sophia seems slightly uncomfortable—shy, maybe? Her skin is a lovely tan, and her dark hair is wavy and full. I think I've seen her before coming out of Spanish class.

She clears her throat. "A few of us met a couple of times. Um, we got to observe some meetings of the model UN for high school students. They're actually really interesting, and they're hoping to do an environmental conference this May. They think our club would

be great to help organize it, if we're interested. And thanks, Darius."
She pauses to smile at a guy with round tortoiseshell glasses and a
fade who's sitting next to Mr. Mendoza. "He organized the meetings
with them and represented our club really well."

"Thanks, Darius and Sophia," Jake says. "I guess the only things
we didn't manage to do from last year were the documentary nights
we talked about. We thought we could even get some professors
from the community college to do a bit of a discussion afterward, if
that's still of interest?"

I look around. No one seems particularly enthusiastic about
watching documentaries.

"Um, right," Jake goes on. "So we're looking for volunteers to help
with that, and we can use the rest of the meeting today to plan. We'll
also need to elect new officers to lead the club this year."

Mr. Mendoza clears his throat. "I believe the only candidates so far
are Darius for president and Marina for secretary. But, of course, others are welcome to run! As we have some new joiners, Darius, would
you like to tell us some of the things you'd focus on as president?"

"Happy to, Mr. Mendoza." Darius stands and tugs at a corner of
his button-down shirt. He's taller than I thought. His skin's almost
as dark as Grandma's, and his wide nose turns down. "I'd like to build
on the stuff we learned at the model UN and work with them to
hold a mock COP—a UN climate summit."

Ummm, what?

"I think it'll be a great way to delve into the policy options and
explore the dynamics at work in negotiating solutions to the climate
crisis."

I have no idea what he's talking about.

"And it will look great on college applications," he ends, smiling
confidently.

My eyebrows shoot up, crinkling my forehead. What good is that?!

"An ambitious plan, Darius," Mr. Mendoza says when Mr. Model UN sits back down. "It would undoubtably be an interesting discussion, and again, other members are welcome to put themselves and their ideas forward. If we have more than one, we can hold an election."

That . . . can't be the only plan?

"Great," Jake says. "Well, anyone who wants to work on the movie night, stick around. Otherwise, we'll end the meeting here and see you all in two weeks."

That's it? I stand up slowly, perplexed. A couple of people move toward Jake, and Mr. Mendoza goes over to introduce himself to some of the new members.

I don't know why, but I'm suddenly furious. My palms sting, and I feel like I'm repressing the urge to scream. I can hear my heart beating in my ears. Without a word, I turn on my heel and storm off toward Mrs. Vethanayagam's. I'm positive Kat will still be there; I haven't been gone long.

Back in the studio, it takes me a moment to find her.

Everyone's spread around the cavernous space, which is now full of giant tentacles. They hang over the long tables and chairs that students move throughout the day. They cover the windows at the back by the paint cabinets and industrial-size sinks. And they stretch through the door that leads to the kilns and storage area, where I can hear people working. Kat's on her hands and knees at the far end of the room, painting a truly enormous pair of sun star legs.

"That was quick," she says when I throw the notebook I didn't need down next to her. "How was it?"

"Fine," I basically shout.

"That good, huh?" Kat looks at me questioningly, but I don't say anything else. Why am I so angry?

"Oh, I've been meaning to ask if your mom's cooking for her boss this weekend? Want me to come to the restaurant and help?"

That does it.

"She's not doing it—again! She couldn't find the fish she wants, and she says the oysters she bought aren't good enough. It just sucks!" I fume, the floodgates opening.

"It feels like it's coming at us from all sides, you know? We're stuck under this fucking immovable heat dome, and instead of getting everyone to talk about how we live in a world where we can't buy food and have to worry about our homes going up in flames, all we can think to do about it is practice making speeches at a fake UN?!"

Kat puts down her paintbrush. "So . . . I guess you wanna talk about the meeting, then?"

I didn't realize how much this has all been building up inside me. How the relief I felt at suddenly being in a room with other people who seemed to feel the same way I do about the climate crisis came crashing down after Darius's speech. For about five minutes I'd felt hopeful. And now, even that's gone.

I let out a tremendous sigh and sink down to the floor next to Kat. My shoulders slump forward in defeat and disappointment.

"It did start off good," I say at a normal volume. "Some girls introduced themselves by talking about things they're scared about, and how they wish they knew what to do. But then none of the things the club is planning seem to match that. The incoming president is more concerned with rounding out his college applications than making a real difference. And there were, what, like ten of us?"

"That many?" Kat scoffs, reaching for more paint.

"I just think this is something we all care about. I wish we could all sit down and talk about it together, you know? Like have a real conversation and come up with a plan."

Kat is looking at me quizzically again, but I'm too worked up to stop.

"It wouldn't even take that much," I brainstorm aloud. "We could get that punk band to do a song at the assembly. Or get the vegans to cook something we could give out at lunch. Anything to get people talking about what's actually happening! The crisis we're all living through."

"And the fake UN thing? What's that?"

I reach for a brush, studying the legs she's doing so I can start replicating them. "I have absolutely no idea. But that's what the guy who'll be the next president wants to do. Have a model UN climate summit."

"Is that a thing?" Kat asks.

"Apparently."

"Who's this guy?"

"I don't know him. Think he's a junior, too, though. Darius? Cute. Wears glasses. He thinks this model UN stuff is great, when literally anything related to our actual lives would be so much better. What's the point in hosting a *fake* climate summit—how is that going to help anyone? And he's the only one running for president this year!" My voice has gone up in volume again.

"Screw that," Kat says. "*You* should be the president."

"What?!" I snort.

"Oh, come on, Isa. Your ideas are *so* much better than that, and you've only been ranting about it for five minutes."

"My ideas?"

"Yes—*your* ideas!" She sits up and puts her brush down. "A climate concert—I'd go to that. Vegan food feed. Yes, please." Her face is frustrated. "You sound like your mom, you know. All these ideas and all this talent, but are we eating her food at a restaurant yet?"

My mouth falls open.

"Run, girl." Kat looks me straight in the eyes. "Run!"

CHAPTER 3
UNEXPECTED ENTRANT

Darius

CHAD'S EYES ARE CLOSED, AND HIS HEAD'S TILTED UP TO THE sky. "God, I love the rain."

I hurtle to a stop and bend over to rest my hands on my knees. "I'm just glad we can run outside again," I wheeze. When the rain finally started last week, the entire cross-country team jumped off the gym's now-overused treadmills to welcome it. I can't remember being so happy.

"Rain over smoke any day," Chad breathes. "I hope the rest of the fires stop soon." The area east of the mountains always gets less rain than we do, and their fires aren't out yet.

He twists his right wrist to read his watch. "Six miles in thirty-eight minutes. Nice."

Chad's a machine. Senior captain of Lakewood High's cross-country team. Rumor has it he gave himself stress fractures at age twelve from pounding the pavement.

When I slowly straighten up to standing, he thumps my shoulder. "Well done keeping up, middle distance. I bet you could get your splits down to 5:30, if you set your mind to it. Don't want to push it too hard before this weekend's meet, though."

That *wasn't* pushing it? I feel a bit sick.

My ideal races are measured in meters, not miles. For me, cross-country's a good way to keep fit for the spring track season. Before I can respond, Chad's in motion again. He jogs toward the empty football stadium to do the grass laps that will mark the end of our practice. I catch up when he stops to unlock the turnstile. He's the only one Coach trusts with a key, and to validate my miles.

My breath's still not back, but I gasp out what I've meant to say all morning. "Thanks again for coming out early."

"It's every other week you need, right? Or does Coach want you to do this every Friday?"

"No. Every other Friday's fine. I'm an officer of a club that meets this afternoon during practice." It's almost true; naming me president is just a formality. "I can't miss the meetings, but I still want to be on the team. Coach said I could run Friday morning instead."

"What club is it?" Chad asks as we stride over the AstroTurf in the center of the football field. The covered stadium seating looms hazily in the mist. These laps are supposed to be a cooldown, but Chad's still moving faster than me.

"The Environmental Justice Club," I pant. "It's not very big. Mr. Mendoza's the advisor. He's the science teacher with the mustache."

"I've never had him," Chad says. "I'm still stuck with Mrs. Goldman. I'll be lucky if I pass biology this year."

"Oh, I've got Mendoza for AP Bio."

Chad finally slows to a stop. "So you're a brainiac, then? That explains why I never see you around. Too smart for us, right?"

I shrug, copying his movements through the cross-country team's series of standing stretches.

"The captains always host a team party for homecoming. You should come."

"Ah. Great." Nothing makes standing around at a Lakewood High football game more fun than standing around at an awkward party beforehand. And I'm just rolling in free time.

"So you'll be there?"

"Yeah." I nod. I can't really say no. The guy literally woke up at the crack of dawn to run with me. "I'll be there."

Chad's watch beeps. "Fifteen-minute warning," he says. "My stuff's in my car. See you around, Middle D!" He takes off running—again.

I follow Chad out through the turnstile at a more leisurely pace. Even though keeping up with Chad may kill me, at least I'll get to school before anyone else.

I push open the doors to the athletic complex, the end of Lakewood High's campus with the basketball courts. It's the entrance nearest to the football field. Coach Kerry and the zero-hour weightlifting crew are still in the gym, so I shower and change in a nearly empty locker room, then take out my phone to look through the day ahead.

My calendar is a marvel. All deadlines, dates, and tasks are colorcoded into neat precision. My Advanced Placement classes, extracurriculars, practices, and meets. Planned study times. The first sitting of the PSAT in a few weeks. Every moment's been accounted for, and nothing's been overlooked. It's truly a thing of beauty. If I stick to schedule, everything should get done.

I fuckin' love school. I always have.

The first bell takes me back to the present, and I head for homeroom, down the long corridor that connects to the main atrium. I make it to B Hall well before the second bell.

"Sup, D?"

I turn to see Levi jogging toward me. He claps me on the back like we're besties outside of Ms. Patten's room. "Rumor is that the leader board's already up in Mr. Davis's class. Only three weeks in, and the competition is on."

The side of my face pulls up in a grin. "So how much do I have you beat by?"

"Oooh! As always, not lacking in confidence. Too bad you couldn't hold me off over the summer."

He makes it sound like we were training for the Olympics. Nope. When most kids turn sixteen, they get jobs. Our advanced degree–holding parents sent us to math camp. But hey, a competition is a competition, and unlike distance running, nobody beats me at this. I. Am. Number one.

"Who's at the top?" It's Marina.

I hold the door open for her, letting her pass through first. We're technically early, and we're still the last to arrive. The twenty-five kids starting the day in Ms. Patten's AP US History class are the same ones I'll spend most of my year with. We're the high-achiever crew, and the older we get, the more classes we have exclusively with each other. Junior year has us herding between college prep and honors classes in a pack.

"I haven't seen it yet, have I?" Levi answers her. "But my money's on Lucas—he always comes out ahead in Calculus, and that's the only test we've had so far."

Since freshman year, some teachers have made a show of ranking us for top of the class. I don't really understand why. This group's not exactly in need of extra incentives to overachieve at school. I've never questioned whether I'd go to college. I will go to *a lot* of college. It's what matters most to Mom and Dad. They only rarely make my track meets, but they're always at my parent-teacher conferences. Mom booked my PSAT slot herself.

"As long as we all know that I'll be taking the stage as valedictorian, I don't see why Lucas can't have this one," I say.

Levi scoffs and walks to his seat.

"Hey," I say to Marina.

Though I'm a foot taller than her, the oversize flannel shirt she's wearing looks big enough to fit me. Marina tilts her chin up so that I can see her face, her curtain of chin-length black hair and bangs falling back slightly.

"Morning." She smiles. She hands me a blue reusable lunch bag. It's the same one Mrs. Takahashi has filled for me since Marina and I met at age seven. In elementary school, we were the only kids of color in the gifted program. I'm glad that changed once we got to middle school. There are lots of us now. When we met, we were also the only two kids wearing glasses, which is what I remember. That, and that Marina liked the same anime I did. We've been friends ever since.

The snacks inside banish any embarrassment over the fact that at sixteen I'm still eating out of a kid's lunchbox. Mrs. Takahashi packed her homemade dorayaki, my favorite red bean pastry, and a couple of filled rice balls wrapped in nori. And some matcha KitKats. Score!

"Your mom is insane, and by that I mean the best!"

"She's something." Mrs. Takahashi can be a lot. I understand that what I think of as amazing, Marina finds suffocating. "The onigiri are pickled mustard greens and salted salmon today. Did you finish the essay for Lit?"

"Nope. I passed out last night before I could text you back. I'll finish at lunch today."

I take the seat next to her, surreptitiously unwrapping the dorayaki under my desk as Ms. Patten stands to start. We're on the evolving relationship between the Nisqually, Puyallup, Muckleshoot, Suquamish, and Cowlitz tribes prior to the Treaty of Medicine Creek. Ms. Patten never gets as far into her lecture as she means to, because we've all already done the reading and ask too many questions. She's still not through her PowerPoint presentation when the bell rings.

"By Monday, I want essays describing the continuity and change in the relationships between the tribes prior to the Puget Sound War in 1855. Please pay particular attention to changes in fishing rights and the influence of the American concept of Manifest Destiny and European concepts such as the tragedy of the commons."

The hall is filling with students, but no one in this room moves. Her last sentences are always the most important.

"They'll be key to understanding the conflict, which culminated in the US government's hanging of Chief Leschi in 1858."

Got it.

The herd moves on to Honors American Literature. Then I split off to Spanish III before lunch, most of which I spend in the library trying to crank out my Lit essay. It's not due until Monday, but I told Marina that I'd finish it so we could focus on the vocab for the PSAT this weekend. Even with the summer prep course, I'm nervous. Those scores mean everything. Well, the SAT scores do. But the PSAT is still an important test—a great result could mean a finalist position for the National Merit Scholarship. Even if you don't need the money, finalist status looks incredible on college applications.

I haven't decided exactly where I should go for undergrad.

Mom's pushing for Princeton, where she went to law school. Dad says I should go to UCLA so he can visit whenever the Lakers are playing. I used to be dead set on going to Harvard Law School someday. There's just so much you can do with a law degree. I don't want to be a criminal lawyer or a politician. But I've got this West Wing vision of myself advising people in the oval office, one of the guys with glasses and stacks of paper. Writing legislation. It's not a clear picture yet. Right now, all I know for certain is that I'll apply to at least ten schools for undergrad and get through that before worrying about law schools. Between my extracurriculars, college prep, and honors classes, I should have some good options.

"Big D!" Levi hollers when I cross the threshold of AP Calculus. He's pointing to the leader board.

I walk over to get a closer look at the piece of paper taped to the wall. I'm at the top—and by several percentage points, which makes sense. Math and science are my strongest subjects. Like Dad, I'm good at anything with numbers. My ability to memorize things is good, too, which makes history and Spanish easy enough. Honors American Literature, however, is a different story.

The day ends with AP Biology. I've had Mr. Mendoza for science since freshman year. He has posters of environmental justice heroes hanging on the walls in his lab. They were one of the reasons I started attending club meetings. This year, Robert Bullard grins over me from his place on the wall. As the bell rings, I catch myself reading the quote on his poster: WHEN YOU DON'T PROTECT THE LEAST IN YOUR SOCIETY, YOU PLACE EVERYBODY AT RISK.

My mind races through all of the work I've already got piling up, not to mention coordinating the mock COP—when am I going to finish my essay for Lit?

I really need to get faster at writing.

"Who's sticking around for the Environmental Justice Club?" Mr. Mendoza asks.

A few people give halfhearted waves. I stretch my hands over my head, then stand to help Marina arrange some lab stools into a loose circle at the front. Levi calls Mr. Mendoza over to ask him questions about the weekend's homework assignment, which he clearly doesn't understand.

"We should have carpooled today," Marina tells me. "I forgot you don't go to cross-country practice on Fridays."

"You wouldn't want to come in that early. I met Chad at like six thirty this morning."

"Hey, Marina," Collin Hwang interrupts. "What'd you get on the second question?"

Collin definitely has a thing for Marina. He's been coming to the Environmental Justice Club meetings for a while, but whenever I ask him what he wants to focus on, he doesn't seem to know. Marina, apparently.

"I got that the heat-shock protein translated from mRNA I plays a greater role in refolding proteins than does the protein translated from mRNA II." We spent the lesson learning how a gradual increase in the water temperature of a krill's habitat may ultimately affect its ability to survive. "I'm pretty sure that's right," Marina says.

"Right, 'cause the concentration of mRNA I rose most in the krill exposed to the warmest water. Brilliant." Collin smiles. "Hey, do you want to study together this weekend?"

I cover the laugh that escapes me with a cough. Marina is *not* going to like that.

"Umm," I hear her flounder. "Darius and I usually study at Gravity on Saturday afternoon."

"Oh, that's near my place." He's determined. "What time?" Collin says loud enough for me to hear.

"I actually can't make Saturday. I've got a cross-country meet."

Marina narrows her eyes in my direction. I turn my attention back to arranging stools, trying not to laugh.

"Just you and me, then." I can practically hear Collin beaming. "Three o'clock work for you, Marina? I can do later, if that's better."

"'Sup, Darius?" Jake interrupts my eavesdropping. "Think we're gonna need more stools."

I'm surprised. Several people I don't recognize are following him in with Sophia and her friend Lily. When Tyler, José, and Julián join, they're with several more people I don't know.

"You're going to have a bigger club to lead than I did," Jake tells me. He's right. There are like twenty people in here, and another clump of students coming in. I can handle it, but still.

Jake starts writing up an agenda on the whiteboard. I walk over to where Mr. Mendoza's gesturing over Levi's notepad.

"You can take my stool, Darius," Mr. Mendoza says. "But I think Levi's going to need his a little bit longer." Levi looks comically lost. "If you want to try number two again, I'll check it after you're done."

Back at the front, I get the sign-in sheet out and send it around while we wait for everyone to claim a seat. Eventually, Jake calls us to order.

"Alright, everyone, I thought we could start by debriefing movie night. Then we can move on to planning out this year, and Darius, maybe you'll want to do that?"

I give Jake a thumbs-up. I've already noted the points I thought we should cover in the notebook I'm holding, ready and waiting.

"Great. So, movie night," Jake says. "For those of you who couldn't make it, we showed *The Future of Energy: Lateral Power to the People* in the auditorium on Wednesday. I thought it went well." He shrugs. "There weren't many questions at the end, though, so I felt a bit bad that Professor Clark from the community college came all the way out. What did you guys think?"

There's a beat of silence. I'm so looking forward to doing more than educational stuff under my presidency. A girl with turquoise streaks in her hair raises her hand. I noticed her at the club's first meeting. Girls that pretty are hard not to notice.

Jake points at her. "Ah, yes. Sorry. I don't know your name."

"Oh. I'm Isa. Hi, everyone." She waves.

"Hi, Isa," Jake says back like he's at an AA meeting.

Isa laughs. "I enjoyed the film, and I learned a lot about renewable energy. But, to be honest, there weren't many people there."

She's not wrong. Isa and her friends made up most of the crowd. It's hardly worth putting on a movie night for seven people.

"No offense or anything, but I think maybe the club should focus on getting some more members? Nobody seems to know about it or what it does, or that there's a space where we can talk about what we're concerned about."

Her shoulders and her tone go up while she talks, so I'm not sure if she's asking a question or making a statement.

"Like, I know Harper's really stressed about the red tide. And lots of us started coming to the club because of the wildfires. I think it'd be really great to have a school-wide conversation about all the things that are important to us, so we can talk about what we can do about them."

A blond girl next to her whoops, and Isa laughs in her direction.

"I think that's a really great idea," Jake says.

What?

"It'd be good to get some new members in and have a bit of a conversation. What were you thinking, like using the next meeting?" he asks her.

"Well, I think getting more people to know about the club is what we should do first," Isa answers. "Maybe we could do some canvassing at the homecoming dance?"

The dance? Congrats on the world's worst idea. What is with people and liking homecoming?!

"And the club seriously needs some social media presence," the blond girl says.

"That too, especially in the run-up," Isa adds. "Oh, and that would be a great way for people to write in if they can't make the conversation. Anyway, everyone will be at homecoming, so it'd be good to make a splash. Plaster some flyers around, talk to people and invite them to come."

"Yeah." Harper nods, jumping in. "And can we meet some time other than Friday afternoons? It's only hard-core nerds who stay at school during the weekend."

"Preach!" Collin yells. Really? Even Collin?

What is happening?

"That's a good idea," Isa says. "I just think so many of us care about the environment and the climate, but it all seems so big. So complicated. If we could just talk about things that are bothering us, we could focus, you know? Bring people in and work together. It'd be so much more real, and we'd be more empowered to do something about it." The longer she speaks, the quicker her words tumble out.

"Like for me, I know the city wants to build a natural gas pipeline at the port. That makes no sense. We couldn't even go outside this summer, and they're building another pipeline? I mean, I don't want that to happen—but what can I do? My guess, though, is that lots of us don't want that to happen?"

She looks around. Several people nod. From the back of the room, Levi starts clapping.

How is he still even here?

"So anyway, I think movie nights are great, but what I'd really like to do is get everyone talking. That's all."

Isa sits back down, and I can't help blinking in her direction.

"That sounds amazing," Jake says, his voice saturated with sincerity. "I'm totally down. What does everybody else think?"

A few others clap, and people start talking over each other: throwing out ideas for how to bring others in; different times the club could meet; things they're worried about. And everyone's looking at this Isa girl. Not at Jake, who doesn't even seem to mind. He's just as engaged in this chaos as everybody else.

I put my hand up and clear my throat. "Oh, ah . . . Darius?" Jake says loudly enough to register over the babble. "I guess we are getting a bit ahead of ourselves."

"Yeah." I try to keep the irritation out of my voice and wait for the remaining chatter to die down. "I mean, it's a good idea and everything. But we already have a plan for this year. We're going to work with the Pacific Northwest conference of the model United Nations and host a mock COP—a UN climate summit."

No one responds. If there were crickets in the room, I would have heard them. I look at Sophia and Marina, but they don't say anything.

I realize I'm killing the mood and that I should say something nice, even if I don't really mean it. "I guess it's a good idea to get more people interested in the club. But we do already have a plan for what to do this year."

"Right, um," Jake says. "Well, I suppose it's up to the club?" He seems unsure about how to handle this turn of events.

Mr. Mendoza steps in. "Really great conversation starter, Isa. And you're right, Jake. It looks like we have two bids for president this year."

That's not how to handle it! *Two* bids?

Isa's hand goes up. "I wasn't suggesting I be president," she says quickly. "I just think opening up the conversation is a good idea. A good first step. If people want to do the mock COB, then great! If they want to do something else, then the club can do that. As long as we're bringing in more people and choosing something we all care about. I just think that's most important."

I struggle not to roll my eyes. It sounds like someone's not willing to do the actual work. And does she not know that every year the UN climate negotiations, the real ones, convene a Conference of the Parties? I'm pretty set on the *COP*—no matter how pretty Isa is.

"Okay, well, why don't you and Darius talk about it and see if we have two bids or one," Mr. Mendoza says. "First, though, it seems like raising awareness about the club is something everyone's interested in. Jake, why don't you take that forward, and we'll hold an election—if necessary—before the next meeting."

"Perfect!" Jake says. "Any volunteers for doing some club canvassing? Maybe get a social media presence going?"

Nearly everyone's hand goes up. Marina looks like she's the only one as surprised by what just happened as I am. People start gathering up their things and making their way over to Jake.

"Darius? Isa?" Mr. Mendoza says over the noise. He waves us toward him, and we assemble close enough to hear.

"Perhaps you two want to discuss how to take things forward? See if your ideas are complementary or if you have separate visions? Of course, you don't have to run against each other if you don't want to. Collaboration is always welcome!"

Another bell rings, the one that marks the end of extracurricular hour, after which you have to be accompanied by a teacher to remain in the building. Mr. Mendoza turns to everyone still in the room.

"We need to clear out, folks. Enjoy your weekends!" To Isa and me, he continues, "Just let me know if we'll need to hold an election before the next meeting. Either way, these are some great initiatives for the club to be working on."

Marina's hovering, waiting for me and pointedly ignoring Collin, who is waiting for her. I wave a goodbye in resignation, then gather up the rest of my things so I can leave with the new girl. We're the last ones out the door.

"So, hi," Isa says. "We haven't really met yet."

"Hey." I nod.

"Um, want to grab coffee? I know Kat and some of the others are heading to Starbucks?"

"This shouldn't take that long."

"Oh, okay," she says. "Walk you to the parking lot, then?"

My forehead crinkles in confusion. Where else would we be going? I match her pace, and we walk together through the empty building while I try to think of the best way to start this conversation.

She starts talking before I do. "I don't think we've ever been in class together before. Have you lived here long?"

Another weird question. "I've lived here all my life." Let's get this back on topic. "This is your first year in the club." I mean to ask this, but it's a statement, really. I know it is.

"Right," Isa says. "I only heard about it the day of the first meeting. It does seem really cool, though, and I'd like to be involved. I didn't mean to step on your toes or anything. Just throwing ideas out there."

I knew she wasn't serious about this. "Yeah. I've been working on the model UN thing for a while now, and I don't want to give that up. It's taken a lot of effort to make those connections happen. If I'm honest, I'm not really open to other ideas."

"Oh . . . okay." She pauses, and we walk in silence for a few steps.

"I don't know anything about the model UN or what a climate summit would look like. Can you tell me what we'd actually be doing, if we did that? How it would, you know, help?"

If we did that? She's been here all of five minutes and it's suddenly her decision? I sigh. This isn't how I want to spend my Friday afternoon. "Um, that'll take a while, and I'd really like to get going."

"So . . . you don't want to work together?"

We're outside the front doors, facing each other under the awning rather than continuing out into the rain. Her turquoise streaks frame her face as she smiles uncertainly. She doesn't seem to be getting this.

"Look, I've been in the club for years, and I've been planning this all summer. I don't want to discourage you from coming, I just think there's way more momentum behind my idea than yours. If you want to focus on getting more people to join the club, go ahead. But, like I said, I'm pretty set on the mock COP—which, by the way, stands for Conference of the Parties to the UN Framework Convention on Climate Change."

Her eyebrows inch up as I speak, and when I end, she keeps them raised. The dimple in her left cheek has disappeared. That might have been too direct. I take a deep breath.

"You seem nice and everything, and I don't mean to be rude. I just don't have time for this." That probably could have been phrased better, but it's the truth.

"Okay, then," she says.

"Right." At least that's done. She's cute and she does seem nice, I just doubt she'll be back. "Maybe I'll see you around."

I turn and jog through the rain to my car, a Volvo 'cause my parents are obsessed with safety. Inside, I throw my stuff in the back and use my sweatshirt sleeve to wipe condensation from the windshield while the vents get going. My phone's attached to the auxiliary cable and the volume's up before I'm out of the spot. The only thing left to do today is pick up Jordan. Then I'm going to crash so hard.

The rain has picked up by the time I reach my tree-lined neighborhood, whose roads curve as they wind around the lake nearest Lakewood High. Instead of turning right onto my street, I turn left onto the street after and pull into the Takahashis' driveway, getting as close to the front door as possible. While the familiar doorbell sounds, I bend over and start untying my shoes.

Marina's the one to answer. She puts her hands on her hips, which would look more threatening if she weren't so tiny and didn't have to stop to roll the sleeves of her giant shirt up. She stands over me while I slip my shoes into their designated spot. "Way to leave me with Collin earlier. I can't believe you did that!"

I laugh. I'd forgotten about that. The thing with Isa pushed it out of my mind.

"Marina, what did you get for the second question?" I try to imitate Collin's voice crack, wishing I could time it better, but I'm laughing too hard.

"Stop it!" Marina says. "I'm going to reschedule for Sunday. There's no way I'm studying with Collin alone."

"If you can't bring yourself to say no, he'll get you alone eventually." Marina never says no to anyone.

"Who'll get Marina alone?" Mrs. Takahashi asks from around the corner.

"No one," Marina mumbles.

"Collin Hwang, a guy in our class," I say loud enough for her to hear. We head toward the kitchen, where Mrs. Takahashi's voice is coming from. She's wearing a frilly apron, not a hair out of place even though she's surrounded by boiling pans.

"Oh! He's the one who likes you, right? You should give him a chance, Marina. I haven't dressed anyone up in ages!"

"Yes, you have," Marina retorts. "You helped me with my Totoro costume for Sakura Con."

I laugh. Mrs. Takahashi definitely didn't mean that and Marina knows it. I can't remember the last time I saw Marina in a dress.

"Seeing my daughter as a giant bear who carries an umbrella is not what I had in mind," Mrs. Takahashi says.

"Totoro is a forest sprite, not a bear," Marina huffs. "You never listen to me."

Mrs. Takahashi plows on with "Just one date, Marina! You could finally wear that skirt I picked out."

"Oh please, Mom," she groans. "I'm not Akira! That's never going to happen."

Marina's stunning older sister left for UW over a year ago. Guys were forever asking Akira out and stopping by to pick her up. Mrs. Takahashi lived for doing Akira's waist-length hair and choosing her clothes. She cried when Marina chopped her hair off this summer.

"You could really like him."

"Nope," Marina says. Then she locks eyes with me and laughs at her bad joke. Being able to tell her mom no wasn't what I meant, either. Part of me wonders why Marina doesn't say yes to Collin. He's good-looking, and he's clearly interested. Maybe she doesn't date just to annoy her mom.

"And what about you, Darius? Anyone caught your eye this year?" Mrs. Takahashi asks.

"Yeah, Darius?" Marina piles on, hands on her hips again.

Crap. I shrug, feeling awkward. It's not like I haven't liked people before. It just never seems to go anywhere. If I'm honest, my first massive crush was Akira. From age twelve to fourteen, I worshipped her. Followed by Jade, a girl on the cross-country team who moved away freshman year. I never worked up the nerve to talk to her about anything other than what she got on our language arts test, though. Asking someone out seems like the most cringe thing ever.

They're both still looking at me expectantly. All I can think to say is "Haven't noticed anyone."

Marina rolls her eyes. Mrs. Takahashi lets out a frustrated sounding sigh. She's shaking her head at both of us.

I hear a muffled shout from the basement. That must be where everyone is. It's raining hard enough that even the boys aren't out playing basketball in the back.

"Is Jordan downstairs?"

Mrs. Takahashi nods. "Are you guys staying for dinner?"

"No, thanks," I answer. "We're supposed to be having dinner at our house tonight."

"That's good. A celebration dinner? I saw your mom won her case." My mom's a trial lawyer, one of the most media friendly in the area. People usually know more about her work than I do. Especially adults who watch cable news during the day.

"Er, yeah. I think we're getting takeout." I don't actually know. Friday night dinners together are a new Dad idea.

I follow Marina to the stairs that lead down to their finished basement, my socks squishing into the thick salmon-colored carpet. "How'd the chat with the new girl go?" she asks.

"Fine. I don't think it'll be a problem. She said she's just throwing ideas around."

"Really? People seem to like what she has to say, and she had a bunch of people with her."

"Yeah, a bunch of people who've never been before and who aren't going to stick around for meetings on Friday afternoons. We'll see who's really committed when it comes to doing the work." Which reminds me: "Are you still free to meet the Model UN officers next week? They emailed me the place today."

"Yup. It's at six fifty, right?"

"Yeah, gives us an hour before school. I'll send the details around to everyone." We've reached the rec room at the back, where two old sofas are pushed recklessly close to a large flat-screen TV. And there, transfixed by the game it's projecting, is my younger brother.

"Hey, Jordan, you ready? We're leaving in five."

"What? We just leveled up!" he says at the same time that Marina's brother, Ken, shouts, "Play us!" Marina's cousin Yuto is over, too, and not one of the three has turned from the screen.

"Come on, Jordan. You know Dad said we're having dinner at ours tonight."

"So?" he answers. "They won't be home for *forever*."

Then, before I can open my mouth, the three of them shout, "Ten more minutes!" in unison. It's a trick they've perfected over the years.

Jordan, Ken, and Yuto are all fourteen and have been virtually inseparable since kindergarten. That's when Mom insisted that if I was going to be spending all my afternoons at the Takahashis', then Jordan would be, too. While Marina and I—the nerdiest of our families—were content with studying, Jordan, Ken, and Yuto played ball. Sometimes, they'd manage to pressure us into kickball or baseball games. They could even get Akira and Haruto, Yuto's older brother, to play, too . . . before they became too cool for us.

When it pours like this, though, it's video games. Hours and hours of video games.

Marina folds herself down onto the floor. And I give up the idea of leaving anytime soon. "I don't want to play *Halo*," she says. "Dance off?"

"No!" Ken scoffs. A wise move. Though we've all tried, Marina's unshakable reign as *Dance, Dance, Revolution* queen continues unabated. "*MarioKart*?"

"Or *Smash*?" Jordan asks.

"No, let's rock!" Yuto's impassioned expression makes me laugh. Fierce competition led Marina's parents to invest in several group games, including *Guitar Hero* and *Rock Band*, that are meant to get us to work together, not apart. It's hilarious that—in a room where no one plays a musical instrument—we now take fake performing so seriously.

Guitar controllers, drum pads, and karaoke mics appear out of the set of IKEA bins that line the room. Jordan and I push the sofas back, and Yuto loads our warm-up set. Marina and Ken grab mics, and soon we're all singing and performing with a ridiculous intensity. Some of my best moments have been spent in this rec room, acting completely silly.

As the tracks get harder, my fingers race against the guitar controller. Jordan belts out lyrics next to me. I'm only vaguely aware of time passing until Mrs. Takahashi materializes in front of the screen. She can sometimes be persuaded to sing with us, but apparently not tonight. And when she says time's up, she means it.

"Dinner," she announces, and that ends it. The controllers drop, and we all troop out of the basement together. My stomach growls at the smell of the food waiting on their table. Too bad we're not eating here tonight.

"Bye, Darius. Bye, Jordan." Mrs. Takahashi waves. "Tell your mom well done!"

Jordan and I retrieve our shoes in the entrance way.

"I'll message you about Sunday," Marina tells me. "About studying with Collin."

I laugh. I'm fairly certain she can handle studying with Collin alone, but if they're doing PSAT vocab, working together could be helpful. We'll see how the weekend goes. Jordan pulls the door open, so I click the button on my keys to unlock the Volvo.

It takes all of two minutes to drive to our house. Both garage doors are closed when we pull up, and all the lights are off.

"They aren't back yet," Jordan pouts. "Did Dad text?"

He's been all mopey about Mom and Dad lately. I don't know what he expects. They both have jobs, and we're not little kids anymore. "He said to be home for dinner. They're probably just running late."

"Or not coming," Jordan mutters. "We should have stayed at the Takahashis'."

He slams his door and heads straight into the house. I'm too tired to yell at him about it. This car will be his when I graduate, anyway.

Just as the closing garage door reaches its final rung, it pulls up again, and Dad's headlights slide in through the rain.

Dad gets out and stretches his arms up. "Hi, guys! Just getting in?" He takes his glasses off and rubs his face, scratching the graying hair on his chin. Sometimes I catch myself doing the exact same thing when I'm tired. The rubbing my face part. I don't have hair on my chin.

"Yeah, just pulled up. Mom's not here yet."

"She messaged and said she'll probably be late. They're all out celebrating the win. They didn't expect the jury to come back so quickly. But don't worry." He turns toward the door into the house, which Jordan left open, and raises his voice. "I picked up ribs."

"From J's?" Jordan's voice echoes from inside. I can hear him moving at top speed.

Dad winks at me. He reaches into the back seat and grabs two clean white bags. Jordan's through the door. Dad holds them over his head, acting like he won't let us have them. He's been doing that since we were kids, but it doesn't really work anymore—I'm taller than him. And even though Jordan's only fourteen, he's making steady gains on Dad's six-foot height. So now, instead of letting him jump for it, Dad pivots to sling his arm, bags and all, around Jordan's shoulders, which has them both laughing as they fight for control of dinner.

By the time I make it inside, they've got the Lakers game on, and they've settled onto the media room sofas, ribs in hand. Mom would never let us do this, but she's not here. The sofa curls around me, urging me to finally relax—no thoughts about mock COPs, PSATs, or valedictorian speeches, and definitely not about infuriating, pretty girls with turquoise streaks in their hair.

CHAPTER 4
FALSE START

Darius

"WHAT IF WE COULD REALLY DO THIS, DESIGN INTERNATIONAL policy?" Ava says, excited. She has to raise her voice over the noise of the old espresso machine behind us. Even though the Model UN crew got to Gravity before 7:00 a.m., the tables by the counter were the last standing. The local bookstore–coffee shop combo is a town favorite.

"What if we could write what the world did about climate change?" The rickety machine lets out a blast of steam that has her reaching up to hold her hijab in place. Ava goes on undeterred. "How cool would that be?!"

I sip my latte, leaning forward. "It'd be freaking awesome. A justice-centered treaty!"

"Totally achievable. Not a lot of work at all," Charlotte scoffs. She's the one tasked with organizing conferences and always adds a depressing note of realism.

"Come on," Danielle tells her. "Imagine we could take down the man fueling the climate crisis. Write a compliance mechanism that's empowered to hold governments and corporations to account. Put people above profit. Save the world. It'd be wicked!"

This is why I like the Model UN crew—this group of volunteer college students who run the whole region's conferences—so much. Why meeting at the crack of dawn in a busy coffee shop across town is worth it. I've never talked to people who get as excited about the potential of good legislation as I do. Because figuring out how to stop the climate crisis isn't the problem; figuring out how to get powerful people to *do* it is. And coordinating the change we need in time will take policy. Big policy.

Geeks we may be. But our vision is amazing.

"Come on, let's focus on action points," Charlotte says. "What do we need to get done? Danielle and Ava, you're on researching the position papers. Owen, you're starting some draft text based on our research into UNFCCC decisions. And Darius and Marina, you'll get confirmation this week that the Lakewood High club is interested in helping organize this, right?"

"Yup," I say. "Our club meets on Friday afternoon, so we'll get the final go-ahead then." Next to me, Marina looks up from her MacBook to nod.

We end with a round of soy matcha lattes, which has me buzzing as I follow Marina's car through the rain toward Lakewood High. Now that the meeting is over, the PSAT resumes its domination of my thinking. Just today and tomorrow left to cram. The test is on Saturday morning. Coach Kerry isn't pleased that I'll miss a meet, but cross-country's a hobby; that test is the first step toward the future. Wherever that is.

I pull into the school's parking lot, surprised that there's still some time to kill before the warning bell. I check my calendar, task list, and email. The latest is a reminder from Mr. Mendoza to cast any final ballots for Environmental Justice Club president before tomorrow's meeting. I star the email and make it a task. Annoyance at having another thing to do has me out of the car. I flip up the hood of my sweatshirt and jam my hands into my pockets as I march toward the entrance.

I still can't believe he's holding an election.

The first I heard about it was an email on the Monday after talking with Isa. When I asked Mr. Mendoza for an explanation in AP Biology, he seemed surprised by my surprise.

"I thought you two talked about it? Right? Go ahead and send me a paragraph about yourself and your priorities, and I'll email a ballot out to registered club members. It won't take long."

Now the club suddenly has a fancy new web page that includes a message board and members tally. Social media pages materialized, too. Every time I check the new pages, the number of members increases. But what good are followers if nobody shows up to things? I'm sure I've got the election. Mr. Mendoza's emails make it very clear that only people who've attended an Environmental Justice Club meeting can vote.

At least the club's new online presence will be a good way of letting people know about my plans this year.

Guess I should remind the AP crew who haven't voted yet to get on it.

Inside Ms. Patten's room, I see I'm not the only one who's made it before the warning bell. Tyler, who's got fresh cornrows, looks up from his laptop and waves at me. Hai and Abigail are there, too.

"Hey, Darius," Abigail says. "Why are you early? I bet you're not freaking out about the PSAT. You've always got your shit together."

From my seat behind her, I can see the practice test she's got open. "I've still got studying to do. I can't crack 1400 on the practice exam."

"1400! I'd kill for that," Hai says. "Well, actually, my mom would."

Abigail slumps down in her chair. "As long as I qualify for the National Merit Scholarship, I'll just be happy to have it finished."

"Right, so you can move on to the SAT in six months," Tyler chips in.

"GAHHH!" Abigail groans. I don't want to think about that either.

"Hey, have you guys voted for Environmental Justice Club president yet?" I ask them. "I haven't seen you at a club meeting this year, but you all used to come, right?"

"Yeah, too much to do this year. But I got the ballot," Tyler says.

"Me too," Hai nods. "I didn't know there'd be an election. Who's Isa? She's not in any of our classes."

"Yeah, she's new to the club. Can you vote for me? I really want to lead this year." Not the most elegant campaign pitch, but they all say that they will. Everyone I ask in the AP crew does. Over the past two years, Mr. Mendoza's gotten most of us to attend at least one meeting. Marina and the others who've been coming for ages should have my back, too.

By the time I'm moving the lab stools into a circle on Friday afternoon, I feel nothing but confident. I wonder if I should have invited Charlotte and Ava from the Model UN to this meeting so we can get things started. I'm scribbling a list of actions in my notebook when Mr. Mendoza calls us to order.

"Thought we'd kick things off with the election results. Drumroll, please!" He waits for everyone to slap their hands against their knees and build to a crescendo. There are more people here than there were at the last meeting. More than I've ever seen.

Isa's sitting across from me in the circle, trying her best to hold a poker face. The turquoise streaks that were in her hair are now lavender. It's a shame she's about to be sorely disappointed. I almost feel bad.

"In a shocking turn of events, the election is a tie!" Mr. Mendoza announces.

What?!

"Exactly fifteen ballots were cast for Isa, and fifteen were cast for Darius," he reports. "That's the most interest we've had in this club over its entire history. Very well done, everyone!"

A few people clap. I've stopped breathing.

What does that mean?

"Now, I know this is unprecedented, but I'm going to propose that—given the amount of interest—we proceed with two co-presidents this year rather than having a president and a secretary."

It takes me a second to process. Mr. Mendoza wants us to lead *together*?! He cannot be serious.

"So, many congratulations to Darius and Isa, the new co-presidents of the Environmental Justice Club!"

CHAPTER 5
ALL IN

Isa

WHAT? *WE TIED?!* A STARTLED LAUGH ESCAPES ME, AND I HEAR Kat curse under her breath. Thankfully, the clapping that's echoing off the lab surfaces covers the sound of both. I blink at Mr. Mendoza, who's looking at Darius and me with nothing but enthusiasm. I suddenly realize he's waiting for us to say something.

Darius looks like he's been stung by a bee. At least I'm not dealing with his smug, condescending little smirk.

I don't have much of a better handle on myself, but I catch Susie's eye and remember that she voted for me. Half of the people in this room did. And it worked. I'm president—kind of.

I stand up, and the people left clapping stop. "Ah, wow. I wasn't expecting that," I say. "Thanks, everyone, for your votes. They really mean a lot to me."

Darius still looks like he's recovering. Will he even agree to this? He made it very clear that he doesn't want to work with me. My mind goes blank, and I can't think of anything else to add.

"Let's get you both sworn in." Mr. Mendoza waves us forward and hands me a piece of laminated paper. It's bordered in the same red, orange, and green color scheme as the posters with the heading ENVIRONMENTAL JUSTICE HERO hanging around the room. Darius stands up next to me. Does he want to hold it, too?

"Read on." Mr. Mendoza smiles, like this is the most natural thing in the world. Darius starts reading aloud the bold text on the sheet I'm holding, and I scramble to keep up.

> *As president, I recognize that environmental justice is the fair treatment and meaningful involvement of all people in the development, implementation, and enforcement of environmental laws, regulations, and policies. All people means all people regardless of race, color, national origin, or income. Environmental justice will be achieved when everyone enjoys the same degree of protection from environmental and health hazards and equal access to decision-making processes to have a healthy environment in which to live, learn, and work. I will lead the club's efforts, recognizing the legacy of nonviolent civil disobedience toward these goals.*

What a mouthful. I'm tempted to ask Mr. Mendoza if I can hang on to this, so I can reread it and think through what I just said. But he takes it from me when we finish.

"Congrats again, Isa and Darius," Mr. Mendoza says. "I know I'm certainly looking forward to seeing what we can all do together this year. And a round of applause for our outgoing president and secretary! Any other business you want to tackle during this meeting?"

Once we finish clapping for them, Jake says they want to talk about the new web page. The club hasn't quite finished all the updates or added the last of the proposed features. Mr. Mendoza gets it projected, and Sophia mans the keyboard while we click through the list of tasks. I'm too lost wondering how I'm going to lead *with* Darius to really pay attention. The dude might be smart—and cute, as much as I hate admitting it now—but he is *such* a jerk. A jerk who's made it clear he doesn't want to collaborate. Or treat me with basic respect.

"Enjoy your weekends, everyone!" Mr. Mendoza says after the bell rings.

That was fast. I look across the room at Darius. He hasn't said a word since we were sworn in. I know we'll need to talk about how this is going to work, but the sour expression on his face has me guessing that now's not the best moment.

I put my stool back under a lab bench and gather up my stuff. Club members start drifting out of the room. Susie and her boyfriend, Josh, walk over to where I'm standing. They're all smiles, high-fiving me and offering congratulations.

"Kind of the best outcome, don't you think?" I'm astonished to overhear Jake say. "That way they can both lead." He gives me two thumbs-up on his way out the door. My answering smile feels entirely fake.

"Oh yeah, it's brilliant." Kat rolls her eyes.

We head out. In my last glance around the lab, I see Darius speaking to Mr. Mendoza at the front of the room. The East Asian girl he's always with is there, too, arms folded over her chest. I'm positive that I don't want to hear what they're saying, and I abandon all thoughts of talking to Darius today.

Instead, I walk into the empty hallway with the others. I can hear Jake yelling, "Friday!" ahead of us. Josh laughs, cups his hands around his mouth, and hollers, "Weekend!" down the hall after him.

I grin, feeling more buoyant.

"Let's go get bubble tea at that place by the mall," Susie says. "We should celebrate!"

Kat's brother Isaac flips Julián's hat off his head, and they chase each other toward the atrium. Tyler hears them coming and sprints ahead, shouting, "I'll drive!"

"You guys can ride with me," Susie says to Kat and me. "Maybe we can hit the mall after."

"Can you believe that guy?" Kat asks. The annoyance on her face looks ready to give way to a full-blown vent, but before we can answer she suddenly stops and spins, patting herself anxiously.

"Have you seen my LHS sweatshirt? Mom'll kill me if I lose another one." Kat's lips go all thin, like they do when she's stressed out. Money's an even bigger deal for her than it is for me.

"You can borrow my jacket," I offer. My favorite patchwork of denim is folded between the arms crossed over my chest. If Kat needs it, she can wear it.

"No, thanks. That jacket's all you."

Well, technically the jacket belongs to Mom. Or at least it did. In one of our moves, I fell asleep under her jean jacket in the back seat of our car. Afterward, I carried it around like a security blanket. Mom started patching it with mementos when it caught and tore— collecting tokens of every move we made. When I was ten, Grandma sent a Bedazzler for Christmas, so it's now emblazoned with studs and rhinestones, too. It's so much, and I love it.

"I swear I had it today." Kat's still worrying. "I had my sweatshirt when we got to club, right?"

"Just go back and check," I tell her. "We'll meet you in the park-ing lot."

Once Kat heads back to the lab, Susie tries to pick up the conver-sation pre–sweatshirt loss. "Did she mean that guy, Darius?"

"Yeah," I mutter. "He seems less than thrilled to be working with me."

"I'm sure you guys will figure something out," she says, unfazed. She slings her arm around my shoulders and squeezes. "I'm so happy you won! I've never been in a club before, and now I know the president!"

"One of them." I laugh. But her enthusiasm is catching.

I've never really been part of an actual LHS club, either. I've certainly never led one. I'm glad that Kat talked me into this. Glad that Susie and everyone else came with me. And excited to have a group of people to work with. I catch myself beaming, despite the unexpected outcome.

When we get to the parking lot, Susie's brother shouts, "Isa for president!" out the window of Tyler's car as they drive off. I laugh, and the rest of us load into Susie's car, saving the last seat for Kat, who—sweatshirt in hand—jogs over to catch up.

Susie's got the radio up, and we all start singing along as loud as we can. I can't stop smiling. It's the weekend. I'm with my friends, and we did it.

Sort of.

"'Oh, the overwhelming, never-ending, reckless love of God! Oh, it chases me down, fights till I'm found, leaves the ninety-nine . . .'" I sing.

Outstretched hands extend skyward, filling the church with fives as the congregation sways in time. I'm hot under the nylon of my purple choir robe. Next to me, Gladys's arm touches mine as she lifts her hands up. I smile. She can never help herself.

"'And I couldn't earn it, and I don't deserve it, still You give Yourself away. Oh, the overwhelming, never-ending reckless love of God!'"

We sing the last bars, finishing off the worship part of service. The pianist plays softly on to cover the choir's descent offstage. While I wait my turn, I spot Grandma in the front row. She's still standing. Mom's tugging on her, trying to get her to sit down. Grandma catches my eye and waves so hard her upper arm shakes.

I don't know who wishes she was up here with me more—me or her.

The choir line winds its way to our dedicated pews on the side of the stage, and I take my seat, settling in for Pastor Scott's sermon. I watch the Sunday morning sun seep through the skylights and look for Kat among the crowd. Her grandma's easy to spot. The hat she has on today is blue, but I can't find Kat, her mom, or either of her brothers sitting in the pew with her.

Uh-oh.

Pastor Scott starts preaching. Today, it's the gospel according to Matthew. I go back to looking for Kat. It takes me several minutes to search carefully through each pew, including the seats at the side and the handful of people up in the balcony. Nope. No sign. I glance over at Kat's grandma again. She checks her watch and turns to face the door, expectantly. They're late, and the sermon's well underway now. Her face pinches, and even though she's not my grandma, her disapproval makes me squirmy.

I really do try to like Kat's grandma. She's kind of the reason Kat and I met.

I can't believe that was three years ago. In a classroom of the long double-storied recreation building just across the parking lot, where neither of us was paying attention. Both of our grandmothers have called this church home for a long time, so before I'd even started school in Lakewood, I found myself in a summer confirmation class. Doodling.

He needs claws, someone said, over my shoulder.

I couldn't get the parrot I was drawing to look right, no matter how many feathers I added. From the row behind me, Kat saw what I couldn't. That the poor, unbalanced bird had no feet.

We spent the rest of the lesson passing her back and forth, adding the Amazonian jungle that became her home. The things Kat's pencil brought to life seemed almost magical.

My favorite thing to do is paint, she told me after.

The walls of her childhood bedroom were painted so often that Kat's parents had given up disciplining her for it. Back when they lived together. She isn't allowed to do that at her grandma's, though. I never had to ask why she was staying there; the sadness in her voice said enough. It took her parents forever to finalize their divorce. Kat's mom is even younger than mine, and splitting up meant moving in with Grandma. And all of her rules.

I'm not sure exactly what the deal is, but I know Kat's grandma still helps them with money. Grandma was the one who got them into the town house last summer and is paying for Kat's mom to get the degree she studies for at night. Grandma is the one who says, loudly and often, that Ms. Nelson can't raise three kids working part-time at a grocery store. That she never should have married Kat's dad in the first place. Grandma's unhappiness has serious consequences, and Kat doesn't say much whenever she's around.

But, at twelve, I also learned that Kat's whole face changes when she has a paintbrush in her hand. Engrossed in her creation, she smiles without thinking about it. And the bigger the canvas, the greater her joy. That summer, after we ran out of space and other things to do, we convinced my grandma, who convinced Pastor Scott, to let us paint one of the rec building's classrooms.

He liked it so much that he let us take on an even bigger surface.

The east side of the church's recreation building is directly above Interstate 5. Only a few feet of lawn separate its siding from a low mound of blackberry bushes that disguise the fifty-foot drop to the freeway. Over the years, Kat and I have turned this patch of grass into a shared escape. Our conversations muffled by the noise of the unseen cars passing below. The murals we create on the building's side are proudly displayed to everyone driving south on the interstate.

This is what I assume Kat is working on whenever I can't find her. And, just a few minutes before Pastor Scott ends, when the back doors swing and Ms. Nelson—who looks like a brunette version of Kat—slips into the sanctuary, it's not hard to guess where she is.

I sing out our last hymn and am grateful the choir gets to exit first so I can slip my robe off and sneak out the side, avoiding everyone milling around over cookies and coffee. From the main chapel, I dash across the parking lot to the rec building.

I head for the utility room in the basement, where I can hear a surprising amount of noise. Kat's there going through the paint at the back. She's flinging stuff around with more force than necessary.

"Hey." My smile slowly fades as I process her mood. "What's up?"

"We were super late—again. Grandma's gonna pitch a fit. But we couldn't help that we were up all night. Dad just came by the house yesterday."

"What?!"

"I know. I have literally no idea. Mom hasn't said anything about them being in touch, and Liam was the one who opened the door."

"Oh no." Kat's oldest brother has the least love for their dad.

"Yeah, so they got into a massive fight. He and Dad were scream-ing at each other in the street. Mom tried to break it up, and Liam ran off. The whole thing's a fucking mess!" She stops flinging paint and marches out into the hall.

Most of the rec building's downstairs is a large linoleum-tiled room. Grandma used to come to the dance classes here. Today, all the tables and chairs are stacked to one side, and the only thing visible is the art nest Kat's made herself in the hall's center.

"What were they arguing about? Why was he even there?"

I follow her to where a roll of craft paper's lying across the floor.

Kat doesn't answer; instead she folds herself down onto the floor, cross-legged and scowling. Pencils, pens, and canisters of paint are piled up around the massive sketch she's been drawing. It looks like a universe, but I'm struggling to understand the vortex thing in the middle.

She shades in furious silence until I ask, "What are we work-ing on?"

"Our next mural is a giant black hole that sucks all life from its victims," Kat spits. "I call it *Family*."

"Okay," I say indulgently. "Or maybe something a bit more *love thy neighbor*?"

These days, we have to run our ideas for the side of the rec build-ing by Pastor Scott before we paint. Apparently, quoting Jesus as saying *Totes amaze* was disrespectful.

"Fine," Kat snaps.

I sink down next to her and scoot over to nuzzle my head against her shoulder, wrapping my arm around her. "I'm sorry, Kat."

She exhales, and a sob comes out. I know how much the fight-ing gets to her, how long she's had to deal with it. How her older brother will probably take off for a while, and how she'll worry about him while he's gone. And how the stress of Grandma cutting her mom off will manifest in anxious nightmares spent searching for her mother.

"That really sucks."

"Yeah." Kat cries for a bit, wiping her eyes on the back of her sweatshirt sleeve.

I look at the paint she's pulled from the utility room and assess the rest of her fevered sketches. Kat always likes doing things she finds beautiful or wants to draw attention to, and her stuff's usually so joyful. When she gave up eating red meat, she featured a cow and her calf, lit up like the nativity. I loved the conversations we had with everyone who asked about that one. The black hole she's got going now, though, might not be the best conversation starter.

"We could still do something galactic. There's a lot of black paint, and Dad's got some more in his truck."

Tama's been supplementing the church's art supplies for years, on an industrial scale. He says there's always half-used paint at the port that no one misses. I hope they never catch him.

"Cool." Kat nods.

We walk out to the parking lot, where many members of the congregation are still talking. I climb up on Dad's sideboards and lift down paint cans and the big Tupperware container he fills with whatever he thinks we'll find useful.

Back in our lair, we stretch out on the floor with a sketch pad and the craft paper between us. Kat's pencil creates a swirling galaxy, with Earth eventually replacing the black hole as the focal point. She still looks a bit out of it, so I start drawing happy faces on the planets to make her laugh. It takes drawing a baseball cap on Neptune to get her to smile.

"What should the mural say?" she asks.

I think, reaching for Pastor Scott–approvable slogans. "We're all in this together?"

"You wish," Kat scoffs. "OMG! I haven't told you yet! I was going to text you yesterday, but then all that stuff happened."

"Tell me what?"

"Friday afternoon, when I went back for my sweatshirt. Darius and what's-her-name were still in Mr. Mendoza's room."

"What?" The image of Darius's face at the end of the club meeting fills my mind again. I haven't heard from him, although it's not like I've reached out, either.

"Yeah, Mr. Mendoza was leaving when I got to the door. He had my sweatshirt and was taking it to the lost and found. Gave it to me and then he left, you know, told me have a nice weekend. But his lights were still on, and Darius and what's-her-name were in the lab, cleaning up or something," Kat says, her words spilling out.

"He was raging. Saying that Mr. Mendoza must have made a mistake, that there was no way you could have gotten as many votes as he did. And she was all like, 'Who even is she?' And complaining that you'd mess up all the work that they'd done for their Model UN thing."

My mouth pops open.

"He said that working together would be a waste of everyone's time," Kat says.

There it is again! He doesn't "have time for this." All the frustration I felt during our first "conversation" (if you can call it that) comes flooding back to me. He didn't take me seriously then, and he doesn't want to take me seriously now. And the dismissiveness of his parting line that first day, *Maybe I'll see you around.*

Some co-president.

"What an ass!" I fume.

Like I'm somehow not worthy. Even after I get just as many votes as he does, I'm still not qualified to work with him? And who knows, maybe he won't even do it, 'cause working with me is such a waste of his time.

"I know," Kat says. "It was nuts."

"Screw that." My temper flares, just like it did after the first time we talked. I don't care what he thinks. This is bigger than some straight-A asshole and his timetable. This is my chance to actually do something, and I'm going to give it everything I have, whether Mr. Model UN likes it or not. I'm doing this.

"I'm going to be the best fucking co-president that club has ever had," I vow.

Suddenly, something clicks in my brain, and I write ALL WE'VE GOT IS THIS PALE BLUE DOT in bold marker across the craft paper.

"Ah, perfect." Kat grins. "And besides, we don't have to do *every-thing* through the club, right?"

This surprises me. "What do you mean?"

"Well, my friend, I've got some ideas of my own. I think it's time we took this paint show on the road."

"I'm in!" I tell her. Darius be damned.

🔥

"Waste of time," I mutter aloud over my laundry. The words Kat overheard have run through my head all afternoon. I'm sitting cross-legged on my bedroom floor, attempting to fold and stack a mess of dryer-warmed colors. Tama's watching a football game downstairs, and outside it's raining so hard that I can hear the gutter overflowing in a constant stream under the dark sky.

I inhale the sweet smell of Tide dryer sheets, trying to calm down. It works for about thirty seconds. *Waste of time.*

That's it!

I get up and snap open the Chromebook lying on my bed. My fingers click angrily across the keyboard. It's easy to find Darius's email address in the school directory. I can't find it in me to be rude, but I also can't manage to be nice.

> Hi Darius,
>
> We should find time tomorrow to meet and talk about how we want to lead the club together. I've got first lunch, if that works?
>
> Let me know,
>
> Isa

Good. That's over. I take another few deep breaths and move to slide the computer off my lap, only to hear the inbox ping. He's already replied.

> Let's meet in the library—that's usually where I am at lunch. Do you know where it is? —D

Is he trying to piss me off? Alright, I may never go in there, but I'm not an idiot. Also, who spends their lunches in the library?! No wonder I've never noticed him before.

He's such a jerk!

By the time I get to school on Monday, I'm ready. More than ready. I've never been so ready for a conversation in my life. At lunch, I find him sitting at a table in a back corner of the library. He's hunched over a ginormous textbook and has his laptop open to one side so that he can type without taking his eyes off the page. Intense much?

I bite my lip, suddenly nervous. Even though I'm well prepared, I don't want to fight. It takes a beat to gather myself. Then I square my shoulders and march over, swiftly pulling out a chair across from him.

Darius jumps a bit in surprise.

"Oh. Hey." Despite the fact that it's dead quiet in this corner, he hadn't heard me coming.

"Hi," I start, sitting down. "Thanks for meeting me. I figured we'd better work out how we want to do this, if we're going to be running the club together."

"Um, right," he says.

"I think it's clear from the conversations we've had that we should get more people involved. Everyone seems to agree that raising the club's profile is a good first step."

Darius looks slightly dumbfounded. His hands haven't moved from the laptop. Eager not to repeat our first conversation, I've thought through everything I want to say.

"I think there are several ways to do that," I go on. "The club's school web page is looking good, but I'd like to add a few other features. I think it should have profiles of both of us, so people know who they can talk to. I also think the club should up its poster game, and homecoming's a great time for that. I know several people said they were interested in working on it."

Darius closes his laptop a bit. "Okay."

"Then there's picking what activities the club should focus on, which I know we have different opinions about." This seems to register with him more, but I manage to continue before Mr. Model UN can get any words out. "I think the best way forward is to choose whatever has the most support, so that we can work together on something we all care about."

"So, vote on everything?" He doesn't wait for a response. "I don't think turning the club into a popularity contest is the right way to lead. The mock COP is an excellent thing to focus on, and several club members are already working on it."

"Sure, but I don't think the mock COP is what *most* people want to do." His mouth's already open, but I don't stop. "And the only reason I've heard you give for why it's a good idea is that it will look good on college applications, which isn't what the club is for. Mr. Mendoza said that working with the Model UN will require a tremendous amount of effort, so unless everyone's behind it, it's not going to work."

I'm shocked that Darius doesn't try to argue. I use his hesitation to charge on. I've almost gotten out everything that I want to say.

"I think that neither of us expected to be co-leading the club. If we're going to make this work, we'll have to do things differently than we planned. And if we're going to do things together, we'll need to compromise."

He sits back in his chair, and his arms fold across his chest. I hadn't realized how far forward I'm leaning over the table. I don't move away.

"First, we get more people to know about the club. Then, we host a school-wide conversation that gets everyone talking. Then, we make a plan that most people are excited about," I summarize.

"And if that's the mock COP?" he challenges.

"As long as we're bringing in more people and choosing something that we all care about. Something that actually addresses what everyone's worried about, then fine," I say. "Because that's the most important thing, right?"

He blinks at me, and there's a pause before he answers. "Right."

"Great." I can't believe I did that! "I'll email the club."

The bell rings and I push back my chair, not pausing to wait for him. I know I shouldn't, but I can't help adding, "Maybe I'll see you around."

The satisfaction of watching the shock that I quoted him register on his face is utterly amazing. I wave, grinning, and walk triumphantly out of the library.

Waste of time my ass.

CHAPTER 6
BLAZING

Isa

"COME ON, KAT! WE GOTTA GO." I STAND UP AND TAKE A last look in her bedroom mirror.

Kat's room, especially reflections of Kat's room, are a strange mind trip. Her family lives two streets over from mine, and their town house is essentially identical to the one my family lives in. Only, because their apartment is on the other side of the dividing wall, their layout is the exact opposite of ours. So even though the Nelsons have lived here for over a year now, I'm still constantly turning the wrong way to look for the wrong room.

"I thought we agreed that football is stupid and we're just showing up for the dance," Kat says.

I roll my eyes. "No, we agreed that we needed more time for our hair but to make at least the last quarter so I can check in with the Samoan crew."

Football is a big deal to Samoans. Most families will have arrived before the game, Dad included. He left hours ago.

"I thought you were just going to the dance with what's-his-name? We have to watch him play, too?"

"I'm not going to the dance *with* Robert. We're both going to the dance. Not like you and Logan, who are going to the dance *together*," I correct her. "And since when are you so into him, anyway?" Kat's latest crush has escalated quickly. I didn't even know it existed until last week.

"Nice try. We're supposed to be talking about you and Robert. That's the whole reason I told you to come over here to get ready. And then you show up with your mom!"

I laugh. "Was that why you told me to come over? You should have said!" My house is our usual designated hangout 'cause Mom loves doing hair. Before she left for the restaurant, she helped us redo our dye. My highlights are now the hottest of pinks, and Kat's ends are Halloween orange. Mom also helped us finally decide what to wear—black jeans and glittery, sequined tank tops that will be fun to dance in—and experiment with colored eyeliner until it looked on point. Since she left, we've taken about a billion selfies and have eaten way too much candy.

"Come on!" Kat begs. "Spill! Tell me everything about you and Robert."

"There's nothing to tell." I laugh at how disappointed she's about to be. "He dances at the community center, and his uncle is apparently a distant relative of my dad's. His high school is playing ours tonight, so his whole family is going to be there, and he asked if he could come to the dance after. So, I said yes."

"You make it sound so boring!"

"What do you want me to say?" I giggle, working up a fantasy. Kat "falls in love" every few months, and I've never understood how she can get so into people so quickly. She'll love this.

"I saw him dancing across the room, his chest glistening, and thought . . . I want him! I *need* him!!" I start gyrating ridiculously.

No one else is home, so I'm free to scream "I love him!" at the top of my lungs.

Kat's choking with laughter by the end. She gasps for breath and wipes tears out of her eyes.

"Come on. Let's go!" I pull her to standing and we head out, locking up behind us.

We cycle over to Lakewood High in the late October mist, arriving minutes into the third quarter. The stadium is packed, and the stands are buzzing as everyone eyes the scoreboard. The cheerleaders and the marching band are working hard to hype people up, but with the score as close as it is, they don't need to do much. I scan the crowd and eventually find Tama sitting with a group I recognize from the community center. They're up in the stands under the cover of the overhang, out of the rain. Dad introduces Kat, and she seems pretty overwhelmed by all their crushing hugs and handshakes.

When the game clock hits ten minutes remaining, I tug on Kat's sleeve.

"It's time," I remind her.

No one notices us slip out. We've already got our school sweatshirts on under our coats, so when we meet the others we'll look as "pep squad" as possible. It's not like anyone's guarding the school during the last few minutes of the game, but we don't want to answer any questions, either. This hasn't strictly been approved.

Through art studio, Kat's had a hefty stack of posters printed, which she takes out of her locker now where the other club members are assembling. The green-and-blue posters are even in Lakewood High shades, so they'll blend in with the homecoming decorations.

"Right." I start passing out the rolls of tape I've been carrying in my bag. Mia's wheelchair comes to a stop next to me. "Everybody knows where to go?"

Lily and Harper nod as a few others round the corner.

Kat counts out sheets of paper and gives small stacks to the outstretched hands. The posters announce that at the next Environmental Justice Club meeting everyone is welcome to share what they're worried about. WHAT KEEPS YOU UP AT NIGHT? (EW, DON'T BE GROSS) AND WHAT DO YOU WISH YOU COULD DO ABOUT IT? There's even a QR code that leads to the club's web page, where people can comment if they can't make the meeting.

"Great." I smile. "See you soon!"

Club members fan out through the hallways, passing under balloon arches in Lakewood's school colors and giant glittered paintings of the school's mascot, Ottey the fighting otter. Our mission is to tape our posters up in every restroom—on every mirror, on the back of every stall door, and above every single urinal.

Kat is a genius.

D hall is silent, not a person in sight. Susie and I break into a run as soon as we realize the coast is clear. We're too excited not to. My feet thud down the empty corridor in an exhilarating rhythm. When we slide into the first bathroom, I can't help laughing out loud as we start plastering our message all over the place. Everyone is going to see this!

"This is so great!" Susie giggles. "I bet people will comment from the toilet tonight."

We high-five after we finish our assigned restrooms. I stash the extra rolls of tape in my locker, and then we surreptitiously make our way toward the line forming at the ticket table by the entrance to the gym. The other members trail in not far behind. Mission complete.

"Hey, where's Darius?" Collin asks. "I thought he and Marina were coming."

"Nope," Jake tells him. "He had some cross-country thing, so he couldn't come early."

Working *with* Darius over the last several weeks hasn't exactly materialized. After our chat in the library, we've taken a divide-and-conquer approach, which means everyone else in the club's been helping me plan this while he and Marina continue to meet with the Model UN kids. Whatever. At this point, I'm just glad he didn't try to stop us.

Kat and Isaac round the corner and walk slowly toward us. We were short on guys, so Kat enlisted Isaac to help cover all the bathrooms. Kat's got her phone out and is smiling down at something on her screen. I bet they're the last to finish because she was texting Logan. Fourteen-year-old Isaac slings his arm over his sister's shoulders, probably to get her to move faster and rub in the fact that he's taller than her. Kat reaches up to ruffle the tuft of hair he's becoming rather precious about, and the bridges of freckles across their noses get all scrunched up as they tussle.

"We did it!" I whisper-shout to everyone when they're close enough to hear. "And it only took fifteen minutes. Done! Go forth and dance, people!"

I'm pumped. It feels so good to be doing something.

"And if anyone asks," Kat says, "tell them that it was the homecoming queen's wish to end climate change. You had no choice."

Homecoming isn't a formal, so after we buy tickets, our group sticks together. We pass under the balloons and crepe paper until we find a good spot to set up a dance circle, throwing our jackets and sweatshirts into a pile in its center. Pop music is playing over the standing speakers that are spread around the gym, and party lights fill the space with moving spots of color that catch the sequins of my tank top.

A giggle bubbles up from my chest, and my body moves with the music. We've spread the word about environmental justice, and now I get to enjoy the dance with my new friends.

The football players don't show up for a while, and when Robert does, he's with a few guys I recognize from the APCC. I introduce them to our circle, which now also includes Logan, who's basically attached to Kat.

Robert's a good dancer. He starts throwing in some Samoan moves and getting the others involved.

"Lakewood High, we now present your homecoming court," a voice calls over the speakers. A giant spotlight shines on a senior couple standing in the middle of the gym. Oh, right. I forgot this party was meant to be about them—them and the football team. I don't even know who won the game.

In the spotlight's glare, I see Darius across the room. He's dressed nicely, in dark jeans and a crisp button-down under his letterman jacket, standing with some guys I don't know. They're in a loose line, not dancing even when the music starts again. They must be the cross-country team. I'm about to rejoin our circle when I realize he's walking toward us. Oh man, I was having such a nice night.

Darius comes to stand next to me and says something, but I can't hear him over the music.

I lean in closer and raise my voice. "What?"

"I saw the posters in the bathroom," he shouts too loud. "Sorry!" he says, and leans closer, too, moderating his volume. I've never stood this close to him before. He smells like a homey combination of laundry detergent, coco butter, and the leather of his letterman jacket. It's nice to find something I like about him.

"The posters are actually pretty smart. They're really noticeable. I saw two guys scanning the code."

I roll my eyes. Does he *try* to be rude, or does it just come naturally? But I don't want to spend my evening fighting with Darius. I'm having too much fun.

"That was Kat's idea. She's brilliant!"

I point over to where she and Logan are moving. Darius's eyes take in our dance circle, and he waves at Susie's brother and some of the other club members. I can't tell if he wants to join us or not. Aside from the cross-country team, he doesn't seem to be with anyone, and I suddenly realize who's missing.

"Is Marina here?" They're so rarely apart. "Do you guys want to dance with us?"

"No!" he says, too loud again. The girl next to me moves. I lean away slightly and can see his forehead's all crinkled.

"I mean, Marina and I aren't here together—we're not together—she's not here." This all comes out very fast.

"Okay?" That wasn't what I was asking, and I still don't know if he wants to join us. I don't really know what to say. We stand awkwardly, looking at each other while the song changes, then someone's hand takes mine and turns me away from Darius.

I don't mind at all that Robert's spun me back into the circle.

CHAPTER 7
WORLD'S WORST RACE

Darius

I SWERVE AROUND THE MAN AHEAD OF ME, PUSHING UNTIL I'm the only cyclist on the trail. This weekend is supposed to be recovery time for the cross-country team, perfect for some easy STP training with Dad and Jordan. Yet I've been cycling for hours, pushing it since we first got out here. Even though the Seattle-to-Portland bicycle ride isn't until July. Even though we only brought one car, and it's already started to rain.

There's just way too much to think about. I have about a billion essays to write for US History and Honors American Literature, and I still have AP Calculus homework to finish. The PSAT went pretty well, but I just can't stop obsessing about what I'll score—and we won't get the results for another month. An entire month! And then there's last night's homecoming dance. What a hot mess.

I keep seeing Isa's face. The neon-pink streaks running through her hair and the withering look she gave me as her date spun her away to dance. Her forehead crinkled with the effort of raising the inner corners of her eyebrows in, what, exasperation? Why didn't I just say yes? For fuck's sake, I like to dance! And it's not like I don't know most of those kids from Environmental Justice Club. The ones she's hanging out with. And I'm not. Not to mention the way I blathered on about not being *with* Marina, even though she obviously wasn't asking about that.

I thought Isa would bow out, fade away once the actual work began. I thought the club would stick by me and everything we started this summer. But instead, everyone's been working with *her*. Helping her. And it's *working*! I also cannot stop thinking about those football jocks I overheard in the bathroom last night, talking about the climate crisis. How did *that* happen?

This is not how this year was supposed to go. Now I have to pitch the mock COP to the entire school?

I mean, Isa's not wrong, which made it annoyingly impossible to argue. Marina and I can't host a Model UN conference by ourselves. It will take the entire club for us to pull this off. And apparently, they're all way more interested in Isa's plan. Whatever that is.

We're supposed to host a Model UN conference this year so that we get invited to observe the collegiate Model UN conference senior year. This change of plans might blow the entire extracurricular portion of my college applications. I probably need to think of another thing to get involved in, in case this all goes wrong.

Another thing to do. Another thing I don't have time for. And all because of her.

My feet press down on the pedals, rocketing me forward. As the rain picks up, I inhale the smell of pine needles and moisture, the wetness of home. The low waves of Puget Sound drum against the pebbled beach. I don't care that the headwind has picked up, too. It means hardly anyone else is out—I can fly down the paved part of the trail at a reckless speed. My family and I train on the network of old railroad tracks the city's turned into cycling and hiking trails.

They crisscross the western part of Washington State for hundreds of miles. But Dad and Jordan are long behind me. I guess there's nothing like stress to power a training session.

By the time I decide to turn around, it's showering relentlessly. My shoes are full of water, and my feet slide against the pedals. It's getting dark, especially under the trees, which grow closer together the farther inland I cycle. Dad parked where the trail connects to the state park nearest town. Where there are toilets and an old army structure that's been converted into a skate park.

I'm happy that the skate park's mostly empty when I roll through. I don't want comments on my cycling clothes. Being a guy in span-dex makes you an easy target.

Only one of the bowls is covered and lit, so rain usually sends most people home. That bowl is under the bones of an old building that's now entirely covered by graffiti. The only riders not in it are a couple of guys with a death wish who are attempting the slick rails.

The last time I was close enough for Dad and Jordan to hear me, I told them not to wait. That if I didn't catch up to them, I'd cycle home. That was before my underwear was soaked through, though. Back when I could feel my fingers. I do a lap of the parking lots and pray they didn't hear. The cold I hadn't noticed before hits me. I realize I'm shivering just as I see Dad's headlights flash on.

Yes!

"Thought you'd want a ride," he says. Dad gets out and opens up the back so we can get my bike loaded. He throws me a few towels to sit on before I drench his car. Inside, he turns on my seat warmer and tosses the book he was reading into the back seat.

"Hard at it today, huh?"

"Yeah, I guess." The clock on the dash says it's almost five. I probably did close to fifty miles, and I'm still wound up. "School's a lot. We've got tests coming up."

"You'll walk them, and you're always top of the class to me." Dad grins.

I practically throw my shoes off, and he gives me some side-eye. "How was last night? Who won the game?"

"We did. Close one, though, didn't clinch it until the end of the fourth quarter: forty-seven to thirty-six."

"Nice. Weren't you going to the dance after? You were home before Jordan and I got back from the movies." I can't remember which one they went to. Dad loves a superhero film.

"Yeah, I didn't stay long." Just long enough to be awkward with Isa and her date. "Can we pick up pizza? I'm starving."

Dad laughs. "I knew you were a genius. Call Pizza Pizazz and order three. Get a salad, too. Even though she's out of town for the weekend, Mom will know if we don't eat any greens."

As I walk up to Marina's house late the next morning, I'm greeted by the sound of her little cousins chasing each other through the front room. I can hear them shouting even before Marina opens the door.

"Full house today?" I ask her. There are more cars than usual in the driveway, too.

Marina's eyebrows push together as she crosses her arms. The oversize black T-shirt she's wearing today seems a stark contrast to her cousins' laughter. "It's been quite the morning."

The sound of her mom and aunt talking follows us through to the dining room. Marina's books and laptop are spilled over the far side of the table. I set myself up a similar station a few chairs over.

Their dining room looks out over the backyard, where her cousins are continuing their game of tag.

"Would you like some tea, Darius?" Mrs. Takahashi asks through the swinging door to the kitchen. A lifetime has taught me that no matter how I respond, a small pot of green tea will arrive within minutes. I thank Mrs. Takahashi when it does and am surprised to see Marina's uncle sitting on the other side of the door. I've only met him once. Weirder still, he switches to speaking Japanese when he sees me.

Marina's buried in our AP Biology textbook, giant noise-canceling headphones over her ears, so I write *What's going on?* on a piece of paper. Then I ball it up and throw it at her. She slides the headphones back and lowers her voice to a whisper.

"They've been at it for hours. Akira's in there, too."

"Your sister's home?" Even though Seattle's only an hour away, Akira doesn't come down from UW much, especially when it's not a holiday. "What's wrong?"

"Oh, it's not her," Marina whispers. "Remember Haruto, Yuto's older brother?"

"Yeah." I should probably be embarrassed that I know Marina's extended family better than my own. I see way more of them than I do mine. Though Haruto is certainly the cousin I've seen the least. He only rarely hung out at the Takahashis' after he started high school.

"Haruto started at Washington State this year. Not even a semester in, and he's dropped out. Apparently, he was thrown out of the dorms for drugs three weeks ago and he didn't tell anybody."

"What?!"

"Yeah. We only found out this week because he got pulled over and given a DUI. The police called my uncle."

"Shit." I can't even imagine my parents' reaction to something like that. It would not be good.

"I know. My uncle's livid, and my aunt's really upset. They've been here most of the weekend. Aunt Yamada asked Akira to come talk to Haruto, have an intervention or something. We knew he was drinking before he moved away, but there it's gotten out of control."

"Wow—that's intense! What's he going to do?"

"Shhh!" Marina's eyes get all wide, and she looks with trepidation at the door to the kitchen. I guess I was a bit loud. My mind flashes back to Isa's grimace when I practically yelled in her ear at the dance. I need to work on my volume control, apparently.

Marina lowers her voice even further. "They *can't* know that you know. My uncle's insistent on keeping the entire thing a secret. So worried about what people will think."

She gives the quiet another second before going on.

"Akira says they should get him to go to AA or send him to rehab. That there's no point in him going back to college until he's sober. My uncle doesn't want to let him out of his sight. He's been sleeping in our basement. That's why everyone's here. Haruto doesn't want to go home, but he doesn't have any money to go anywhere else."

Man, that would suck. "Wait, so he's going to live here now?"

Marina shrugs. "I don't know. I mean, I don't care if Haruto moves into Akira's old room. If I were him, I wouldn't want to go home, either. It's just that if he's here, my uncle will never leave."

Just then, the kitchen door swings open so that her younger cousins can chase each other through into the living room. The two little girls are the daughters of Marina's youngest aunt, who I gather is also over.

Marina sighs. "Can we study at your place today?"

"No one's there," I remind her. Mom and Dad probably wouldn't mind Marina coming over. I just don't want to hang out in my empty house all day. "Isn't Jordan out with Ken and Yuto?"

"Neither of your parents are home? It's the weekend."

I shrug. "Dad went golfing, and Mom's away. They said they'd be home for dinner."

"It's like the opposite of here."

An email alert flashes across both our phones at the same time.

"Shoot," Marina says. "We have got to get the Model UN some answers. What happened with the club at the dance?"

I sigh. "I don't even know, but the school-wide conversation thing is definitely going ahead. Friday's the special club meeting."

"Why did you even agree to that?"

I throw my hands up. "What choice did I have? You know we can only do the mock COP if the club sponsors it, and how was I supposed to know that getting people interested at *homecoming* would actually work?"

Marina's curtain of hair swishes back to her textbook before she asks, "What if no one wants to do the UN thing?"

"No one? You're not going to say anything?" For all the work she's done, Marina still hasn't said a single word at the club meetings. I'm tired of being the only one defending the mock COP.

"I mean, I can," she equivocates. "But it's not like one of us is going to be enough."

Suddenly, I don't want to talk about this with her. "Let's just see what happens," I say, trying to keep the frustration out of my voice. "I'll stall the Model UN crew until it's over."

I've always been able to count on Marina. For so long, it felt like we understood each other so easily. Wordlessly. It still feels like she's the only person who takes school as seriously as I do. She was right behind me on the leader board when it was last posted. But . . .

I don't know. The jittery, worked up feeling I had last night resurfaces. I can't figure out what my problem is.

We study in silence for a while. Marina slides her headphones back into place. I delve into the logical world of AP Calculus, sipping tea and turning pages. Until another email alert brightens Marina's phone.

"It's shipped!"

I look up to find Marina beaming and holding the phone up so that I can see. There's a picture of Coco from *Witch Hat Atelier* on her screen. But it's not the usual drawing of the anime character—it's a costume.

"Since when are you so into cosplay?" I ask. It's not like Marina won't look good. She's just getting so . . . into it. Way more than I am.

Marina's shoulders rise and fall in a quick motion.

"Sakura Con was really fun all dressed up. I don't know why you won't even try it. Qifrey would be an easy character for you to do. You already wear glasses. We just need to darken one lens." She smiles. "You like *Witch Hat Atelier*."

"Yeah." I laugh. "I like watching it."

Marina leans forward in her enthusiasm. "Being it is better! You full-on get to be someone else. It makes it more real. You sure you don't want to?"

"I'm sure," I say confidently, then remember. "Hey, there's a new episode out! Do you want to watch it?"

Marina's lips pull up in a sly grin. "Thought you'd never ask."

"This Friday, the Environmental Justice Club is hosting a special meeting to discuss climate change and what Lakewood High students can do about it. All are welcome. Please email Mr. Mendoza or visit the club's website for more information." The principal moves on to the rest of the announcements, but I'm no longer listening.

Now our club is being publicized on the school announcements? And it's a week-long campaign, at that. Another thing I wouldn't have thought to do. Isa's withering look, those pink streaks framing her face, flashes through my mind—again. I also overhear Abigail mention that the members tally on the club's web page is up to forty, and that the page has over a hundred views. When I pull it up to check for myself, I see that people did comment on homecoming night.

Mr. Mendoza seems aware of the hype, too. On Friday, he ends AP Biology five minutes before the bell and dismisses everyone not staying for the meeting.

"For those who are staying for the Environmental Justice Club, could you help with getting more stools from Ms. Johnston's lab? It looks like we're going to have a crowd."

He walks over to me. "Darius, do you know exactly how many we should expect?"

My eyes bug. Why does he expect me to know? This is Isa's thing. "Um, I haven't exactly been keeping up with the numbers."

"Well, there are more stools in the storage room at the end of the hall, if fifty's not enough."

Fifty?!

I stand, stunned, and follow Mr. Mendoza and a few others across the hall to grab more seats. We've moved most of Ms. Johnston's stools over by the time people start arriving. Regulars first, then lots of people I don't recognize. And they just keep coming.

I stop counting at thirty-five, when the lab is fuller than the AP crew ever sees it. Some of these kids have to be in middle school. They look super young.

When she arrives, Isa's chatting with another group of people I don't know. I've claimed a stool off to the right. Mr. Mendoza waves Isa and me over, his eyes twinkling. Isa looks . . . nervous?

"Um, Mr. Mendoza," she tells us. "Do you want to start? Maybe say something about the club?"

Does she *not* have a plan? I'm only just realizing that we probably should have talked about how she wants to do this.

Mr. Mendoza smiles. "Sure, Isa, but I'm happy for you or Darius to start. I don't want to steal your thunder."

"No, that's okay." Isa's got her back to the room and is just looking at the two of us. She's chewing on her lower lip, and she keeps touching her hair. I didn't peg her as someone who doesn't like public speaking.

"Alright," Mr. Mendoza says. "I'll start by introducing the club. What would you like to happen then?" he asks, looking between us.

"Well," Isa answers. "Then I guess we can go around and get to the sharing bit? I know people have commented on the webpage too, so maybe I can ask Kat to read those?"

"How many have written in online?"

"About twenty, I think?"

"Twenty, plus everybody here? That's really very well done, Isa," Mr. Mendoza tells her.

She smiles. "Thanks, Mr. M." I don't miss that the conversation is now entirely between them.

"Darius." Mr. Mendoza says, seeming to read my mind. "Perhaps you can take notes? We'll need a way of capturing what's said."

"I'll ask everyone to do hand gestures, too," Isa says, at the same time I get out, "You want me to take notes?"

"That's right," Mr. Mendoza says, "and we better get started. If we've got fifty people sharing, there's going to be a lot to get through."

How did *that* happen? I'm secretary to Isa's lead? She still looks like a deer in headlights. When I stalk off to get my laptop, Marina tries to catch my eye, but I don't have time to complain.

"Welcome, everyone, come on in and have a seat!" Mr. Mendoza announces. "Feel free to move the stools around and grab more if we run out."

He starts his spiel, and I take a place by Isa at the front. While he's introducing the club, Isa grabs a whiteboard marker and writes up:

What does environmental justice mean to you? What are you worried about? And what should we do about it?

I reluctantly type her questions into a blank Word document. When Mr. Mendoza finishes, he turns to Isa expectantly. I'm suddenly nervous that she won't say anything and I'll end up having to chair *and* type.

Isa takes a shaky breath.

"Thanks everyone for coming," she tells the room. "I just thought we should start the year off by finding out what we all care about? And that will help us find something to work on?"

Is she asking us?

She stops to clear her throat. When she speaks again, she sounds more decisive.

"I really encourage everyone to share, and if someone says something you agree with, please do this."

With a deliberate movement, Isa makes jazz hands up by her face. Then she laughs.

"I know it's ridiculous, but it makes it really easy to tell if people think the same as you do. If you only kind of agree, do this." She turns her jazz hands into a "maybe" at her waist.

"If you disagree, don't do anything." And here, she drops her hands.

"So, let's practice," she says. "I *love* peanut butter chocolate."

Almost everyone laughs. Then people start waving their hands, moving them to the right place. It does look ridiculous, but it also does make it surprisingly easy to tell what people think.

"See, most people love peanut butter chocolate!" Isa giggles, summarizing. "Um, so anyway, we better get started. Who wants to go first?"

"You do!" Jake calls.

This has Isa laughing, too. I try not to notice how much I like the sound. She's got a bubbly kind of giggle. It's infectious. Sweet.

"Okay, I'll go, then," she says. "Well, I'm really worried about climate change. I think it affects us so much. Probably most obviously with the wildfires."

Susie stands up and lifts her jazz hands as high as she can. This prompts nearly everyone else to raise their hands, too. I start, but then I remember I'm supposed to be writing this down. My fingers fly into action across my keyboard.

"And I'm tired of not talking about it, and not learning about it and not really understanding what I can actually do to stop it," Isa continues.

More hands go up.

"I think what brought me here, though, is my dad's job. He works as a longshoreman, and his hours have been cut because they're building a natural gas pipeline down at the port. The natural gas isn't even for us! The pipeline will ship it out east somewhere. And it will only make the climate crisis worse. I'm just so frustrated, and I don't know what to do about it."

She's talking so fast, my fingers have to move to get it all down. Everyone's hands are still up and waving when she finishes. "Damn, girl!" someone says.

She cracks a smile. "Yeah, so I'm here because I want to be with other people who care, and because maybe if we all work together, we can really change stuff. So, that's me."

I didn't know any of that. It's like I've never really seen her until just now.

"Jake, I think you're up next," she tells him.

"Alright, guess I earned that. Really good to know about the pipeline. My dad works at the port, too, but I didn't know that's what they're building. That makes no sense. Also, I totally agree about the wildfires, and that's why I'm here. I've got asthma, and I nearly died staying inside all summer."

Susie's still got her hands up and jumps in next. "Yeah, I started talking to Isa about this when the fires were still burning. My cousins in Snoqualmie lost their house, and I really want to do something for them. And I really don't want anyone else to lose theirs."

The guy next to her reaches out to hold her hand. "I'll go," he says. "I'm just generally worried that we, you know, won't have a future. Animals are going extinct. There are like hardly any bees anymore. And way too many forest-killing pine beetles. The seasons don't start and stop at the right time. It's crazy!"

The few hands that had stopped waving start again. I type on.

"My family is from Hawai'i, and sea level rise is a real thing. It's really unfair. They're relocating entire island nations, and it's not like they caused the problem. I saw the case Vanuatu brought before the international court of justice. Like, where are they supposed to go? What the fuck!"

"Language," Mr. Mendoza chides. "I know this is a hard topic, and I do understand the sentiment, but school rules still apply. Julián, why don't you go next?"

"Yeah, a lot of my family works in agriculture, and during the summer it's fucking boiling out there. ¡Mierda! Lo siento, señor." The two guys he's always with wave their hands emphatically.

Before Mr. Mendoza can say anything, someone adds, "My dad's a contractor, and he had roofers collapse of heatstroke this summer."

Another girl starts with "There's a red tide again, which I'm really upset about. My family has an oyster farm, so we can't sell anything. Unless, you know, we want to poison people. A whole family died this summer from eating bad shellfish."

"Yeah, and there's never good news is there? I'm genuinely worried that the world is ending. That like major tipping points are being crossed and we aren't doing *anything* about it. Nothing governments are doing is truly reducing greenhouse gas emissions."

Trying to capture the conversation is taking most of my energy, but I realize that this is probably the best opening I'll get. I stop typing and put my hand up.

Isa smiles at me. She's never smiled directly at me before, and for a second I'm lost in the dimple in her left cheek. Her eyes search mine.

"Hi, I'm Darius," I tell the room. "I'm one of the co-presidents of the Environmental Justice Club. I'm really concerned that the world isn't doing enough to stop climate change, too, and I want to better understand how countries make international decisions."

Several jazz hands go up.

"I think it's a really good idea to do this by holding a mock COP—a Model UN climate summit. The club could host it, bring all the regional Model UN clubs together and really get into the weeds of understanding how climate policy is made."

Marina's hands are still waving, but she and Sophie are the only ones who look sold. How does Isa make getting people interested look so easy when I'm the one with an actual plan?

The girl next to me has got her hand up and starts talking before I can add anything else.

"I'm really worried about eating animals and the strain that puts on the planet. I want us to push the school to have more vegan options in the cafeteria."

More hands go up for her than did for me. Seriously?

One guy talks about the snow on Mount Rainier, while another kid brings up fracking. The conversation goes on well past the extra-curricular bell. When people stop chipping in, Isa asks Kat to read the comments on the web page, which kicks off another round of discussion. My fingers are going to fall off. I've organized the comments into a spreadsheet—grouping like things together and tallying up the jazz hands in support. It's immense.

A girl I haven't seen before raises her hand. I bet she's a freshman. She looks absolutely tiny, her eyes almost too big for her face.

When she starts talking, she's so quiet that I can't understand what she's saying. When I raise my head to ask her to speak up, Isa's walking over to her.

The girl is crying. She's sobbing so hard, she's shaking.

Isa puts her arms around her, then rubs her back.

"I know, it's really scary," she says.

The only sound in the room becomes the near noiseless motion of fifty people waving their hands.

Mr. Mendoza stands up.

"Thank you, Jessica, for sharing that. This is a very difficult conversation to have, and I'm very proud of everyone for engaging in it. Environmental injustice and the climate crisis are among the greatest challenges we face. I'm sorry that these crises are yours to grapple with, too."

He pauses. Jessica seems to have a better handle on herself. Isa lets go, and the girl next to her, Mia, pats Jessica's arm.

"I think we should bring this session to a close," Mr. Mendoza goes on. "If you didn't get a chance to speak or if you think of something else, please add it to the comments section on the club's web page. Please also take care of each other and yourselves this weekend. And many thanks to Isa for convening us and Darius for taking notes. Let's give them and everyone who shared a round of applause!"

A chorus of clapping fills the room before everyone starts moving. In the dwindling chatter, Mr. Mendoza waves at me.

"Darius? Isa? Let's have a quick chat."

Isa extricates herself from the group forming around her and slowly makes her way over.

"Congratulations on a truly excellent discussion," Mr. Mendoza tells us. "That's the best conversation I think this club has ever had. I really don't want to lose the momentum here—or, in my case, forget what was said."

He pauses to laugh at his dad joke, and Isa gives him a small smile. "What did you have in mind in terms of taking this forward?" Mr. Mendoza asks her.

Isa's deer-in-the-headlights look returns. "I, um, hadn't thought through the next part yet," she admits.

"Well," I say. "I've done a spreadsheet of the notes." I turn the laptop open in my hands around to face them, so they can see the screen. "I've color-coded and sorted things by preference. Perhaps we should review that and look at the options?"

Isa blinks at me.

"That's great, Darius!" Mr. Mendoza exclaims. "I hate to leave this for another two weeks until the next club meeting, but I'm loath to add things to your schedules. I know, Darius, that you have practice after school and commitments in the morning. I'm not sure what your schedule looks like, Isa. Any suggestions?"

"Lunchtime early next week? We could meet in the library?" I offer.

"Excellent. Let's do Monday, then. You both have first lunch?" Isa and I nod in time. "Great. I'll see you there. And congratulations again on a job well done!"

As Mr. Mendoza says this, he pauses to put a hand on each of our shoulders.

It feels very weird to be congratulated for something I didn't do. Something Isa did. She's looking up at me now. The accusation I expect to see isn't the emotion most visible on her face, which makes me feel even worse. She looks almost . . . grateful?

I can only meet her eyes for a second before looking down at the floor.

CHAPTER 8
WE'RE DOING THIS

Darius

WHEN MR. MENDOZA AND ISA FIND ME IN THE LIBRARY ON Monday, they're chatting about his kids. He has five; I had no idea. We start by looking through my spreadsheet of notes, which I already have open on my laptop.

"The things in green got the most support, then yellows, and then reds," I explain.

They both lean forward to take a closer look at the shaded rows. Mr. Mendoza starts slowly scrolling through the entries.

"What I noticed is that there are way more things that people are worried about than activities for the club to do," I note. "The wildfires, for example, are the brightest green."

"Right," Mr. Mendoza says, reading. "People certainly voiced a lot of concern. I suppose doing some mental health work or sessions on environmental anxiety probably isn't what you guys had in mind?"

I shake my head. Isa doesn't look happy with that suggestion, either, though it's a logical next step I hadn't thought of.

Mr. Mendoza and Isa read on, and it's quiet for a few minutes while they process.

"It didn't seem like people were really asking to better understand a particular topic, either," Mr. Mendoza observes.

"No," I say. "And I was hoping the club would move away from doing purely educational work. The mock COP was one of the only actionable tasks. I still think working with the Model UN is the way to go."

I don't mention that I've created a special color for actionable ideas, just to give it more prominence in the spreadsheet.

Isa looks up from the spreadsheet and straight at me. "I don't remember the Model UN getting a lot of support, Darius."

"This isn't a popularity contest," I remind her. "Ideas and attention are great, but someone needs to make an actual plan."

"How is pretending to be at the United Nations an actual plan? I think we want something slightly more realistic."

"Like?" I say, holding out my arms.

"Alright, guys," Mr. Mendoza comes in. "No one said tackling the world's most complex problems was going to be easy. And you've done a lot already."

He shifts his attention back to the screen and takes another few minutes to scroll through the list again.

"Alright," he says again. "Let's think about this. A lot of people are referencing the impacts of climate change: wildfires, rising temperatures, sea level rise, extinction . . ."

"We could do things to raise awareness about that? If more people knew that all these things are connected, maybe we'd make a difference?" Isa asks.

I sigh. "We just said that focusing solely on educating people isn't what we want to do."

"I'm talking about more than education," Isa states. "I'm talking about advocacy. Reaching people who haven't thought about this before. Doing something that really draws attention to the cause."

"But to what end?" I ask. "Unless advocacy is connected to policy, it's pretty pointless. It's just attention-seeking entertainment."

Isa glares at me, her dark brown eyes fierce. "Well, what's the point of your fake UN, then? That's not connected to real policy."

"Yeah, except the whole point is to show us how real people do this so we can make our own policy someday."

"Not all of us are going to be politicians," Isa snaps. "It would be nice if we could all work on something we care about. Something where we talk to real people in our actual community about something that actually affects us."

"*Like??*" I press—again. "For all the dumping you're doing on my idea, I'm not hearing another one."

"Cool it, guys. We're on the same team here." Mr. Mendoza hums in thought for a moment before glancing at his watch. "I may have been overly ambitious to think that we could get this done in twenty minutes."

"Twenty minutes?" I ask. Lunch is a half hour.

"Sorry. I've got to go prep for next period. This is quite the puzzle we've got. Darius, would you mind sending your spreadsheet around so we can all mull it over?"

I nod and reach for the laptop. I've got it attached to an email and sent with a few clicks.

"Shall we all try again tomorrow, or do you guys want to have a go at tackling this yourselves?" Mr. Mendoza asks.

"Try again tomorrow!" we both say too loudly.

He chuckles. "Alright, then. I'll see you both later." I watch him leave, then return to glaring at Isa.

"Well, that was interesting," she huffs.

"Yeah," I say in a voice thick with sarcasm. "Any bright ideas?"

"What?" she glares.

"You were the one who wanted to do this."

"You know, you could try to be helpful. Pushing the same *one* idea isn't going to get us anywhere. We said we'd have to compromise. Remember?"

I can't think of a counterargument before she pushes back her chair and storms out of the library. How does she keep doing that?

The three of us spend the next several lunchtimes in the library, and even when Mr. Mendoza's present, we don't seem to get anywhere. We comb through what was said and Mr. Mendoza identifies a theme—the environmental injustice of climate change on islanders and people of color, which is something we're all interested in. Then we try to think of something the club could do about it, and the conversation falls apart.

I eventually give up on pushing the mock COP and try throwing out ideas in the name of compromise. That only seems to make things worse.

I'm talking through the connection between policy and nonviolent civil disobedience when Isa suddenly snaps, "Yeah. I know, Darius. You're not the only one who knows how to Google things."

"If it's so easy, then make a plan!" I fume.

I'm so annoyed every afternoon that Chad essentially becomes my running partner during practice. If the club's not doing the mock COP, why am I even leading it? I can't think of a better idea. Not one that we would both be happy with. Yeah, maybe my ideas aren't actually going to change things right now. But can't we do that when we actually have some agency?

"Whoever she is, man," Chad says next to me, "she's great for your splits." He's looking at his watch as we run through the coldest November rain yet.

"What?" I hadn't realized we were going that fast, or that the source of my frustration was so obvious.

"Your splits are down to 5:30. Keep this up and you'll be coming to the state cross-country meet with us."

Chad ups the pace and I match it, too caught up to respond. Isa keeps talking like she wants to do something real. Something now. Not sometime after grad school, when we're real adults who have things figured out.

Days become a week. Marina starts asking what's taking so long, and Mr. Mendoza gives us some time off to think things through independently. And then two weeks have passed, and we've essentially left it for the club to decide.

The next Environmental Justice Club meeting is packed. Lots of people who came for the conversation are back, and several have brought friends. Mr. Mendoza helps Isa and me summarize where we've got to in trying to decide what to do with everything the conversation brought up. Then Isa asks the room for help.

That does it. People start pitching ideas completely unrelated to what we discussed last time. Others throw new ones into the mix. And, surprise, surprise—no one says anything that's an actual plan. It's such a hot mess. Everyone's talking over each other, and I can hardly hear myself think. Exasperated, I slump down on a stool. I'm not even taking notes. I wanted to lead a club, not host an environmental talk show.

"I've got it!" Mr. Mendoza suddenly shouts over the noise.

I'm not the only one that freezes to stare at him. The room goes from mayhem to silence.

"You want to address climate change and its impacts, and limit pollution in Puget Sound. That's what most people were talking about. Engaging with the plans for the new natural gas pipeline at the port addresses all of that."

I blink at him and suddenly remember that Isa started the whole conversation off with that two weeks ago.

"Engaging with planning permission means going to city council, examining their policy," I say. For the first time since the Model UN, an idea I'm excited about comes together in my mind.

"That's brilliant. And we'd need to raise awareness about the pipeline in order to get people involved!" Isa shouts.

"I must admit, I'm out of my depth about what a group of high school students can do about a pipeline," Mr. Mendoza says. "But it does seem to be the thing that connects to almost everyone's interests."

I raise my hand. "My mom's a lawyer, and her last case was against the city. She'll know what options we have."

Isa stares at me for a moment, and I don't look away. Her brown eyes brim with a catching enthusiasm. I feel more hopeful than I have in a long time.

"It's perfect," she says. "We do something about the pipeline. We raise awareness with the school and the community. And we influence policy. I love it! What does everyone else think?"

The entire room fills with jazz hands, and I put mine up, too.

We're doing this.

CHAPTER 9
TAKE YOUR MARK

Isa

MY HEADLIGHTS ILLUMINATE THE RAIN THAT'S STARTING TO fall as I pull into a large, curved driveway and park in front of one of the three garage doors. Disbelieving, I double-check the address to confirm that I'm in the right place. I am. Darius Freeman lives in this massive, lakefront house. Of course he does.

I still can't believe that this is where I am on Thanksgiving. Though I am grateful that having plans forcibly removed me from the mountains of irresistible food at my house. With good cooks in the family, I've always enjoyed Thanksgiving too much. Way too much.

We finished eating hours ago, and I continue to feel like I'm about to burst. My family still has people over, and Kat refused to come with me.

"You're seriously going over to Darius's house? Now? Pass." I wanted to push her, but she had only just stopped venting about "stupid, ghosting Logan" and how she'll never speak to him again.

She and her brothers were playing a loud game of Cranium with my parents, a mother and daughter that Mom knows from the restaurant, and a Samoan guy Dad works with. Grandma and her friends were drinking tea and playing a raucous game of cards in the kitchen.

I announced, "I'll be back in an hour," and reluctantly closed the door on the smell of a turkey none of us could eat any more of. And now I'm sitting here in front of Mr. Model UN's giant house.

Another car pulls into the driveway behind me, and I watch Mr. Mendoza step out into the drizzle. I pick up the gift Grandma insisted I bring and rush to meet him on the porch so that we can ring the doorbell at the same time. After he presses it, the chimes seem to echo deep inside a cavernous space.

Darius opens one of the French doors.

"Happy Thanksgiving!" Mr. Mendoza says. "I really hope we're not disturbing your celebration."

Even though coming tonight was Darius's idea, it does feel strange. I look around the entrance. A curved staircase leads upstairs, and I can see a sitting room off to the right. Framed canvases hang on the walls. There doesn't seem to be anyone in the house.

"Not at all," Darius says. "We finished a while ago. Mom's in the kitchen; I'll take you through."

He leads us purposefully down a hall and around a corner. An immaculately clean kitchen opens up to a glass-walled sitting area. It's dark beyond the windows, but I can see lights on in the houses across the lake. I bet the view from in here is phenomenal during the day. Wait . . . do they have their own dock? Seriously?

Standing in the kitchen, Darius's mother is wearing a smart black dress, her laptop open on one of the sparkling marble countertops. Mrs. Freeman looks exactly like what I imagined a lawyer would look like, even on the holidays. Her no-nonsense expression is framed by severely straightened hair and immaculate makeup, her dark skin practically glowing. She must be close to five foot eleven.

Darius introduces us. "Mom, this is my science teacher, Mr. Mendoza, and this is Isa—she's co-president of the Environmental Justice Club."

I copy Mr. Mendoza, who steps forward to shake her hand.

"Thank you very much for having us and for giving us some of your valuable time," Mr. Mendoza says. Darius told us that the only time we would catch his mom at home was today, when her office is closed.

"I made you a pie," I offer. "Well, my grandma did—she's the baker. It's pecan!"

This makes Mrs. Freeman smile. "I can't remember the last time I had a homemade pecan pie." She takes the box I'm holding and lifts the lid. "It smells absolutely delicious. That's so kind. You didn't have to do that."

"She insisted." I smile. Then, I can't imagine why, but I start imitating Grandma. "You're seein' lawyer Freeman, from the news? You can't thank her enough. And you can't go to someone's place on Thanksgiving and not bring pie!"

No one reacts. I laugh nervously, wondering why things feel so formal.

Mrs. Freeman doesn't exactly laugh with me, but she waves us toward a table. "Please, sit down. Would anyone else like a piece? Darius, do you like pecan pie?"

Darius shrugs. "I don't know. Probably?" Mr. Mendoza puts his hand up politely.

"No, thank you," I say. "I'm still stuffed. I've already had three slices of pie today."

"Darius, why don't you go ask Dad and Jordan if they want some? I'll get this served up." Darius turns without a word and walks back down the hallway. It's weird seeing him at his house, acting like a teenage son and not a know-it-all honors student.

"Now," Mrs. Freeman says, moving around the kitchen. "From what I understand, you want to petition city council over the planning permission for a natural gas pipeline being constructed at the port."

Mr. Mendoza nods. "That's right. I'd like to admit how very out of my depth I am here. Any advice you could give us is more than welcome."

"And what exactly is the nature of your objection? Why should city council not allow the pipeline to proceed?"

My mind goes completely blank. No wonder Darius talks like he does.

"They'd both like pie, and Dad says, please can he have his warm with ice cream?" Darius's voice rounds the corner before he does. I think he's walking up a flight of stairs?

"Of course he can," Mrs. Freeman says. "Will you get the ice cream out of the freezer? I was just asking about the nature of your objections to city council."

"Well, I think we could approach it from several angles, but perhaps the most compelling is that constructing the pipeline goes against city council's stated environmental protection goals," Darius rattles off.

Man, what an intimidating family! Who talks to their mom like this? It's like watching a debate club. One that meets in designer slippers.

"Hmm . . . that's one angle to take." Mrs. Freeman considers. "I'd first question the city council's jurisdiction versus the port authority's. If planning permission has already gone through, as I suspect it has, we may well need to take that political line of argument you suggest. But first we'll see if we can object based on process."

She's set slices of pie down on the kitchen table and takes one out of the microwave for Darius to add ice cream to. Then her fingers return to the keyboard of her laptop.

"I'll have an intern look into jurisdiction and procedure. As well as how far along the pipeline is in the approval process. Does anyone know?" Her head swivels to look at us. "Have they already obtained planning permission?"

I blink, terrified again.

Darius sticks his head out of the kitchen door to holler "Pie's ready!" down the hall. A boy who looks like a younger, cooler version of Darius seems to materialize out of nowhere, only to collect the two slices on the counter and disappear without a word. I guess Darius has a brother?

"Isa?" Mr. Mendoza asks. "You mentioned that construction's already started, right? That your dad had his hours changed?"

"Uh. That's right, but so far they've just blocked off the dock they want to retrofit. I don't think they've actually started building anything yet. Or at least, that's what my dad says."

Mrs. Freeman smiles at me. "We'll look into the approval process, then. If that's already progressed, you're right, Darius, we'll examine this from a political angle: How are the council's actions not acting in accordance with city principles and the mayor's stated objectives? It's a weaker argument, but it may be the best we have."

She and her laptop join us at the kitchen table. She hasn't touched her pie.

"Now, how to get on the council's agenda and make them take your objections as seriously as possible?" she muses. "You'll likely need to raise a petition—the more signatures you can get, the better."

"Getting signatures shouldn't be a problem; everyone at school's behind us," I say.

"To have the most impact, you'll need the signatures of people eligible to vote. Adults, over eighteen, who reside in the area."

"Oh, right," I mumble.

She goes on. "And once you've generated around a thousand"—*around a thousand?!*—"I think the club's best bet would be to make a public comment, which you'll need to prepare and deliver, as a party of record. That will allow you to appeal the council's decision, if you wish."

Mr. Mendoza chokes on his pie. "Uh, I doubt we have the funds necessary for the appeals process."

Mrs. Freeman laughs. "Of course. My apologies, I'm forgetting who I'm talking to. An appeal does have an expense, so we'll need to make the most of this and see how far the council is willing to move."

I feel a bit shell-shocked. This is all sounding very serious. Across the table from me, I realize that Darius is taking notes. He hasn't touched his pie yet, either. This family is so bizarre.

"Alright," Darius says. "So, action points: The logical next step, while we wait for further confirmation, is to brief the club and get their go-ahead; raise awareness about the pipeline; prepare a petition and collect signatures; draft a statement for the public comment—"

"I'll get an intern to help you register as a party of record," his mom interrupts. She makes another note, probably directly into an email that's about to ruin some poor soul's holiday weekend.

There's a pause while they both finish typing. Then they look over at Mr. Mendoza and me.

"This is quite the undertaking," Mr. Mendoza eventually says. "It's very impressive, and I'm sure the students will want to be involved. Thanks again for your time, Mrs. Freeman, and for that of your interns."

I manage to smile. "Yes, thank you."

I can't think of anything else to say, and the room goes quiet while they all eat their pie.

"It was so, so weird," I tell Kat. "Like being at a board meeting."

We're under the dripping eaves of the covered section of the skate park. It's a misty Saturday morning, and Kat's practicing spray painting shadows on a concrete curve that's already covered in color.

"Well, that explains his social skills . . . or lack thereof," Kat says. "I wouldn't mind his lakefront view, though. I bet he doesn't have to share a bathroom with his brothers."

"Yeah, but whose mom doesn't know what food they like?" I still can't get over that one. My mom knows me better than anyone else. And action points, at the kitchen table? So bizarre.

"That's looking amazing, Kat." Using only black and white, she's managed to create a giant hand that looks like it's reaching through the wall.

Our plan to expand our mural enterprise has really come together over the last month. It's felt good to be doing something, even if it was just practice, while the club did nothing but argue. Or at least, while Darius and I did nothing but argue.

These murals are our chance to spread our message. I want to hit the convenience store by the Emerald Queen Casino. It has a great south-facing wall that everyone sees from where the freeway connects to 705. It's more prominent than the church's rec building, and it's a bigger surface, too. We'll need taller ladders to fill the space.

We've gone back and forth about the design for weeks, and Kat's nearly perfected the spraying technique she wants to use in between rain showers and watching Isaac board. We've been mocking things up in the skate park for the past few weekends. What we don't have yet is permission.

Kat finishes with a final shake of the can, then steps back to take in her creation.

"Yup, I think I've got this." She smiles. Her phone comes out and she starts taking pictures. "Do we really have to ask? Can't we just paint it at night?"

I laugh. "How many times, Kat? The store's open twenty-four hours. I'm pretty sure someone would see us. Besides, we've never done anything this big. We don't know how long it will take. I think getting permission is pretty important."

Even though I know this, I haven't pushed us to do anything about it yet.

"Fine, then let's go ask. It's Mr. Sue, right?"

"That's what my dad says, but I've never met him."

"So get your dad to ask him," Kat suggests.

I wish. "He doesn't *know* him know him. He just stops in there when he works nights 'cause it's one of the only places open. And usually it's Mr. Sue's son that's working then. He's never met the older Mr. Sue."

"Well, then we're just gonna have to go and try. We're cute, and you can talk to anyone," Kat says confidently. "It'll be fine."

"Sure." I'm not nearly as certain. Coming up with ideas is way easier than actually doing them sometimes. "And if it isn't? If he says no?"

Kat shrugs. "Then he says no. It's not like waiting any longer is going to change things. And then we'll have an answer and can look for somewhere else to paint if we need to."

It takes another week and another failed attempt at trying to persuade Tama to ask for us before I work up the nerve. Finally, on the first cold Saturday morning in December, Kat and I drive over together in Grandma's car. The convenience store we want is part of a gas station. No customers when we pull up, so now is probably a good moment to ask. I've always wondered why the convenience store is two stories, because the inside isn't. Maybe the building was a house before?

Kat looks both tired and nervous. Before I can ask—again—for her to do the talking, she reminds me that she's the artistic talent and I'm the one who has a way with words. I don't exactly consider the gift of gab a skill, but I guess I did get an A in English last trimester.

"And you're the one who insisted we wear our Lakewood High sweatshirts and look presentable at nine a.m. on Saturday morning. So clearly"—she yawns—"you've got this all figured out."

I take a deep breath.

"Fine, let's do this!" I say with as much enthusiasm as I can muster. We make silent screaming faces at each other and then slowly climb out of the car.

A bell tinkles when I push open the door. I'm surprised that there are a couple teenage guys inside. How did they get here? They're at the Slurpee machine, but otherwise the shop is empty except for a man with gray hair sitting behind the counter. He's reading a newspaper and looks like he has time to talk.

I walk timidly forward. Here goes nothing. "Hi there. Are you the owner?"

He looks over his glasses at me. There are wrinkles around his eyes, and his shirt is stretched across his stomach. "I am."

"It's nice to meet you." I push my hand forward, and though he looks bemused, he shakes it lightly. "My name is Isa, and this is Kat.

We're students at Lakewood High School, and we'd love the opportunity to paint the back of your store for you."

This opening surprises him. "What's that?"

"Well," I say. "We're really concerned about climate change and have been painting some murals around town to raise awareness. Do you know the City Church? The one you can see from I-5?"

He doesn't seem to and doesn't say anything. Just as I'm about to start talking again, someone says, "You painted that? Really?"

Kat and I turn around to take in the guys behind us. They look like they're about sixteen, too. One's all legs and arms, like he just had a growth spurt. His hair is more curly than straight. The other isn't as towering and has an expressive face, and he's looking at us curiously. They both have dark hair and light brown skin and are wearing jackets with the Emerald Queen Casino logo on them. The Slurpees they're holding are nearly overflowing.

"Yes." I smile. "That was us."

"What did they paint?" Mr. Sue asks, seeming more interested now.

Kat pulls out her phone and passes him a picture of our galaxy mural. It's turned out to be one of our best and is still up. I give her a meaningful look while Mr. Sue enlarges the photo on the screen.

"I'm hoping to go to art school one day," Kat tells him. I wish that were true. But Kat's terrified of ending up reliant on her grandma, and going to school for art isn't a sure path to financial independence. No matter how good she is. We decided that the aspiring artist line was probably the clearest sell here, though.

It's the guys who respond first. "That's so cool!" the shorter one says. They've walked closer, and we're all huddled around the counter now. "Have you done all those murals?"

Kat nods, sticking to the aspiring-art-student lines we discussed.

"I've been painting since I was little, but it's hard to find spaces that will let you create."

"You've seen those murals, haven't you, Mr. Sue?" the taller guy asks. They must know him.

Mr. Sue seems to choose his words carefully. "Huh, I suppose I have. And what's this? You want to paint one on my shop?"

"We would love the opportunity to," I say. "It would be different than what's on the church, but a similar theme. We were thinking something like this."

Kat pulls out her sketchbook and slides it across the counter toward him. It's already open to the right page. The guys lean over to look, too. The drawing centers on the face of a little girl laughing with delight. She's on the beach and jumping for her dad, whose bent arm is in frame waiting to catch her. His bare arm is covered in a sleeve of Samoan tattoos—modeled on Tama's. The black lines form turtles, sharks, seabirds, and other marine life in traditional Polynesian design. Hanging over the scene, the words PROTECT THEM are written on the giant picture's upper left corner.

"That's sick!" the shorter guy says. His face is all lit up, and he looks approvingly at Kat.

I catch Mr. Sue's eye, pleading silently. He doesn't seem entirely convinced, so I look around at the other guys for help. The taller one smiles at me.

"The message is amazing," he says, reading the slogan. "Mr. Kiona would love it."

"Really?" Mr. Sue asks.

"Of course. You know the tribe's been working to clean up Puget Sound for ages."

"Ah, that's right. Your aunt leads that campaign, yes?"

The guy nods, and that seems to clinch it for Mr. Sue. I'm

suddenly very curious about who these guys are and itching to ask how Mr. Sue knows their aunt. We talk through the details of how and when we're allowed to paint. The guys pay for their Slurpees but hang around through our effusive round of thank-yous.

When we leave the store, they follow close behind. "Thank you so much!" I continue telling them. "That was really nice of you."

"No worries." The taller guy smiles. "We're part of the Puyallup tribe and work at the casino, so we're in here all the time. Mr. Sue seems curmudgeonly, but he probably would have let you do it without our help. I'm Nathan and this is Eliyah, by the way."

"Hey." Kat and I wave at the same time.

"Do you want help with the mural?" Eliyah asks. I haven't missed that he's looking only at Kat.

"That depends," Kat says arching an eyebrow and putting on what she considers her prettiest face. Nose in, lips out. *Here we go.* "How are you with spray paint?" she asks.

"I'm amazing," Eliyah answers, puffing out his chest.

Nathan bursts out laughing. He looks at me and rolls his eyes. "He's literally never held a can."

"Yes, I have!" They swing for each other, showing off. Their Slurpees nearly go flying. Kat's watching Eliyah as he tries to force Nathan off the sidewalk in their mock fight. They give it up a few seconds later and reclaim their spots next to us.

"Seriously, I painted my neighbor's garage once," Eliyah says.

"A masterpiece!" Nathan mocks, reverently. Kat and I laugh with them now, too.

"Do you have a ladder?" Kat asks.

"Or two?" I add. "We could definitely use some help with that. We've never painted anything this tall before." Now that we'll actually get to do it, the two-story building looks immense.

"Oh, we've got ladders. We'll hook you up!" Eliyah offers. "When do you want to start?"

After we exchange numbers and they get into another play fight, Kat and I get back into Grandma's car. Before I even pull out of the gas station, Kat says, "So, *that* just happened!?"

"I know! We got permission!"

"And met Eliyah! He's gorgeous!"

I laugh, loud, with relief and the high of doing something new. "Keep it in your pants, Kat! Do you think they'll actually show up?"

She laughs. "They better!"

The next weekend, the weather's dry enough to paint. We text Mr. Sue, Nathan, and Eliyah before rolling up bright and early. The cold nips at our noses, but Nathan and Eliyah are there waiting in a truck that has several ladders and wood planks sticking out the back.

They rig up a makeshift scaffold, their movements quick and sure like they've done this before. It's steady enough that even I don't mind climbing up—to the first level. Together, we roll paint on the largest canvas that Kat and I have ever done. Mom and Tama stop by, bringing sandwiches. Isaac, too—he's always liked helping Kat with her creations. In the weak December sun, everybody helps with the base painting.

Once it's dry, Kat gets out a bucket of sidewalk chalk and draws the outlines of the entire mural. Then it's essentially a paint-by-numbers game. We use the drawings in her sketch pad as the key and spray the appropriate colors into the right parts. Kat does the shade work and detail, telling us which sections she'll handle herself. I'd thought it would be a long weekend, with a whole day spent mocking up the mural and another painting it, but we make good progress.

Nathan and Eliyah have to come and go for their shifts at the casino. Between all of us, things go quicker than I imagined they would. When Mr. Sue comes out to inspect our progress on Sunday, he likes the mural so much that he sends his son out to help finish the job.

A few minutes later, Nathan laughs. "He didn't last long." I look over just in time to see the younger Mr. Sue slipping around the corner of the building, away from the shop.

"Guess it's not for everyone." I bend to retrieve my next color, pausing to shake the can. Nathan does, too, and the Emerald Queen logo printed on his jacket blurs with the movement. "What's working in the casino like?"

"Well, we don't exactly work *in* the casino. We help manage the parking lots. It's nice to officially work for the Puyallup tribe, though, now that we're sixteen. My aunt's a council member. Eliyah's family, too."

"Nice." I smile. That explains their connections. "Getting paid is the best."

Nathan nods. "Yup. The tribe's got a lot going on. I'm hoping to do more environmental work, but nothing's paid at the moment. Guess I've gotta start somewhere. How'd you get into this?" He lowers the can of spray paint and points his masked chin up toward the others on the scaffold.

Above us, Eliyah asks, "Hey, Kat, do you wanna do the details here?" He's got most of the arm finished, but the finer points of the tattoo need shading. With each passing hour there's less base painting for us to do.

"You can give it a go, if you want," I hear Kat say.

I smile under my mask. Eliyah's talented, and Kat knows it. Now that she's seen him work, they have a serious vibe going. Nathan's looking at me, and I realize I haven't answered his question.

"Um, how did I get into painting, or environmental stuff?"

Nathan shrugs. "Both, I guess."

I think for a moment, spraying the sand of the beach with a steady movement. "I got into painting through Kat. The environmental stuff, I've thought about for a long time. I just never knew what to do about it. Then my dad, he works as a longshoreman now, said that they're building a new natural gas pipeline at the port, and I don't know, something just snapped."

Nathan lowers his can. "You know about the pipeline?!" he says. "No way! Nobody outside the tribe's been talking about that. Well, I guess not no one. I've just never met anyone else who knows about the petition."

"What? There's already a petition against the pipeline? Really?!" I ask, unbelieving.

"Yeah—I can send you the link." He pulls out his phone. "My mom's the one who's been helping with it. This environmental organization asked to come talk to the tribe about it months ago. Have you heard of Halve by 2030?"

"Uh, no." I never thought to look into other groups that were already working on the pipeline. This is brilliant! The link Nathan sends me now, to a real petition that already exists, has me welling up. I'm thrilled that we're not the only ones rallying against the pipeline.

"And we should totally do a mural about it. We should ask the tribe, too," Nathan suggests.

I blink at him. This is all actually happening. The mural, the club, the petition. Meeting Nathan and Eliyah seems almost too good to be true.

I smile so wide I can hardly see over my cheeks. "Definitely!"

CHAPTER 10
SOMETHING TO PRACTICE

Isa

"THE MURAL'S GETTING SO MANY LIKES!" KAT EXCLAIMS, scrolling through her socials next to me in A Hall. She flicks between the platforms open on her phone. She's posted our mural everywhere. "The next time we paint, remind me to get more footage of it actually going up."

I pull out my phone, all jittery with a strange, hopeful energy. "Wow. It hasn't even been up that long. This is so great!"

I've been riding a strange high all week. When I got to school on Monday and told Mr. Mendoza and Darius about Halve by 2030's petition, they seemed palpably relieved, too.

After Thanksgiving, Darius and I explained to the club what doing something about the pipeline will actually take. Darius rattled through a never-ending list of action items, and I noticed people's eyes glazing over at about step four. Not that the club's reaction deterred Darius in the slightest. He just continued going on about all the tasks ahead of us. I swear, he must have his whole life mapped out in a spreadsheet.

He stood there, laptop open, assigning things like we were

members of a law firm and not a group of high school kids who care but have no idea what we're doing. And no one looked thrilled about being tasked with preparing a "well-researched" public comment or drafting a petition. Mostly because none of us has ever seen either of those before, let alone prepared one.

"Why don't we invite members of Halve by 2030 to come meet with us and talk us through what they've been doing?" Mr. Mendoza suggested. "Perhaps we can join forces. Can you email them, Isa?"

I nodded, excited. Later, when I sat down to write, I may have gotten a bit carried away. Their website looked so amazing that my email quickly turned into fan mail. It got so long that I added my phone number at the end, in case speaking was easier than reading my entire love letter.

"This way, Kat," I tell her, moving to follow the rush toward the door in the Friday exit surge.

When Kat and I reach the sidewalk outside, I scan the crowd. "I probably should have asked for a picture or something. I don't know what they look like." A chatty woman named Debbie called me yesterday. She sounded busy but happy to drop by the club meeting.

Kat's head bobs up for a second. "I'm guessing that's them." Her thumbs have already returned to typing on her phone.

"What? Who?"

She doesn't even raise her head. "Grandma and Grandpa over there. The ones getting out of the electric car."

"Oh, right." I wave at a silver-haired couple, emerging from a Golf parked in one of the visitor's spots. They're wearing khakis and matching raincoats. The woman smiles when she waves back.

"Hi there. You must be Isa," she says when they're close enough to shake my hand. "I'm Debbie, and this is Doug."

I nod. "Nice to meet you. This is Kat, another member of the club. We'll take you to the meeting."

Debbie starts chatting almost immediately as we head toward reception and get them signed in. While we walk through the quickly emptying halls, she tells us how much the school's changed since their kids went there. That they're a retired teacher and veteran, and that back in the dark ages they went to LHS, too. She talks so constantly that I have trouble nodding at the right places. Doug stage-whispers to me that she does that and smiles affectionately at her.

I like them.

They follow us to Mr. Mendoza's lab, where the club's assembled. It's good the meeting hasn't started yet. Mr. Mendoza shakes their hands and asks them if they want to kick things off.

Debbie doesn't waste time. She's started talking before I've even claimed a stool. Doug clears his throat loudly enough for everyone to realize they should pay attention.

"Hi there. We're with Halve by 2030, which is a campaign working to end the age of fossil fuels and build a world of community-led renewable energy for all."

So awesome!

"We're named Halve by 2030 because we must cut greenhouse gas emissions in half by then to limit global warming to 1.5°C—the limit we hope will prevent extreme and irreversible climate catastrophe. That's why we're passionate about preventing the construction of the new natural gas pipeline, which I understand you all are interested in stopping, too."

"That's right," I jump in without thinking.

"The more the merrier," Debbie encourages, unfazed. "Doug here has created a petition on Action Network. I think you all have the link already. We'd love your help collecting some names and email addresses of residents against the pipeline! Once we hit our goal, we'll be taking it to city council."

I've never met adults who actually work on this stuff. Who care, and who are doing something about it. It's ... empowering. Most of the club's on the edge of their stools. Debbie stops for questions, and Darius's hand is first up.

"Thanks for joining us," he says. All the smugness and arrogance he usually wears is gone, replaced by cool, collected focus. "Could you speak more about what you're planning to say during your public comment?"

Doug, who apparently has petitioned the council before, gives us some amazing pointers. Darius's fingers don't stop typing. No doubt updating his list of action points. The amount of stuff he's put together for the public comment is staggering. The only people brave enough to work with him on it are Marina and some of their friends who were in the club last year. Most everyone else is working with Kat and me on spreading the word about the pipeline. We've updated the club's web page again and have done some posts on social media.

By the time Doug starts putting his raincoat back on, Debbie's still talking. "Last thing before we go. Halve by 2030 is collecting signatures outside Safeway this weekend. We'll be standing out front next to the bell-ringing Salvation Army volunteers. You're very welcome to join! It's slow work, but it's worth it. Once you've seen us in action, you can help with our pre-holiday push. We've organized a door-knocking campaign and can include you in the roster."

"That's a very welcome offer," Mr. Mendoza says. "Thank you."

"Well, we won't take up any more of your meeting time, then." Debbie smiles. "Really nice to meet you all." She and Doug wave as they close the door behind them.

"What do you guys think?" I ask. It's the last official club meeting before winter break. Attendance has definitely gone down, but I'm always so happy that people are willing to give up their Friday afternoons to be here. "Personally, I'm down to help, but I know signature collecting and knocking on doors isn't everyone's thing," I tell the room. "I know we're already doing a lot preparing for the public comment."

Mr. Mendoza is the first to speak. "I want to emphasize that no one is to go out collecting signatures alone. And you'll need to take a shift at Safeway before you go door knocking. We'll need multiple people who are willing to go out together, and I'll need permission forms signed before you do."

That cuts the enthusiasm in the room, but Jake and a few others raise their hands.

"Can't hurt to try," Jake says. I love that he always seems to be in a good mood. "I've never door knocked for a petition before. Makes a change from raising money for the baseball team. Should be fun. Sophie, wanna come with me?"

Sophie blushes and looks down. Huh. I've been wondering if there was more to them than just former president and secretary. "Sure, Jake. Just can't stay away, can ya?"

I laugh and write their names up on the board. Susie and Josh are the next pair up. Julián and Tyler say they'll go, too. That's more than I thought we would get. I don't need to ask Kat to know she's not interested. Most of the social media kids won't be, either, though they'll help spread the word about the petition online.

"I'll take a shift," Darius says as the bell rings. He gets up and moves to stand next to me.

"Oh," I say, surprised. I hadn't pegged door knocking as something he would be excited about. Though I guess it is Democracy 101. My hand moves back to the pairs on the whiteboard and I realize that I haven't put myself up there yet. He watches me write *Darius & Isa*. "I guess it's you and me, then?"

He nods. "I guess so." Maybe *excited* isn't exactly what he's feeling.

"For everyone on the board," I tell those left in the lab. "I'll ask 2030 which streets we need to cover and send them around."

"Right, two three. Left, two three!" Mrs. Leota calls. My feet slide across the wood of the newly constructed stage at the APCC. The hall is buzzing with the noise of rehearsing and setting up for the Christmas show.

"Sina, move a bit forward. That's right, in line with Isa." A large grid has been laid across the stage floor in blue painter's tape. Ms. Tilo helps Mrs. Leota move people to the correct places as we work through the formations of our routine.

Mr. Young, who teaches the guys, restarts the music and gives a loud, vocal cry, the signal for us to clap in time as we change formation. The crowd will get involved with this cheering and clapping, too. Pockets of people echo Mr. Young now, even though it's just rehearsal. I can hear Tama's call from farther down the hall, where he's helping set up stalls.

I move in time, making way for the guys to come forward and start their dance. We're not quite in our final costumes, but we're dressed like we will be during the show. The guys perform shirtless, with a wrap over their shorts and strings of grass tied to their legs just below the knee. The girls will wear long patterned wraps and tunics, flowers and feathers in our hair.

In my head, I count the beats. Halfway through the song, I move forward. Wave right arm, wave left arm. Swivel the foot, heel to toe. Step. Step.

I move until I'm right at the center, first in our four rows of four. I kneel down and watch my fingers and wrists dance in graceful waves, lost in the music. I can hear Mom cheering—she must be standing by the front of the stage—but if I look at her, I'll get distracted and forget the choreography. Instead, I keep my eyes focused on following my hands.

The formation shifts again, and four rows of guys move in between our four rows of girls. I smile at Robert, who's dancing opposite me at the front. Even though he's a nice guy, and a great dancer, we haven't talked much since homecoming. He chants, and then we clap in unison. Someone calls out, and the formation shifts. I can hear Mr. Young instructing their side. The song changes with four claps and another chant.

"Louder!" Mrs. Leota hollers at us, not satisfied with our efforts. Robert grins, and with everyone else, we belt cries out to each other.

"Good!" Mr. Young says, restarting the music. "Now, knees up, knees up. Move, move, move!"

We shuffle into a wide circle as the music changes to a fusion with hip-hop, making way for the best guys to take center stage. Robert and his usual backup dancers are first in. Mrs. Leota cheers and moves forward, mimicking the aunties that will come to throw money at the dancers during the actual show.

When we step to the group formation that starts the last song, Ms. Tilo and Mr. Young join her. They move through our lines, patting our shoulders. We're to keep dancing, to not get distracted. More aunties and uncles will come onstage to join us, tucking money into our collars and sleeves in appreciation for our dance and to raise money for the center.

We end with a raised volume of clapping and cheers. When we stop, the crowd will go absolutely wild. I finally look for Mom and find her standing right beneath the stage, cheering her head off.

"Go Isa!!" She beams up at me.

Mom's helping with the food for the Samoan stall. She and Grandma have been market hopping, baking, and boiling all week. The whole house smells like coconut rolls. My family will spend most of our Saturday here. Mrs. Leota's giving us some last instructions, so I move closer to listen.

Mom's still up front watching when we're dismissed. She claps again as I climb off the stage to laugh at her. "Rein it in!" I giggle. "Are you crying? It's just rehearsal!"

"I can't help it. I love watching you dance!" She hugs me and squeezes my shoulders, still beaming. "I have to remember to bring cash to the show, so I can go up onstage and join in."

"You can just give me the cash."

"Nope." She shakes her head. "You'll have to earn it. I'll bring my tips from the restaurant."

We walk over to where all the Samoan society's stuff is piled up at the side of the hall. I sit down on the floor next to my bag and hunt for water. Mom sits down next to me. Another dance troupe (the Korean group, I think) is taking the stage for their rehearsal.

"Does Jay have shifts for me this weekend?" I ask after a bit. I started working at the restaurant the week I turned sixteen, busing tables and helping pack takeout orders. Jay sometimes has extra shifts when it's busy, and with the holidays coming, things are picking up again.

Mom's watching the dancers on the stage. "I'm not sure."

Weird. "What do you mean? Did you ask him? I thought you liked me working at the restaurant."

We had a blast this summer. I've hung around the restaurants Mom's worked in all my life. Making money for it is so nice. Ever since school started, though, I've had to bug her for shifts. I thought it was just because things slowed down. Maybe not?

"You know I like having you around, but you should focus on school," Mom says.

"School's fine," I tell her. "Besides, we need the money."

She exhales. "We don't need your money, Bo. Even though he's working fewer shifts, Dad's earning more now, and we're still saving living with Grandma. Things are fine. Better than they've been in a long time."

"I want to help. I'm sixteen. I can pay for gas and stuff."

Mom cuts me off. "Trust me, you have your whole life to worry about money. Focus on school. Figure out what you want to do. You don't want to end up like me."

I turn my head to stare at her. Mom's my everything, and I *do* want to be like her. "What's wrong with being you?" I ask defensively.

She looks me in the eyes for a moment. "Nothing," she finally says.

I'm not convinced she believes that. "Your life could be different, if you wanted it to be. You could cook. Jay will definitely hire you once he tries your food."

"But that's my life. What's yours?" she snaps.

And we're suddenly mirror images of defensive frustration. Lately, something like this happens whenever we try to talk about the future. It's been months, and Mom still hasn't cooked for Jay. Every time I ask her about it now, she avoids answering by asking me about school. Like that has anything to do with her cooking?

It's so frustrating. And the problem of hanging my future on Mom's dream is that it might never happen. Where does that leave me?

I sigh and fix my gaze back on the stage. The truth is, I don't want to think about that. My dream *isn't* to waitress with her.

I don't like restaurants or cooking nearly as much as she does. And I know the money's crap. Even with Dad's income, we've never had enough. We've always lived in not-nice places, driving not-nice cars. The town house with Grandma is the nicest so far, and it takes all three of them to pay for it.

But we'll keep living together . . . right?

I actually have no idea what I want to do. Not right after high school and definitely not for my whole life. Thinking about it is so overwhelming that I actively try not to, which makes me feel a combination of sad, frustrated, and helpless. And unlike when we talk about anything else, Mom and I just seem to annoy each other when we attempt to discuss the future. Hers. Mine. Money, college, career. I just want to be with my family. Is that so bad?

Onstage, a woman in an elegant hanbok is moving gracefully to the sound of drums. I have to stop myself from swaying in time. I do love to dance, but who makes a living from Samoan dancing? Ms. Tilo works for the school district, helping with special needs kids. Mrs. Leota has a day job, too. She's some kind of accountant when she's not here teaching dance and Samoan language classes.

There are definitely things I don't want to do. I'm really squeamish about blood and guts, so being a nurse or anything in medicine is out. And with my math skills (or lack thereof), I'm not going to be an accountant or engineer, or anything like that.

I let out a frustrated sigh. Then a movement across the hall catches my eye.

Mom sees it, too. "Robert's looking nice," she says.

Robert and some of the other guys have tackled Mr. Young. They're laughing and jumping around. We can't hear what they're saying over the Korean dance troupe's music.

"Yeah." I shrug. "He's fun to dance with."

"He's cute, too." Robert's powerfully built and has a mop of black curls that fall asymmetrically across his forehead. He's still shirtless, muscles out for all to see.

"He is." I nod. "But everyone thinks he's cute, and he knows it. They're saying he'll probably be quarterback of his football team next year." Since we go to different schools, we only really see each other here.

"Oh, Mr. Popular, huh? Not your thing?" Mom deduces.

I shrug again. "I don't think so. I like him, but I don't think I *like* him like him." Saying it aloud, I suddenly realize that it's true.

My arms wrap around my knees, and I rest my chin on them. I've never really dated. I get asked to dances, and I went to the movies with a guy just before we moved here. But we were always gone before I really got to know anyone. It was hard enough making friends, let alone dating. Maybe just being around isn't enough. Robert and I message each other, but it's emojis and GIFs. I don't know anything about him. Not really.

"He's not for you, then," Mom says.

I giggle at the certainty in her voice. "How can you tell?" I ask sincerely.

She laughs. "If you're anything like me, if you want to be with someone, then you'll really know that you want to be with them."

"What, like love at first sight?" I make googly eyes at her.

"No." Mom laughs. "It's not like in the movies, and it certainly didn't happen for me right away. It's more like you can't get someone off your mind, and the more you get to know them, the more you *want* to know them. Don't waste your time on Robert. Go out with the boys you want to kiss."

I laugh in shock. "Mom!"

"I mean it," she says. "If you actually get to know someone and you still want to make out, they're the ones you should go out with."

"Thanks for the pointers." Mom's still annoyed that my first kiss was from this terribly pushy kid in sixth grade who planted one on me during final assembly. She was standing close to the stage that day, too. Her purse hit him right in the gut.

I smile at the memory and find Robert's form in the tangle of guys across the room. He's laughing. Perfectly nice and handsome. Everything you could ask for, really, and nothing in me wants to kiss him. I laugh thinking about the conversation Kat and I had before homecoming—how I played up throwing myself at him after seeing him dance. It was so funny because it all seemed so ridiculous.

Mom's looking at me for an explanation. "Guess Robert's not for me," I echo.

She shrugs, smiles, and says in the same certain tone, "Someone else will be."

The rainy weekend drums on away from the APCC. By the time I meet Darius on Sunday morning, everything's wet. The trees and café awnings drip with rain, and the lawns of the suburban streets we're meant to cover look like they'll squish water when stepped on.

Darius is waiting outside the Starbucks on the corner, looking overdressed and miserable. Who wears a dress shirt to go door knocking? While we haven't actually fought in a while, we're not exactly friends, either. I'm not entirely sure what we are. I walk toward him, but as soon as I reach him, he turns toward Cherry, the first street on our list. Okay. Apparently, we don't say good morning or chat.

Standing together waiting to cross the street, a thick silence hangs in the air between us. It continues as we start down the sidewalk. I think something's wrong.

"So, how are we feeling?" I ask him from under my umbrella.

"Like I'm a Black man in America and this is the dumbest idea I've ever had because I'm about five minutes away from getting shot."

I stop walking. It takes him a second to notice, but when he does, he turns around to face me. "You don't have to do this," I say. "I know it's scary. . . ."

"I'm not scared," he snaps. "Stating the obvious isn't fear, it's factual."

"What?"

"Nothing," he says. "Come on, let's get this over with."

"Hey," I say, unmoving. "If you're going to do this, do it because you want to. You don't have to be here, and a crappy attitude is going to make this way harder. Why don't you try smiling and wishing people a good morning? It might lead to a nicer conversation."

"Seriously?! Smile? Is that all you've got?"

Apparently, we are still fighting.

"I'm a girl, Darius—a smile's all that's expected of me," I snap. Then I flash the brightest, most insincere smile I can manage and hold it. It's surprisingly therapeutic.

He almost laughs, and we both take a breath while I rearrange my face. "Sorry," he says eventually. "I've never done anything like this before. I guess I'm just nervous."

"That's okay. I haven't exactly done this before either." I shrug.

All the club members interested in helping showed up at Safeway at essentially the same time yesterday morning. We just couldn't help moving in a pack. No one seemed particularly confident, even after watching 2030's approach to collecting signatures. My biggest take away was that it looks like a slow process.

Halve by 2030's goal is less ambitious than what Mrs. Freeman suggested. But the signature counter on the petition's link is still nowhere near it, which made them all extremely grateful for any help we could give. That still doesn't mean any of us know what we're doing.

I clap my hand on Darius's shoulder. "If you get shot, I promise to call 911."

This time he does laugh. "Thanks."

Our eyes lock, and I feel … something. I realize my hand is still on his shoulder and snatch it away.

"Ready?" I ask.

He nods, and I march toward the closest door. Several houses later, someone finally answers. It's a woman in a bathrobe, a baby on her hip. She looks like she hasn't slept in days.

"Good morning." I smile empathetically. Baby Devon next door had a terrible night last night. It was difficult to sleep through, even with the dividing wall. "My name's Isa, and this is Darius. We're students at Lakewood High."

She interrupts me with "Sorry, hun, I've already given to the football fundraiser."

"Nope. We're not fundraising," I rush to clarify. "We're collecting signatures and giving out candy canes." I put it this way because I notice the toddler, who's rapidly making his way toward the door.

"Oh, right," the woman says. She takes the clipboard I'm holding without bothering to look at it. There are a couple explanatory paragraphs at the top, followed by lines for information: names, email addresses, and zip codes. I've filled in a couple to keep it from looking like a blank page. I won't enter those when we add the info we collect to the online petition later. I figured it would help people take a stand, though. Knowing that they're not alone.

"Is it alright if he has one?" I pull a bag of the little individually wrapped candy canes out of my backpack and hand it to Darius. Since he'd rather not make conversation, he can be on candy cane duty.

The woman laughs; the kid's already tapping at Darius's shin impatiently. "Sure, no stopping him. Luke, what do you say?"

Darius bends down to hand him one, and Luke thanks him in a very small voice.

"You're welcome," Darius tells him.

"What are the signatures for?" the woman finally asks.

"We're terrified about the climate crisis and what it will mean for our futures—and Luke's," I add. "We've heard that the mayor is planning to build a new natural gas pipeline, which will make the problem worse. We'd like him to reconsider."

This is clearly not what the woman was expecting to hear. She bites her lower lip in thought before asking, "Won't the pipeline mean more jobs?"

"Not for us. My dad's a longshoreman, and the construction's already disrupted his shifts. The gas won't even stay here. They'll pump it out east."

"Hmm . . ." Her pen hovers over a blank line.

"Mom! It's bubble gum!" Luke's mouth has already turned blue. He waves a sticky hand up at her and wraps the other around her knee.

"Yum, bubble gum's my favorite flavor, too," I tell him. I turn back to his mom. "We'd really appreciate your support. All we want is to talk through the options with the city council. You're welcome to come. We're hoping to raise enough signatures to get a discussion on the agenda."

"Mom—look!"

"Ah, alright, then." She scribbles her name down.

"Thank you so much," I beam. "I hope you all have a Merry Christmas. What did you ask Santa for, Luke?"

The promise of candy canes gone, Luke suddenly moves behind his mom. "What? You're being shy now?" She laughs. "If you don't say what you want, maybe Santa will bring you underwear?"

"Or a pair of socks?" I tease, enjoying myself. This gets him.

"No! Pokémon!" Luke shouts. "Pokémon!"

"Pokémon it is, then." I smile. "Thanks again, and happy holidays!" I wave to Luke until we're back on the sidewalk. Darius puts the bag of candy canes into the pocket of his rain jacket. He's watching me with a funny look in his eye.

"How are you so good at talking to people?" he asks.

The intensity of his sincerity surprises me. "You talk in front of people all the time," I remind him. Confidence is certainly not something he's lacking. At least, not usually.

"Sure. But that's public speaking, and they teach you how to do that. I've got Honors Speech and Debate spring trimester." Well, that explains a few things.

"You connect with people," he goes on. "You can get a whole room to do jazz hands like it's the most natural thing in the world. Do you practice what you're going to say? I always have to write things down beforehand."

I stop and turn to look at him. "What?!"

He pulls something out of his pocket. They're flash cards. He's written out flash cards, with bullet points on them.

"No way!" I laugh, taking them from him so I can read them. "You wrote down exactly what you were going to say today?"

He at least seems to recognize how over-the-top this is, and he starts laughing, too. It's a full laugh, with a rich sound. "How else do you remember?!" he asks.

"You were really going to tell people that the facility will include an eight-million-gallon storage tank and two tanker loading stations? And that the methane leaks from fracking natural gas are as high as 7.9 percent?" I'm so completely bewildered.

The things he's written *are* interesting. It's the way he's put them that doesn't make any sense. Why wouldn't he just say that the process of getting natural gas makes it worse for the climate than coal? You don't need decimal points to explain that.

"We're talking to normal people, here. And yeah, sure, I sometimes think about what I should say." I suddenly remember the weekend I spent muttering things to myself—preparing to argue with *him*. "But this isn't Honors Speech and Debate, Darius!"

We're both laughing. Hard. For the first time, it feels like we're genuinely talking to each other. I dab at the moisture building in the corner of my eyes. "All you have to say is why you care, and why you think they should."

"Why I care?" The perplexed look on his face has me laughing, again.

"Don't overthink it! It's not hard! You're a person. She's a person. You've got a lot in common. We even all speak the same language. And kids make things way easier."

"Easier?!" He's putting it on now, trying to be funny. And it's working. I cannot stop laughing.

"Yes—easier! They're kids. They don't care at all about what you have to say. You literally just gave candy to a baby. It's the easiest thing in the world."

He's wiping his eyes, too, by the time I finish. And it takes us a few more minutes to sober up and start walking again. At the very least, he doesn't seem at all offended that we've both been laughing at his expense for about five whole minutes.

"People skills," I finally say, collecting myself. "Really helpful when working with, you know, people."

I pat him twice on the upper arm. I'm aiming for the movement to be jokingly consoling, but on the second beat I have the oddest impulse not to let go, to sling my arm through his. Weird.

I tilt my umbrella back so I can look at his face. "Maybe something to practice."

CHAPTER 11
RUNNER'S HIGH

Darius

"THAT'S TIME," MS. PATTEN SAYS. WITH A JOLT OF ADRENALINE, I punctuate my last sentence. "Pencils down, please, and blue books in the basket. Pencils down, Levi. You've had forty minutes. On the AP exam, you won't get more for an essay question."

I close my blue book and stand up so I can toss it into the basket at the front of the room with the others. History is DONE. Only four more classes stand between me and winter break. I crammed for today practically all of last night, so during my one hour of sleep I dreamed that Confederate soldiers were made to write essays about Mary Shelley. It wasn't the worst idea.

When the bell rings, I trudge off to Honors American Literature and what should be my last timed essay of the day. I manage to get my reflections down in another blue book before the time goes there, too—just barely, but I make it. Now only Spanish III, AP Calculus, and AP Biology. Then two glorious weeks of sleep.

I did better than I expected on the PSAT, but I've slipped off the top of the class leader board. There's just too much going on. The list taunts me after I hand over my AP Calculus exam—early, of course—at the front of Mr. Davis's room. I should get things back on track during spring trimester, when my Spanish class is replaced with Honors Chemistry. I try not to obsess about it and instead watch the slush fall outside the classroom window. Everyone's been praying for it to turn to snow all day.

I'm barely conscious when the last bell rings in AP Biology. "Have a great holiday break!" Mr. Mendoza tells us as he circles the room, collecting exams.

Marina walks over to my lab bench, shaking her head. "That was terrible!"

"Really?" I ask. "I didn't think it was bad."

"Of course you didn't. You always ace science."

"Bet you did better than me on the Calculus exam," I tell her. "And all the essays. I'm sure of that."

She smiles. I shoulder my bag, and we walk toward the parking lot together with the rest of the herd. The halls are full of kids looking very happy. The AP crew looks like we're minutes away from passing out. Although Collin somehow still finds it in him to stare longingly at Marina when he thinks no one's looking.

"What are you doing tonight?" Marina asks me.

"I have big plans to do absolutely nothing." I grin. "What about you?"

"Family dinner. Everyone's coming over, meaning my aunt and uncle are coming over to check on Haruto."

I take off my glasses so I can rub my face. "Did he get that job?"

"Yup, I hope he's okay there. At least he's officially living with us now that he's working and going to rehab. I still feel bad for him. He's not even allowed to borrow a car."

"Oh, right." I forgot about the DUI thing. "Does he need a bike? He can borrow one of mine." I don't think the Takahashis are that into cycling. I've never seen Ken or Yuto on bikes.

Marina shrugs. "I'll ask, though I doubt they'll be thrilled about it. You can come over for dinner if you want?"

"No, thanks. I don't plan on leaving my house until Sunday."

"What's on Sunday?" she asks me.

"I'm meeting Isa. We've got our last round of door knocking to do, for the petition. It's almost got enough signatures." I yawn. We're parked next to each other, and Jordan, Ken, and Yuto are waiting for us by our cars.

"Well, have fun," Marina says sarcastically.

I smirk. Marina's made it very clear that she has absolutely no interest in the petition or anything else she classifies as "Isa's ideas." While it was nice to have her so wholeheartedly on my side at first, it feels different now. Even the Model UN kids understood when we broke the news—they were excited for us, really, and I'm starting to agree with them.

The pipeline thing is so much bigger, so much realer than anything I could have come up with. And spending time with Isa feels different now, too. This door knocking thing has been . . . good. And if I'm honest, that has less to do with the petition and more to do with Isa than I'd like to admit. She is fun. I'm kind of sad this will be our last pre-Christmas shift.

I tear through the red-and-green wrapping paper, crumpling it in one hand as I lift the lid of the box with the other. It's not even all the way off before I'm yelling, "No way! No. Way!"

"Merry Christmas!" Mom and Dad say together.

"Try them on. Let's see if they fit!" Dad's grinning like the Cheshire cat. The cleats were definitely his idea. We've been souping up my road bike for the past few weeks. I saw him messing with my pedals before break.

"What? You got him cleats?!"

"You, too, Jordan, put your cocoa down and open that box—there!" Mom says, pointing.

I step out of my slippers and slide my socked feet into the cycling shoes, excitedly pulling on the Velcro straps to close them. Dad shuffles across the front living room carpet on his knees until he can press his thumb to the tip of my shoe, feeling for the edge of my toes.

"You want a little room in them, but not too much," he says. Mom's doing the same to Jordan on the other sofa. "What do you think? Go on, stand up."

I stand gingerly, feeling the weirdness of the unyielding sole and Dad's thumb. "Yeah, I think they fit. Thanks!"

"Oh, the fun's just getting started." Dad pulls an Allen wrench, a tube of grease, and metal cleats out of the box. "We've got to get the cleats attached to the right place." Dad loves stuff like this.

"After we finish with the presents, babe," Mom tells him, moving over to investigate what's left under the massive, twinkling tree. The whole house smells of pine from the Christmas tree and the fire already burning behind us. Outside, the wind whistles rain through the early light. I smile, wishing I could wrap the coziness of Christmas morning around me like a blanket.

"They've got more gifts to unwrap. Like this one." Mom tosses a soft package at me. Inside is a waterproof thermal speed suit for winter riding to complete my new look.

Jordan bounces forward, still wearing his new cycling shoes. "Can we go out? Can we go on a bike ride??"

Mom looks warily at the rain out the bay window. Dad taps at his Apple Watch. "The forecast says Saturday will have the best weather of the week."

"Still raining, though," she says.

Dad laughs. "Of course."

"Come on, Mom! Let's ride!" Jordan begs. Part of me wants to tell him to stop whining, but a bigger part wants to join in. There's nothing like getting them both to take a break and spend time with us.

Dad's looking at Mom. "Doing STP as a family this summer was your idea, and this will be our last chance to ride together before tax season starts."

I hope this doesn't kick off another one of their silent fights about parenting styles. One that means the house will be empty for weeks. Mom usually works most of the holidays. She even missed the start of midnight mass yesterday. Just as I start to spiral, thinking through all the various possibilities, Mom raises her chin.

She makes eyes at Dad and tosses an identical soft present to Jordan. I'd bet my allowance that it's a thermal speed suit. "Saturday, then," she says.

"Yes!" Jordan pumps his arm in triumph.

I copy him.

Saturday becomes the day. I love when the four of us ride together. We used to cycle a lot when Jordan and I were little, spent vacations camping and riding bikes. Cycling during the winter isn't ideal, but this new stuff is quality, even though it makes me look like an absolute tool.

Mom's got her hair wrapped up under her helmet in a futile attempt to keep it dry. She pushes forward under the icy drizzle, asking Jordan questions to figure out how to make the cleats more comfortable. He's pedaling awkwardly. Like those dogs forced to wear shoes.

I pump forward. Clipping in and out is a pain, but now that the cleats seem to be in the right place the motion feels effortless. On the straightaways, I can basically fly. The speed is fucking amazing. Even Dad can't catch me. He pulls a muscle trying.

It's just Jordan and me after that, going out whenever it's not raining too hard. They've repaved a section of trail by the state park nearest town, and the smooth surface is great to ride on. Jordan still doesn't like the clip-ins, even though this is our fourth ride of break. To prove their usefulness, I race him back to the parking lot. My feet slipping against the pedals is a thing of the past. I've got him well beat when I reach the skate park, so I slow down and turn in circles, scanning the horizon.

I can't even see him in the distance.

"Darius?" a voice I know calls.

Nooooooo!

I do another slow circle and look around. Of course, the day I'm dressed in a neon skin suit is the day that I run into Isa. And all her friends. What are they doing at the skate park?! I wave halfheartedly in their direction. Then I remember that not only am I covered head to toe in spandex, but if I get off, I'll have to clickety-clack over to them in my clip-in cleats. And be *that* guy. Kill me.

Isa stands a bike up and pedals over to me. Kat and a couple guys I don't recognize without my glasses on are standing around the covered skateboard bowl on the other side of the parking lot. I'm glad they don't seem as eager to talk to me as Isa does.

"Nice bike!" she says when she's close enough not to shout.

"Thanks." I clip out and stand astride it. The comparison between my new road bike and the bike she's riding is pretty harsh. Hers is a royal blue mountain bike. From the bits of the frame that I can see—the few parts that aren't covered in stickers—I can tell it's rusting out. It looks secondhand, and too small for her. "Do you do tricks on that thing?"

She laughs. "Only one. Wanna see?"

"Sure." I grin. Anything to get her to stop looking at me in my gear.

Isa pedals away, and then, with a surprisingly sure movement, she pops a wheelie. But when she tries to turn back toward me, the bike wobbles and she bails. Her feet hit the pavement first, then she stumbles and falls, letting the bike crash ahead of her.

I'm next to her when she lands, bum on the wet pavement. I don't know when I started running.

"Are you okay?" I demand.

She's laughing.

"See? I'm not very good." She stands up and wipes at the back of her rain jacket. "I'm okay. Don't worry. I fall almost every time. Kat and her brothers have been trying to teach me that for the past three years. We're here like every weekend, and I still haven't got it. They skateboard, too, but I'm hopeless at that. I like riding better, anyway."

How is she not embarrassed? She looks totally at ease. We're close to a group of trees that mark the start of a gravel trail going off to the right. She pushes her bike under the tallest one so we can stand slightly out of the rain. I retrieve the road bike I left lying on the paved trail and follow her.

"How was your holiday?" she asks. "Guess we haven't seen each other since we finished door knocking."

A smile spreads across my face. "Well, not exactly."

She stares up at me, confusion in those big brown eyes, and I laugh before adding, "I saw you at the Asia Pacific Cultural Center. You were in the Christmas show. You're a good dancer."

Her eyebrows shoot up. "What? You were there?!"

I laugh again. Maybe she does get embarrassed.

"Yeah, I go with Marina's family," I tell her. "The Japanese society always runs a bunch of the market stalls, and the Takahashis make some truly amazing udon."

Marina and I usually just hang out at the market stalls and help—or, in my case, eat. This year, though, they put everything together in the newly renovated hall, which meant that we could watch most of the performances. Even while I stuffed my face with endless bowls of steaming noodles.

So when the lights dimmed and the announcer welcomed the Samoan society, I had a clear view of the energetic troupe that took the stage. They would have been pretty impossible to ignore, given the enthusiasm the audience greeted them with. When their music started, people were on their feet—several ladies moved to the front, like they were ready to join in. Some of the moves weren't unlike the step dancing Mom and Dad used to do in college.

I was on my feet, clapping and hollering with the crowd, when the first song changed, the lines of dancers shifted, and a graceful girl danced to the front of the stage. Her hips swayed to the music beneath her brightly colored skirt. Her dark hair was pulled back in a low bun framed with flowers, and her eyes shone under the lights. She was stunning. Absolutely stunning. And she was also Isa. Isa Brown.

I haven't really stopped thinking about her since.

I clear my throat, suddenly scrambling to think of something normal to say. "I didn't know that the Samoan society has so many people. Your show was amazing."

"Um, thanks," she says. "I can't believe you were there! It was packed this year, and having the performances and the market together was really fun. It's so nice to have such a big cultural center."

"I think it's awesome. I've always been jealous of Marina for that. There are like two Black families in Lakewood." I don't know why I added that last part.

Isa laughs. "There are more than two! Hit up City Church this Sunday and you'll find loads of us. But yeah, I feel really lucky to have a community around."

She looks at me for a second. "You and Marina spend a lot of time together." Isa doesn't ask this as a question, but I think it is.

I nod, finally getting to explain. "Marina lives down the street from me. We met when we were seven and have been friends ever since. I think I spent more time at her house than mine growing up."

"Oh." Isa's forehead crinkles, and she looks away. "That must be lonely."

What does she mean by that? I guess I'm not always surrounded by people the way she is, but I'm rarely alone—which reminds me. "Who are you here with? Was that your dance partner again?"

At the show, most of Isa's dances were with the other girls. I couldn't help noticing, though, that during the partnered dances she was with the same guy she brought to homecoming. That burly football player from Clover Park High. I also noticed that he seemed pretty happy about being paired with her. And that he's way bigger than I am. But she never mentions him, or any other boyfriend.

"Oh, Robert? No, we just dance together," she starts. Is that who she's here with now? I'm hanging onto her words enough to notice her distraction. Then I hear Jordan shouting and the noise of bikes, and I look away from her to find the source. Jordan and another boy are tearing down the path toward us, racing each other.

Isa laughs. "Get him, Isaac!" Then to me she explains, "He's one of Kat's brothers."

"I win!" Jordan yells when he passes us. "Come on, D!" he shouts, still pumping down the paved trail.

Isaac, though, slows to a stop not far from us. He's panting.

"No. Way." He gasps, clutching his chest.

Jordan will be miles out soon if someone doesn't stop him. "I've got this." I grin. "See you later!"

I clip in and cycle off, racing to catch up. By the time we get back to the parking lots, Isa and her friends have left. I never did find out who they were. And as the days pass, I'm itching to know. Occasionally, I take out my phone and bring up the text chain I have with her.

We exchanged numbers before she and Mr. Mendoza came over on Thanksgiving. The only messages we've sent since have been about where and when we're meeting to do petition and club stuff. This isn't the first time I've thought about messaging her, though. After I saw her dance at the Christmas show, I almost did. I just couldn't figure out how to say *I watched you dance* in a way that wouldn't come off as completely creepy.

I feel like I might spend the last day of break taking my phone in and out of my pocket. Until a single line lights up my screen.

Isa's texted.

> Happy New Year!

I laugh in shock, the sides of my mouth pulling up. I send her a picture of our neighborhood fireworks display lighting up the lake. I add:

> Happy New Year!

Then I wait, staring at my phone.

She sends a video of someone lighting a pop rocket in a driveway. A spark catches his pant leg, and just as he stomps it out, someone pours a drink on him. I can hear Isa's laughter in the background.

> *Your fireworks are much more impressive than ours.*

I send a laughing emoji.

> *Yours look more fun!*

> *Thanks 😄 See you Monday!*

> *See you then.*

I put my phone back in my pocket, and for the rest of the night, I can't stop smiling.

CHAPTER 12
CONFUSION AT THE GATES

Darius

MY FIRST MORNING BACK AT SCHOOL TAKES ON A NEW LIGHT now that I'm wondering when exactly I'll see Isa. I'm shocked by how much time I've managed to spend trying to dissect the meaning in six lines of text. After each reading, I come away with an entirely different interpretation. She was just being nice. She probably texts everyone in her phone a happy New Year. Five minutes later, I'm convinced she's in love with me. A thought that has my pulse racing and my mind running through the possibilities.

I blame some of my preoccupation on the lack of change to my school schedule. Winter trimester has me continuing all the same classes I had during the autumn one. And now that cross-country season is over, I won't have an official sports practice until track starts in the spring. Some of the team meets up to run when the weather's not miserable, but nothing's really set. At least I've got new cycling stuff to play with.

And of course, there's the SAT to prep for. I want to give myself at least two tries this year. Marina says she wants three and is going to sit for it this month. My PSAT scores were high enough that I think

I'll only need one, but I want to give myself another shot to be safe. I'll probably take it in March, then again in May. I can't believe by this time next year, I'll have already applied to colleges.

But which ones?!

I don't have much time to worry about that, because each period we get our midterm results back. And an outline of the work that will consume our lives for the next several months, all in preparation for the AP exams in May. Test scores also mean that a new ranking will be waiting on the leader board after lunch.

Lunch. The only time in my schedule when I would feasibly run into Isa. And probably the only day of the year when I haven't already planned to spend it in the library. I'm completely distracted as I join a line in the cafeteria. Craning my neck around, looking for her. Should I ask if she wants to eat together? What if she goes to the library looking for me?

I suddenly realize that I have no idea where she usually sits. What if she goes off campus?

"Hey, Middle D!" Chad calls, joining the line behind me. "How was your break? Get anything good for Christmas?"

He's with a couple other seniors from the cross-country team. They're arguing about who got the best haul. I don't mind that there's no gap to enter the debate. Vishal's loudly trying to convince them that the drone his parents gave him tops the list and that we should use it to film during track season. I follow them through the line and out to an empty table, only half paying attention. Isa isn't in any of the lines, and I don't see her waiting at the vending machines. If she's not here, what did she mean by *See you Monday*?

I finally stop scanning the crowd when Marina sits down next to me. "Have you seen Isa anywhere?"

Marina's chin bobs up, and I watch her raise an eyebrow. "Why are you looking for Isa?"

Guess not. I drum my fingers across the table and try to focus on my as yet untouched food. I doubt Isa would have texted, but I check my phone anyway. Nothing. Should I message her?

"What, are you guys friends now?" The sharpness in Marina's voice makes me look up. She's staring at me, her face full of disbelief.

"Uh, something like that." I actually have no idea. This is all so ridiculous.

I shrug.

"Which should we watch first after school? Rewatch season one or start season two?" The newest series of *Witch Hat Atelier* premiered on New Year's. Marina's dying to watch it and said we should start together. "I can't believe they've only released the first two episodes!"

While she talks, my mind drifts back to Isa.

What if she doesn't even have this lunch anymore? Eager to leave the cafeteria, I make quick work of the food on my tray and excuse myself to do a lap of the library. She's not there, either. The back corners where we used to discuss club stuff are empty. I'm halfway to the parking lots—to look where, I have no idea—when the warning bell goes. I about-face and head to class.

Why am I making this so hard? I should just message her. My phone's already in my hand when I realize *Where are you?* probably isn't the best opening. My thumbs hover over the keyboard as I cross the threshold of Mr. Davis's classroom and am startled back to reality.

Levi chooses to use the moment I enter to announce that Lucas tops the leader board. What is happening to me?!

I put my phone in my pocket and sit down, resolved to refocus my priorities. I have a lot of work to do. I need to spend the rest of the week getting it done—not thinking about Isa. Why am I making this such a big deal?

Concentrating solely on school goes fairly well for the rest of the day. It's not until I'm plugging my now silenced phone into the car's auxiliary cable that that changes.

Isa's texted.

> Hey, sorry not to see you today!

> I've got second lunch now. I was thinking, the club should do a rally like the APCC Christmas show. We could have booths for different groups and music and performances. It'll be like a big green festival!

> What do you think?

> I'll be at the skate park later, if you want to talk about it?

I'm suddenly driving too fast. At home, I rush to grab my mountain bike out of the garage, ecstatic that Marina's family didn't take me up on my offer to let Haruto borrow it. Isa was in jeans when I ran into her over break, so I don't bother to change into cycling gear. I'm at the skate park in an embarrassingly short amount of time.

It's a rare rain-free day, and this week is supposed to be unusually warm for January, with high temperatures of almost fifty degrees. I soak in what will be the last hour of sun while cycling slow circles around the parking lots. I'm too hyped up to wait in the car. And trying not to freak out about why.

CHAPTER 13
A NEW PATH

Isa

"WHAT, NO SPANDEX?" I CAN'T HELP CALLING AS I RIDE toward Darius. I giggle, remembering him in that speed suit he was wearing last time. It's not that he didn't look good. It was just so much information.

Darius laughs. "Thought I'd go for something a bit less formfitting today. I like the new color."

My hair is billowing out from under my boarding helmet, the red highlighted streaks catching the sunlight. "Thanks." I smile, suddenly feeling a bit nervous. And then, like it always does when I'm nervous, my mouth takes off.

"My mom thought red would be good for New Year's. She's gotten really into making Chinese recipes ever since she tried those Szechuan wontons at the APCC Christmas festival, those dumplings with the numbing chili, they were amazing."

OMG. Stop talking!

I pull myself together enough to ask, "Wanna ride one of the trails?"

I don't wait for a response, just start pedaling toward one of the lesser-used paths. Why am I so nervous?

Darius cycles beside me at a comfortable pace. The trail we choose is wide enough that we can ride next to each other and still leave room for people to pass. When someone does, cycling toward us, Darius raises his fingers off his handlebar to give them a wave. I take a few deep breaths.

"How was your first day back?" Darius asks me.

"Um, well . . ." I shake my head and exhale. "My schedule's completely different. The only thing that's stayed the same is Spanish."

"I've got Spanish, too."

"Isn't Señora Flores funny?" I smile. "Did she go on about how she's addicted to the new flavor of gum they've started selling in the vending machines to your class, too? I'm going to have to try it. I forgot to buy some today."

He laughs. "No, but did you see that Mr. Mendoza shaved his mustache? I barely recognized him. He said he lost a bet to his kids over the holidays."

"No way! My dad would never shave for us. That firework singed his beard, and he still wouldn't let Mom touch it." I'm laughing, more comfortable now.

My legs pump against the pedals in easy rhythm. We've never really talked like this before. I guess by the time our door knocking shifts finished, we had started to. Moved on from practicing people skills to just being people . . . It was nice. So different from the first time we met, when he told me he didn't have time to deal with me. I guess that's the drawback of being around someone who's so forthright. He tells you exactly what he's thinking, even the stuff you'd rather not know.

We chat on about changes since the holidays. The light fades slowly under the thinning pines, and I'm surprised at how pleasant it is, being with Darius. I start telling him a funny story about the compliments Mom's been getting on her new hairstyle at J's and he exclaims, "You eat at J's?!"

I laugh. "Of course we do. My mom works there."

"No way! I love J's. That's my family's go-to soul food place. Their catfish! No, their coconut cornbread!" His voice takes on a reverent tone.

"Oh, I *know*!"

"Your mom cooks there?!" he asks in awe.

The question hits me like a ton of bricks, and I have to purposefully focus on the trail rather than on Darius, hoping he doesn't catch the look on my too-readable face. "Ah . . . no," I mumble.

Jay hired a new chef over the holidays. Mom didn't even talk to him about it, let alone apply. And I only found out because one of the busboys happened to mention it while I was working. I can't even with her right now. I don't understand, and it all makes me so angry. Why won't she just go for it?

"She's a waitress," I say eventually. "I work there sometimes, too." I try to bring my attention back, but I'm quiet for a while, lost in my own mind.

The trail curves, and up ahead I can see the edge of American Lake, Lakewood's largest. We've ridden that far? I register with shock that it's getting hard to see because the sun's setting.

"What time is it?! Man, I forgot my bike lights."

"Oh." Darius sounds worried. He clicks on the light attached to his handlebars and we turn around, following its glow on the pavement ahead of us. "Can you get home okay? I can give you a ride. Or cycle there with you?"

"That's alright. It's actually not that far, I probably just need to head there soon rather than go back to the skate park. I can take the next right; that trail up ahead leads basically to the start of my street."

It does seem weirdly darker now that his light's on. I'm bummed, and surprised, that this ended so quickly.

"We haven't talked about your idea for the festival." Darius's voice sounds deeper in the dark.

"Oh, right!" I laugh, nerves creeping into the edges. "I guess we haven't. Sorry, I can be more on it tomorrow, if you want to ride again?" Did I just ask Darrius out?

"Yeah, I'd like that."

I'm suddenly glad the dusk is hiding the expression on my face. *He'd like that.* "Cool." I smile. "I'll see you tomorrow, then."

The next day, I find myself rushing out of school, pumping the pedals to get to the skate park quickly, but Darius still beats me there. He's cycling circles around the parking lots, just like yesterday. Only today he's wearing a fancy Arc'teryx rain jacket. It's not raining yet, but it's supposed to, and this will probably be the last rain-free afternoon for a while. I did at least remember my bike lights so that we can stay out a bit longer. If that's what he wants.

Darius flashes me a wide smile when he sees me cycling over. It's easy to smile back, to enjoy the ease that exists between us now.

I spent the better part of last night wondering if this is a date or not. Trying to decide if he would want it to be. But then, even though yesterday was surprisingly nice, we were supposed to be talking about stuff for the club. Like we are today. So it's definitely not a date. Right? Do *I* want it to be?

I can't make up my mind.

Today, I start talking through my festival idea right away. I'm hoping that if we get the club stuff done first, it'll be easier to see whether this is a meeting or a date or something in-between based on what happens next. Sure. This is what I'm thinking as I rattle through my vision. Darius nods along supportively.

"I think it should be more of a rally, to celebrate taking down the pipeline," Darius says. "But getting the other clubs involved would be amazing. So would having food and music."

I get a flash of inspiration. "The club could hold it during the last Friday of the school year, when everyone gets a half day! Then we could do it in the football stadium before graduation."

The path curves, ready to launch us down a steep hill. This gravel trail is one of my favorites. I don't like racing much and have never been especially fast. Downhills are the only exception. It's so easy to fly!

"I. Like. It!" Darius's voice shakes out in time with the ridges we're riding over.

I laugh, turning to see how far behind me he's gotten. Like yesterday, Darius has cycled beside me while we talked. Weirdly, though, he seems to put on his brakes whenever the trail really bottoms out. Maybe he doesn't love the off-road trails? He does seem to genuinely like the rally idea.

When the trail levels out, Darius catches up, and we continue side by side. "We could get community groups involved, too," I say.

"Definitely." Darius nods. "We should pitch the idea to the club at the next meeting. We'll need all the help we can get." He looks at the trail ahead. "Does this ever go back up?"

We've rounded another bend, and the trail in front of us slopes deceptively down again, but it doesn't stay that way for long. I nod. "It does, after this. Oh! Want to learn how to pop a wheelie?!"

"What?!" Darius brakes so hard I have to turn my head to see his shocked face behind me.

"This slope kicks right on to a steep uphill. It's perfect for getting enough momentum to pop up," I explain. "It's fun!"

He doesn't look convinced. And he's barely moving. I stop and let him catch up, waiting until he meets my eye.

"Wheelies not your thing?" I ask.

"Yeah, no," he says. "I like cycling fast on a smooth, level surface." He looks embarrassed for a moment; then he laughs. "Guess I can admit that the thought of wheelies, and falling off while attempting a wheelie, scares me. I was always that kid who never climbed trees or colored outside the lines."

He's serious. We're like the exact opposite.

"Really?" I laugh with him. "Guess wheelies are out, then."

"Thank God."

I study his face. There are things I've been meaning to tell him about the murals, and about our plans with Eliyah and Nathan. Things I've been meaning to get the club involved in. But I haven't. Something's always stopped me, even now that we're kind of friends.

I bite my lip in thought, then ask, "Have you ever done something that, you know . . . wasn't school board approved?"

It's the closest thing I can think of to get at what I actually mean. He looks puzzled but takes my asking seriously.

"Um. Not really, no. Kids with glasses who are enrolled in the gifted program tend to thrive on following the rules."

Right. That's what's been bugging me, what I suspected all along. Darius wouldn't be cool with it.

"I mean, my parents didn't teach me study mantras for nothing," he's saying.

This snaps me back to the present.

"The PSAT doesn't take itself," he continues.

Darius takes one look at the bewildered expression on my face and laughs. Hard.

"What?" I say. "There's a PSAT?!"

And we're suddenly both laughing at each other. Bent over our stationary bike frames, giggling over the rustle of the wind through the trees. It feels like we've come from complete opposite ends of the earth. To find each other, here, laughing in the mud of this bike trail.

"Come on," I say when I can breathe again. I push off and cycle forward, losing him on the downhill. I resist the urge to pop a wheelie when the trail kicks up and start the slow climb out of the valley.

"That was a joke, right? You've taken the PSAT?" Darius says when he returns to riding beside me.

I throw him a look, but it's not as serious as I'd want it to be, given that I'm climbing. I'm breathing too hard to answer, so I just shake my head.

"No way." Darius's breathing hasn't changed. I guess he is in pretty amazing shape. Not to mention the fact that his bike has about ten thousand speeds. "Where do you want to go for college?"

Not this again. He sounds like my mom. "Don't know." I'm glad I'm too winded to sound irritated. "I'm guessing you know exactly where you want to go and what you want to be?"

"Well, no, but I have a top-five list of universities going. I'll apply to ten to be safe, and I'll probably be prelaw. Major in political science or public policy, and hopefully set myself up for a good grad school."

My eyebrows shoot up, but I can't answer until we reach some flat ground and I've caught my breath. When the trail levels out, I ask, "Really?" between breaths. "I would have thought you'd do research or something science-y."

"Why?"

I shrug. "In my head, you're more like Mr. Mendoza and less like your mom."

"Huh," he says, pedaling forward as the trail starts to climb again. "That's probably true." He looks over at me. "I think you should work for Halve by 2030. You're exactly what they need."

At this point, Darius is several yards ahead of me (really! He must be in some ridiculous shape!) and can't see my stunned face. He goes on, climbing effortlessly.

"You're a person of color who's all about community. You organize without thinking about it, and you can motivate people. You think creatively about drawing attention to the cause, and you have networks the 2030 organizers don't. They'd be lucky to have you. Have you asked about their internships?"

I blink at him pedaling up the hill, oblivious to my various struggles—with this hill, and with thinking about the future.

"You should email them a pitch and your résumé," he says. "Even if they don't have a formal program, I bet they would hire you for the summer."

I'm still staring at him, barely conscious of my legs straining to keep me moving forward. In my mind, something shifts. I had planned to work at J's and babysit again this summer, make as much money as I could. It had literally never occurred to me that all this stuff we've been doing for the club could be a job. What if I could . . . organize? Work to make change *and* get paid?

By the time I get to the top of the hill, wheezing and hot beneath my jacket, Darius is off his bike. He's standing astride it, waiting for me to cycle on, but I stop pedaling and stand next to him. Breathing and thinking for another moment. We've made it back to the paved trails that lead to the skate park.

"You think I should work for 2030? Just, what? Email them and ask for a job?"

"Yeah." He shrugs. "If that's what you want. Lawyers' kids do that kind of thing all the time. Work experience is expected. I'll probably end up at my mom's firm for an internship sometime before I graduate."

This is too good to be true. It can't be that easy.

"Make sure they pay you, though," Darius says.

Knew it. "People don't *pay* interns?" I scoff.

"They should. They don't always. It's really common to ask students to work for free, but Mom's big on Black people never working for free, ever—especially women. You don't grow up in my house and not learn about the wage gap. Or how that wage gap is more severe for women of color."

"Do you think that 2030 would pay, though? I definitely can't work for free." That much I know. Mom may want me to focus on school, but in the summer, paychecks are nonnegotiable.

"You should talk to Debbie and Doug about it, ask them about their career paths and follow up with emails. You're such a natural at the community organizing work they do. And 2030 is pretty right on. If you make a compelling case, I bet they would offer you a paid internship."

Darius smiles as he starts pedaling again, completely unaware of the thoughts he's unleashed inside me.

For nights, I think about little else. I remain deeply skeptical that this will work. That things could be as easy as Darius describes. That anyone whose first priority for employment has to be a paycheck could make interning for an environmental organization work. And yet. I dream of murals and rallies. See myself in classrooms, leading meetings in church basements, and holding megaphones on protest marches. I take to scrolling through 2030's website and reading the profiles of their staff members. They do this for a living, and they get paid real money. Good money.

My head's full of new possibilities that exist right here, in my neighborhood. I could work for Halve by 2030. And this is bigger than the summer. What if this is what I want to do? *What if this is what I want to be?*

Things are suddenly new and surprisingly close all at the same time. Darius rattled off all these things I've never thought of as skills before. Skills they'd . . . need? Kat talks about me like that, too. The way I'm good with words and have creative ideas. Maybe they *would* want me.

An email alert pings on the bottom of my screen, and I almost fall off my chair.

It's from Debbie.

Is she reading my mind?!

My heart races as I click to open her chatty message.

> Hi Isa,
>
> How are you, dear? Happy new year!
>
> Halve by 2030's drive to collect signatures is paying off. We've almost reached our goal! Should we come by and brief the Lakewood High Environmental Justice Club at your next meeting? It'd be good to coordinate our plans for approaching city council. Let me know! Xx.
>
> Warmly,
> Debbie

This is great! Darius and I are planning to talk about the rally idea at the next meeting anyway, so Halve by 2030 coming along too sounds like the perfect opportunity.

The following Friday, everyone seems to like the rally idea, and a brainstorm of all the clubs we should invite ensues almost immediately. When Debbie and Doug arrive, they tell us that city council has announced that they'll hold a public comment period about the pipeline for three weeks, beginning the last week of February. The city council's website instructs that each speaker will be allowed three minutes during the public comment portion of the agenda, unless revised by the mayor. Speakers are requested to submit their comments in writing before the meeting.

This gives us a clear path forward—a definitive opportunity to reverse the city council's decision to proceed with the pipeline and a moment to celebrate that. Darius says he'll follow up with his mom's firm about getting the club registered as a party of record and lead on finalizing the presentation for our allotted three minutes. The shared research document he created for the club to work on its public comment is massive. Determining what will realistically fit in a three-minute presentation is going to take a lot of work, but Darius seems up for it.

I rally the public outreach team. Halve by 2030's petition is still open for signatures, and the more we can collect before the public comment period starts, the better. I also want to get as many club members to attend the city council meeting as possible, as a physical show of support.

"Does anyone want to do some art projects around town? You know, to get the word out to the community?" Kat asks next. I put my hand up, knowing what she's really asking, but I'm the only one who seems enthusiastic. Most people are already working on at least one part of the club's agenda. I don't blame them for not wanting to take on more. But I'm glad that they're excited about capping off the year with the best rally the school has ever seen.

Still, I can't believe that this is all coming together. It feels insanely cool that we're going to contribute to something real. That Darius's ideas and mine are working together like this, and that we're managing to collaborate with other groups, too. Mr. Mendoza's a genius. He says he'll handle getting the principal's permission for the rally. That Mr. Banner is already impressed with the work the club has done this year.

After the meeting, as some students file out cheering about another Friday done while others gather in small groups to work on their action items, I pull Debbie aside. My heart is beating so fast, I can almost feel time slow down as I work up the nerve to ask her about this summer.

"Thanks so much for coming out today," I say. "I've . . . I've been so inspired by Halve by 2030 and all your work, and I'd love to learn about what you do on a day-to-day basis. I'd love the opportunity to work directly with the organization. Do you take interns?"

Debbie beams at me and nods enthusiastically.

I'm encouraged by Debbie's smile, so I continue to the crucial part. "I would love to help out, it's just, I really need to be paid. Is that doable?"

Doug takes a more practical tone, especially once I say that I'll need to be paid.

"We're tremendously impressed with all the work you're doing," he says. "We'd love to have you, but we'll need to do some asking on our side. Especially about the budget—that's not my or Debbie's call. Go ahead and send us an email, though. Lay out what you're thinking, and we'll see what we can do."

It's not the *of course!* I was hoping for, but after they wave goodbye to me and the other club members sticking around to work through their Friday afternoons, I'm jittery with the energy of new possibilities. Of making real change.

We're actually doing this. And we're doing it together.

CHAPTER 14
GAME TIME

Isa

"ISA? ISA, IT'S THIS EXIT RIGHT?" I'M LOST STARING OUT THE truck window at the rain that's pelting the highway, a thousand things going through my mind. Dad flicks his blinker on and changes lanes. The truck sends a spray of water across the lane line.

"Huh? What, Kat?" I answer, distracted.

"Did they text back?"

"Um, I don't know." I've been such a space cadet recently. Grandma tossed a dish towel at me this morning. I guess I wasn't paying her sufficient attention over breakfast.

I wonder what Darius is doing this weekend.

"They were down here last week," Tama says, pulling off the highway. We're in the docklands. The marshy, tidal flow where the Puyallup River meets Commencement Bay. Most of the lots we pass are industrial properties—all concrete bridges and barriers—that lead up to the port.

"Nathan says they're there, and that their session just finished," Kat says. "He shared his location." She hands me her phone from the back seat. It shows the group chat we're in with Eliyah and

Nathan, which has been going strong since we finished the mural.

I zoom in with my fingers. "Yup, up here on the right."

"I see them." Tama slows down, pulling over on the shoulder. The truck crunches in the loose gravel of the pebbled shore as he parks.

Ahead of us, two traditional canoes are pulled up on the graveled bank. Each is covered by a large canopy that's keeping them out of the rain. Between the boats and the water about fifty yards away, a collection of trucks with sleeper tops, tents, and camping canopies are clustered together. Under a canopy in the center, a handful of people are sitting in camp chairs around a small fire pit.

I pull the hood up on my rain jacket as Kat, Tama, and I get out of the truck.

"Kat! Isa!" Nathan stands and waves from under the canopy.

Nathan is next to two women, one of whom has a hat of woven cedar hung on the back of her chair. When he calls, Eliyah appears from one of the trucks. We're here this weekend to meet everyone at the occupation and talk about doing a mural. Nathan and Eliyah said this would be a good time because most of the tribal council is here this afternoon.

I'm excited to meet them. Mom's taken me to protests before, for racial justice. Mostly I remember marching and singing. This looks different. More sedentary. Instead of carrying placards, they have theirs posted around the camp. One has the Puyallup tribe's salmon on it; under it is written WATER IS LIFE.

We walk toward the canopy, trailing Tama. Dad's usually not a fast walker, but he strides out ahead of us to get out of the rain, stopping just before he reaches the edge. We pause, too, waiting.

"haʔɫ sləx̌il," the woman next to Nathan says. She has a round face and shoulder-length brown hair. She bows slightly and gestures for us to join them. "hədiw'."

"Talofa lava," I say echoing Dad's Samoan greeting. Nathan and Eliyah smile at me. Kat looks lost.

"Aunt Bryan, this is Mr. Brown and his daughter, Isa," Nathan says.

"And this is Kat," Eliyah pipes up. The woman closest to him rolls her eyes at him affectionately. They have the same wide, expressive faces. Maybe she's his mom? I watch her elbow Eliyah in the ribs and point her chin at the fire. Next to it is a kettle, and Eliyah busies himself with handing us mugs of coffee.

"So, you all painted the mural at the convenience store?" Nathan's aunt asks.

I nod in time with Kat. That mural is still getting a lot of good feedback—Kat's socials have blown up, and Mr. Sue says people ask him about it all the time.

"It's beautiful work."

"This is Mr. Kiona," Nathan introduces the booming voice. A man with a bushy gray goatee shakes hands with Dad. He's wearing a puffy jacket that says SONICS across the front.

"How's the occupation going?" Dad asks. "They've been talking about it down at the port. Want to send security over and clear you out."

Mr. Kiona laughs. "We're on our land, and we have rights to these waters. We won't be moved."

"The port authority's blaming you, saying the tribe's protest is slowing things down. It's bullshit. It was management that leased the dock to the energy company in the first place. The longshoremen would have never agreed. It's our hours that will be lost with a dock out of commission," Tama says.

The meetings of the longshoremen's union now go on for days. Dad's there a lot. Replacing lost shift hours with organizing time.

"What will you do?" Nathan's aunt asks.

"Some want to initiate 'first in, first out,' but the union's holding so far. We're pushing management to replace the lost wages, and now they're trying to use you as scapegoats." Tama laughs. "Heaven forbid something impact *their* pockets."

"We think another mural might help get more people to notice," Eliyah says. He seems eager to get the mural conversation going, more at home talking about painting than the protest.

Kat and I nod in agreement.

"You think you could do it?" Aunt Bryan asks. "What would you paint?"

That's the question Eliyah and Kat have been waiting for. Our group chat has been mostly them trading sketches with one another, building on each other's ideas. Drawing things together and making us laugh. Now, they pull their sketchbooks out, and suddenly everyone's talking at once.

"This one's good." Aunt Bryan points.

"Not with this slogan," another woman says. "We should use that one."

The books are passed between the council members, and the others come to join the circle. Aunt Bryan and Mr. Kiona do the most talking, but everyone's pitching in with their thoughts. Eliyah rips off some blank pages from the back, takes a seat, and starts on a composite sketch across his knees. Kat kneels down next to him, markers out.

Mr. Kiona nods. "Yes, I like the people profiles best."

"The fish need to be there, though, and it should say *No pipeline!*"

"But it also has to say *spuyaləpabš čəł*," Aunt Bryan says. "We are Puyallup."

Eliyah writes this across the bottom, and I can see it: The collection of faces and animals. What has been and what could be. It's wonderful to see the message come to life, so simply and yet so completely. It's beautiful.

"Where should we paint it?" Kat asks.

"Only one place for it," Mr. Kiona says. He turns to look upriver and all our heads swivel, following his gaze through the drizzle and across to the largest bridge leading to the docks. The one you can see from the freeway. I've never thought of them this way before, but the bridge's massive concrete legs suddenly seem empty—missing paint.

The most prominent leg is on the other side of the river. It's at the perfect angle to be seen from the freeway. I follow it down to its base: It's inside the chain-link fences that mark off the port of Tacoma's property. Last week, I made Dad take me to work with him, so I know that the pipeline's terminal is supposed to be built on the dock closest to where we're standing. The dock closest to that leg of the bridge.

There. The mural has to be there.

CHAPTER 15
WHERE'S THE LINE?

Isa

IF I DON'T DIE OR GET ARRESTED, THIS MIGHT BE THE BEST night of my life. Despite the painters' mask pinching the bridge of my nose, the fumes cloud my mind as I ride the high, giddy from the thrill of the work we're doing.

Until my hand cramps. My right hand, the one holding the canister, contorts in a spasm of pain and I let go, without thinking. I watch in horror as it falls.

"Heads up!" We're supposed to whisper, but I can't help shouting.

CLANG.

Guess there are worse things than yelling.

CLANG.

Can a person die of wincing?

CLANG.

Somehow, the canister manages to hit every rung of the scaffold I'm clinging to on its way down, before finally landing with a muffled thud—too little, too late—on the pebbled shore. I hold my breath in the collective, dread-filled silence that follows.

Cringing, I wait for the shouts of security guards. For the sirens.

Possibly even the Coast Guard. But all I can hear is the gentle lapping of the bay and the distant, predawn bustle at the docks. The background murmur of the not-yet-awake city.

"Sorry!"

The others working beneath me reply to my muffled apology with a mixture of subdued groans and relieved chuckles.

"Nice going," Kat whispers up at me.

"My hand's freaking out!" I look at my twitching fingers. "It feels like it's about to fall off."

"You should've stretched. Or warmed up with one of those stress balls. Are you almost done up there?"

"There's just another bit of the sky, but I've still got the colors I need. Wait. How are you done with another section already?" I wheeze, shaking my head to focus. "I'll be down in a sec."

"We should all be wrapping up," some guy says. I try to remember the name that belongs with that voice. Todd, maybe? There are a lot of people here that I don't really know yet. "Sun's up in an hour. We need to move."

I angle my head to squint at the triangle of sky left unobscured by the bridge. It's the only bit in my line of sight outside the faint and eerie glow of floodlights, which illuminate the piers farther down the bay. The underbelly of the uniform cloud cover has shifted color. The orangish industrial light reflects back against a gray rather than black sky. Galvanized, Kat becomes a whirlwind of action below me, judging from the clack and hiss of paint.

She swings between people on the lower levels, her voice ping-ponging with the movement. "There, the shadow, can you blend it back? No, tighter with the lines or it won't read. Eliyah, can you check it from a distance?"

The wood planks supporting me vibrate as Eliyah descends the ladder rungs. I slither forward, choosing a silver can. Even up close, I know it's turning out better than we imagined. Eliyah's footfalls mark a running rhythm as they carry him away from us. I carefully spritz my last star.

A birdlike whistle chirps through the air. Eliyah's cue that we're all good.

The others shake half-empty canisters and pump raised fists in silent celebration. Some spray or roll a final burst of color. Kat starts climbing down, muttering that she needs to see this for herself. When she reaches the ground, Eliyah is waiting to catch her as she leaps for the bank.

"It's . . . aaaaaweeeesome," Eliyah murmurs, voice full of wonder and a hint of pride.

I can't help noticing that he's still holding Kat's hand. They're so cute! Almost to the point of being gross, but not. How do they make it look so easy?

"That's it. We'll have to call it." The other voice—which I now realize belongs to Dan—says. "We need to get this scaffolding down before security makes their rounds at five thirty."

I scoot backward until I can swing my legs through the slats. Then I close my eyes and start psyching myself up to climb down. Slow. Careful. That's the key. I've been so focused on the agenda, and maybe a little high on fumes, that I forgot an important rule of physics. What goes up must come down.

"Wait." Nathan speaks up for the first time in a while, startling me with how close he is. I'd almost forgotten he was on the same level. "Are we good, or should we disassemble the top while we're up here?"

"No," Mr. Kiona's deeper voice responds. "You kids just bring the paint. If this thing comes down, I don't want it collapsing on you."

"Oh, great, that's reassuring," Nathan whispers, just loud enough for me to hear. "Glad we haven't been hanging off a death trap for the past eight hours."

He's joking, but it's hard to find anything funny now that I'm thinking about falling. I inhale deeply through my masked nose, trying not to laugh. Or panic.

Gingerly, I reach for the first of the canvas bags we've strung through the planks. Nathan and I fill them back up with canisters as we go, navigating the levels together. We have to pass the bags between us to free up our hands to climb down. I try to focus on the handoffs instead of the climb.

"Made it out alive," I breathe when my feet hit solid earth. I give Nathan a weak high five in the dim light, then turn to search for Kat on the bank. She's still Spider-Manning around, recording from as many perspectives as her phone can capture.

"Your scaffolding was perfect, Todd," Mr. Kiona says to the guy who loaned us the setup as the pair moves to replace us on the ladders. Todd's a professional painter, apparently.

Nathan makes an affronted face, and I silently agree with his unspoken complaint. Todd didn't spend all night careening off the ground the way we did, in fear for his life, at the very top.

"Never thought I'd use it for this," Todd replies, smirking. "Tallest house I've done was fifty feet." Then, to me, he says, "You're great with heights. If you ever want to earn some money, I'm always looking for summer help."

I suddenly want to sit down and put my head between my knees. With every passing month, the fear of heights I seem to be developing grows stronger. Even the thought of doing this again has me praising the ground. *So steady. So reliable.* The birds can have the sky.

"No thanks, Todd. I'm good. I think painting something this tall was . . . a one-time thing. Worth it, but still."

He chuckles at me, then starts gesturing instructions to Mr. Kiona, Dan, and the others who have moved forward to help take the scaffolding down. "Loosen the boards left to right. That's it. Lower them down, then the piping. Good. Railing, flooring, then the next level."

On the shore, we line up to receive things as they're handed down. I help stack the boards on other boards. Put the pipes together. Then load the trucks that Aunt Bryan and another woman have backed farther down the shore. The tide is coming in, the shallow water splashing steadily closer to us and stirring a salty, brackish tang into the dewy air. With my painter's mask off, I breathe deep, relishing the fume-free smell.

The water laps at the base of the scaffold just as we're dismantling the last level, adding to the sense of urgency. We're cutting it close to get back through the fence, dry and on time. "We'll never be out of here before the dawn security sweep," Dan mutters. "I heard they've been coming in early."

I don't tell him that I have an inside man on the job. I do quicken my pace, though, along with everyone else.

Kat flits around the cluster of people loading up, her grin teasing Dan for his pessimism, until she suddenly jerks to a stop. "Look," she gasps, pointing.

A hushed cheer rises, and is quickly stifled, as sunlight hits our creation for the first time. My eyes widen as I take it all in. The fierceness of the woman in the mural's center, the woman guarding the future, holds my gaze. She is not the only person the mural depicts. But as my eyes stare into hers, I feel just like her, and I hope others will, too. Eliyah was right. The mural is awesome. We did an amazing job.

I pile into one of the trucks with the others, and we don't stop driving until we're a block from Kat's. They slow down to let us jump out, and we vault over fences until we hit the alley, sneaking in through the back door just a few minutes before the alarm in her mom's room goes off. When we're certain we haven't been caught, we take turns showering and changing into our school clothes. In the steamy bathroom mirror, I'm someone who is both daring and dead tired. Eyes sparkling, but also a little puffy.

I give Kat's mom the perkiest "Good morning, Ms. Nelson!" I can manage at breakfast. It isn't very convincing, judging by her suspicious eyebrows and slight frown.

Under the dish towel tucked into her neckline, she's wearing one of the Grandma-approved pantsuits Kat loathes. Ms. Nelson probably has another job interview today. I pass on the cereal she's put on the table. Kat attempts to cover a dramatic yawn, then follows it up with a guilty smile.

"I told you guys not to keep each other up all night," Ms. Nelson scolds as Kat and I hustle to catch the bus. Isaac and Liam beat us out the door ten minutes ago.

If only she knew what we were really up to last night.

My eyes close for longer than a blink for the first time in what feels like years. I sigh, finally content. The weak sun is warm across my face. The grass is a little damp where it tickles my ankles and pricks through the thin parts of my jacket, but I don't even care. *Hello ground, my old friend; we meet again. So horizontal.* So exhausted.

Across the field, the babble of lunch hour filters through the open cafeteria doors.

Kat's voice sounds far away, muted. "Should we buy something?"

"No, too tired. Sleep is better than food."

"Agree," she confirms.

I breathe deep. I can really conk out when I want to. Without someone to wake me, I could be out here a long time. Mr. Banner, our ever-frowning principal, would probably stumble across me out here after school, or even days later—napping away. I nearly giggle at the look I imagine on his face, but I'm too tired to giggle. I bet he's never been willingly unconscious in public. Much too undignified. Or, actually, maybe the groundskeeper would find me first, by running me over with his riding lawn mower.

"Don't let me sleep too long," I say, drifting. "I don't wanna get mowed."

There's no response.

"Kat?"

I don't want to open my eyes, but missing my next class is a non-starter. The adrenaline that saw me through the morning is gone now. I deeply regret not copying Kat and sneaking some of her mom's coffee before we left.

"Kat, you awake?"

"No." Kat yawns loudly from a few feet away. "Definitely not."

"We'd better set an alarm."

"I'm sorry. I think you meant, 'Kat, my darling, please set an alarm'?"

I recite, "Please. Thank you. I love you."

The sound of Kat rummaging through her bag confuses me. Kat's phone is basically attached to her hand, so much so that my parents cite her as an etiquette cautionary tale. To them, glancing at your phone during a conversation is super rude. It annoys Grandma so much that she makes Kat leave it in the middle of the kitchen table whenever she visits.

"Nooooooo!"

"Hmmm?" I muse half consciously. "What's wrong?"

"I can't find my phone." Her words syncopate with stress, which doesn't confuse me at all.

"You know, for someone who's always on their phone, you sure do lose a lot of them. Is that your second or third this year?"

Kat's too annoyed to rise to the bait.

"I haven't lost it," she retorts. "I just can't find it. I can't *lose* it. Mom says she's not getting me another one if I do. She says I'll have to use Liam's old walkie-talkie."

I laugh at the visual.

She scoffs. "Jokes on you, you'll be carrying the other one. Dang it! I must have left it in first period? No, wait. I know where it is."

"Where?"

"It died this morning when I was taking that last video, 'member? I plugged it in to charge when we got home," Kat says. "I forgot to grab it before we left. Man!"

"I'm surprised you didn't notice earlier. Like, way earlier." This might even be a record. "You seriously didn't check it all morning? I'm impressed. Also worried."

"I've been trying too hard to stay awake," Kat groans, flopping back down on the grass. "I was gonna post pics during History. Mr. Taylor never catches people on their phones."

The image of the mural resurfaces in my mind, and, despite my exhaustion, my eyes pop open as excitement wins. "It's so good, Kat!"

Kat's feet kick up and down, her hands smacking the ground beneath her. She turns her head with a dazzling smile.

"It is good, isn't it!" Kat says, rolling onto her stomach. "Those profiles are inspired. Eliyah is so talented! He definitely downplayed his experience before."

"It's not just good, Kat." I lower my voice in a bad impression of Eliyah. "It's . . . aaaaaweeeesome."

I make sappy eyes at her and reach for her hand with creepy slowness.

"Stop it!"

"You were totally holding hands! And that was after a whole night of him complimenting you and pouring you hot chocolate. He didn't offer *me* any hot chocolate."

"Ugh! He's sooo hot! Why doesn't he go here?" She sighs. "You and Nathan looked pretty cozy, though."

"That wasn't coziness," I retort. "That was mortal dread. We both thought we were going to fall to our deaths up there."

"Come on, you don't like him at all? You're always like this!"

She keeps asking, but I don't think about Nathan like that. It's not that he doesn't have things going for him . . . like his shoulders and his glossy black hair that's almost as thick as mine. The way he speaks to people. There's a lot going on there. But he's not the one I'm embarrassed to admit how much I think about. Unbidden, my mind's eye conjures a face with glasses. A guy who has sometimes annoying habits and looks surprisingly good in a speed suit.

I shrug, and Kat rolls her eyes.

The lunch bell rings.

"Oh, come on!" I groan like I'm being tortured. "What's the opposite of 'saved by the bell'?"

Kat considers for a moment. "Slain by the bell?" She sighs, rolling into a squat. "You've got paint on your jacket, by the way. Did you notice? It's all over your sleeve."

I hold my arms up to the sky, rotating them at the shoulder. Paint stains the right sleeve of the patchwork denim, adding to the overall cacophony for the eyes that is my favorite jacket.

"Aw man," I say. "One of these days, I'm going to remember to roll my sleeves up."

"Don't worry, I doubt anyone will notice. That jacket's already pretty distracting, all by itself." She reaches for one of my out-stretched arms and uses it to pull me up.

"When are you gonna get a Lakewood patch? You've been here three years already."

"I don't know." I consider. "Maybe I don't need one, if we're stay-ing. I can bedazzle your name on the back, though, if you want some representation."

Kat laughs. "Good. It might not be clear to people that we're like, best best friends. The real, permanent, bedazzling kind."

I snort as Kat and I make our way toward the school, finally duck-ing through the doors of the emptying cafeteria.

"Meet you after school?"

"No. I'm gonna skip sixth period, I think, and run home to grab my phone."

"Come on, Kat, you know you can't skip more class. How will I be able to walkie-talkie you if you get suspended? Those things only reach so far."

"Ha-ha," Kat deadpans. "I really hope it's at home. Besides, you know Mrs. Morrison loves me. I'll just, like . . . say I have cramps. Don't you have to meet Darius after school, anyway?"

"Well, yeah, but aren't you coming? We're supposed to do the final check-in before the city council meeting."

Kat scoffs. "What's left to check in about? It'll probably just be another elaborate fifty-point presentation that he and Marina have worked up, which I definitely don't need to hear. I really hope you don't put the council to sleep."

My throat feels thick suddenly. She's right. In all the excitement, I lost track of the day. We're petitioning the city council. Tonight. That was already a big enough deal. Then somehow Darius convinced me that, as co-presidents, we should co-present the club's public comment. I feel slightly sick at the thought, but only a couple of club members can come to the city council meeting, and it wouldn't be fair to make him do it alone. Of course, I agreed to this before the bridge mural plan came together. The timing's a bit of a fail.

"Planning is prudent preparation," I mutter, already heading to class on autopilot.

Kat stops me with a hand on the sleeve of my jacket. "Are you okay? Also. Did you just quote Darius?!"

"Oh God. I did, didn't I?" My laugh is rightfully embarrassed. The study mantras Darius quotes whenever he wants to make me laugh have infiltrated my brain.

She shakes her head. "You've been spending way too much time together. It's not healthy. You're gonna get that . . . what's that syndrome called?"

Now she's just being dramatic. "Listen. Say what you want, but you know it's super impressive that the club managed to pull this off. I'd never have known how to get us in front of city council. And if we can get them to stop the pipeline, that could be huge."

"Sure," she admits. "But do we need to have *another* meeting to talk about it? We've already toted a petition around for months. And gone over what you two should say. Darius even printed out profiles of all the council members. I bet he dreams about them."

I laugh again, more embarrassed for him than me now.

"It's just a little bit much." Kat turns for A Hall. "I'll see you later. The club's meeting at city hall at six p.m., right?"

"Yup. My dad's coming and everything." Tama's knowledge of the port's security schedule was integral to our success last night. He called city council "act two" when I called him this morning.

I head to C Hall, where my next classes are waiting. In Biology, Harper and Josh stare at me as I come in. I smile and wave thinking they're trying to catch my attention, but they duck their heads and look away.

Weird.

The awkwardness doesn't get the chance to linger. I nod off within minutes of Ms. Goff's lesson. I come to when she snaps the lights back on and asks for questions, and I swear Julián is looking at me. Probably because I managed to slump so far forward that my head is resting on the desktop. Staying conscious feels like a lot of work. I start fidgeting to keep awake.

Time drags until the final bell.

After my last class, I swim against the tide of high schoolers desperate to leave. One more practice, then home for a real nap and to change into more presentable clothes. I head for Mr. Mendoza's empty lab, looking for Darius.

I find him leaning against the table at the front of the room, arms crossed and wearing an even more serious expression than usual. Marina is sitting next to him. I didn't think she would come today. She can't make the council meeting, something about a family commitment.

I grin brightly as I approach, faltering when this doesn't alter their dim expressions.

"Hi," I say into the silence. They look at me like I've missed something very obvious, only I don't know what it is.

"Well?" Darius finally says.

"Well, *what*? What's with you two?"

"Don't pretend like you don't know," Marina says.

Super weird.

"What's going on? Did the council announce something?" I've gotten a lot better at reading Darius's face, but this isn't stress or annoyance. He looks . . . mad? Marina shakes her head impatiently.

"Like you haven't seen this?"

She sticks out her phone with an accusing gesture. The club's Signal chat is open. I always forget to check that. We only do our messaging there because Darius insisted that we communicate on a secure platform, and it's not like anyone else I know uses it. And we've mostly used it to talk about getting petition signatures. Without Kat's prompting, I haven't thought to check the chat today.

Marina taps her thumb on a photo, enlarging it.

The picture is grainy and dark. I can only just make out four figures in the zoomed-in frame. They have their backs to the camera and are standing on either side of a chain-link fence.

It can't be.

The only parts of the picture that are clearly illuminated against the darkness are the bits reflecting back the light. A NO TRESPASSING sign bolted to the fence not ten feet from the truck-size split cut in it. And the rhinestones on my signature jacket. The bedazzled one that I'm wearing right now.

I may as well be tagged.

The other people in the shot are undoubtedly some combination of Kat, Eliyah, and Nathan. I can't tell who's who. This is a picture of us entering the docklands last night. Right there on the Signal chat for everyone to see. So much for our attempts at secrecy.

"What the hell, Isa?" Darius interrupts my processing.

"Who posted this?" I stammer.

The picture has no name above it. I know that you can post anonymously on Signal, but I don't know how. I've never done it, and none of the other club members bother with it, either. The chat's a closed group, and we all know each other's usernames.

Darius stands up. A vein on his temple is throbbing. He's crossed his arms so tightly that the veins on his forearms look like they're about to burst.

"Why? Are you going to pretend this isn't you?" he nearly shouts.

Why is he yelling at me?

"It is me!" I shout back.

I take a breath and try to calm down. "I'm not denying it," I say. "But who would post this on our chat? And why wouldn't they say who they are?"

"Why does that matter?" Darius snaps. "What the hell were you doing?"

Crap.

"I'll tell you what it looks like," he says, too worked up to wait for a response. "It looks like our new co-president, *breaking the law* the night before we petition city council!"

"*New* co-president? What, like I'm some outsider?" Heat floods my face and I push myself forward, like I could somehow take him. "News flash: We were sworn in at exactly the same time!"

"And what did we swear?" Darius says in the same obnoxious tone he used to lecture me when we started working together. The one with the thinly veiled subtext of *I think I'm way smarter than you.* "We said we'd lead the club in nonviolent civil disobedience—"

"Yeah, emphasis on *dis*obedience," I snap, all the tension I thought we'd moved past rising to the surface, sleep deprivation preventing any inhibition from stopping it. "If you and Miss Honor Roll over here are too scared to take risks, that's fine. But that doesn't mean that I—"

That breaks his concentration.

"Too scared?" he yells into the nonexistent space between us. "Like I haven't been out knocking on doors for months? Walking up to God knows who to get laughed at and yelled at—working my ass off on the compromise we agreed to!"

"I didn't mean . . ."

"But nooooo," Darius sneers. "That wasn't enough! You had to go and be *radical*. You don't care about rules, or process, or reputation. Maybe we should all be anarchists! You jeopardized our entire club the night before we petition the city council!"

"What are you talking about? I didn't jeopardize the club! No one got hurt. We cut a fence. So what? Where's the harm?"

"It's illegal!"

"So is the climate crisis they're fueling! *Where's the line?!* I thought we agreed we have to do more. We have to do everything we can!"

"Do more?!" I can feel him exhale on my face, but I glare up, meeting his glower head-on. "We can't do what we said we'd do if you get arrested for trespassing or destruction of property or whatever the hell it was you were doing!"

"It's not like that!"

My anger starts to ebb as the magnitude of what the picture could mean starts to become clear. My face is hot and flushed, and my tear ducts sting as the wave of emotion turns.

"Listen to me!" Maybe if I just get it out, he'll understand. They'll see how important what we did last night is. Why the risk was worth taking. "There's an occupation at the port. They've been down there for weeks, but nobody knows. We wanted to make a statement. We—"

"Who's *we*?" His face is stone hard. No hint of the smile I've grown to cherish these last few weeks. No sign of the Darius I know, the one who's my friend.

I can feel tears threatening to spill over. I don't want to say who; I can't say who. Not now that there's incriminating evidence. Not to a face so rigid, a friend who's become a stranger.

Darius throws up his hands. He reaches for his bag, like the conversation is over. "We'll give you until Monday to resign," he spits.

What?!

I look between them. Marina is wearing a ridiculously small, self-important smirk. I wanna knock it off her smug little face.

"Otherwise, I'll take this to Principal Banner myself," Darius says. "I'm pretty sure he'll agree that club presidents can't break the law, no matter how justified they think they are."

My mouth falls open. All I can do is stare at him.

"Now, if you'll excuse me," Darius says, moving for the door. Marina follows close behind him. "Some of us have real work to do."

CHAPTER 16
A FISH WALKS INTO A DINER

Darius

"I STRONGLY OBJECT. THAT'S COMPLETELY OUT OF ORDER, AND if you think I'm just going to sit back and—"

"Bob? A quick reminder that this isn't a courtroom. Also, while the misuse of the library's ramps remains problematic, I'm afraid we'll have to leave the discussion there and pick up on skateboard restrictions next time." Mayor Malone looks fed up.

To my left, the red numbers of the digital wall clock glow 20:41. We're almost there.

"Two hours and forty minutes, folks. It's like we're going for a record here. Apologies that we're so over time. What's left?"

The heads of the few stragglers remaining in the city hall meeting room swivel toward the agenda projected on the screen. We're finally up to Public Comment and Petitions. Lakewood High Environmental Justice Club is one of the handful of listed speakers.

My palms start to sweat. I wipe them on my slacks as I lean forward to pull the full set of note cards from my backpack. I'll present Isa's half. She went behind our backs and broke the law. It's best that she isn't associated with the club. A suspension's not going on my record because *she* can't follow the rules. Marina and the others and I will take this forward. Even if none of them can stick through a meeting this late. I'm prepared. I have my facts straight, and my arguments are well-reasoned.

I can do this.

"Public Comment and Petitions," the mayor says. "Alright, let's wrap these up in five minutes. The game's nearly over, people."

My eyebrows shoot up. Someone behind me laughs like Mayor Malone's made a good joke.

"Marvin, over to you."

Council member Marvin McAllister representing District 3 shuffles some papers sitting in front of him. He tilts his chin up until he can read through the correct lens of his glasses.

"Petition one is approved." Marvin says. "Petition two is denied after due consideration. Petition three is denied after due consideration."

A kind of cough escapes me. Like when you get hit from behind playing basketball.

"And Petition four is approved with thanks to the Girl Scouts for their continued service to the community," Marvin finishes. He looks over his glasses to smile.

I watch a Girl Scout mother return his grin from the other side of the front row. She salutes the council. My forehead aches from the effort of holding my eyebrows up.

I stand. The uncomfortable plastic chair I've occupied for the past three hours squeaks as it slides out behind me.

"The council members would once again like to thank the community for their continued engagement in the democratic process," Marvin continues reading. "Explanations of the council's decision will be submitted to those registered as parties of record via email within a week. Any rebuttals may be submitted in writing."

I don't know what to do.

"That's that," says Mayor Malone. I'm standing fifteen feet from him, but he carries on like I'm invisible. "Any other business?"

Council member Fred Hines of District 2 raises his wrist.

"Fred? Oh, that's right, Fourth of July planning?" The mayor rubs his forehead. "Happy to take that up at the next meeting, there, Fred? You'll be first on the agenda."

Another critical issue swept under the rug.

Councilor Hines nods.

"Good man."

Feeling silly for doing this outside of school, I raise my hand. Pamela Blanch, the city clerk, catches my eye. Mayor Malone still isn't looking at me. Pamela clears her throat.

"Yes, Pam?" the mayor asks.

"The young man in the front row seems to want to say something, Jim."

"Oh?" He glances over, as if noticing me for the first time. "Brief moment for you, sir."

"Thank you." My voice squeaks a little, thanks to being unused for so long. I clear my throat. "My name is Darius Freeman. I'm president of Lakewood High's Environmental Justice Club."

Mayor Malone looks at his watch. A Hublot, like he's some big shot. He then looks pointedly at the clock on the wall.

"We filed Petition three calling for the reconsideration of the LGN pipeline being built at the port." I speak up, pivoting toward the room. "The liquified natural gas transported by the pipeline will add to the climate crisis. It does not align with the state or local government's climate goals, and the environmental impacts will further marginalize vulnerable members of the community."

I notice a few people shuffle uncomfortably at a Black man's use of the word *marginalize*. I'm not the only one who registers that everyone on the council is white. Or that I'm losing them already.

"Yes, Darius, we thoroughly considered your public comment," the mayor interrupts. "You're welcome to read our full response in the written explanation. At present, we simply do not have time to discuss each petition."

He buttons his suit jacket like he's going to stand, but only his right heel raises. It then taps impatiently against the floor.

I'm not finished. My note cards are clammy in my hand, but I have to say this.

I have to try.

"Council members." I lean forward, aiming for persuasion. "I believe citizens have the right to understand the council's decision making—"

"In brief, Darius"—Mayor Malone uses my name like a punctuation mark—"the council felt that the jobs and financial benefits associated with the pipeline fulfill our mandate to restore the local economy. We are also satisfied that the environmental risk assessment put forward by the energy company is comprehensive, and though we, too, are concerned about the climate implications, we must take a balanced approach in securing our energy futures."

I list points as he speaks, then shuffle my cards. One of them has the economic tally the club worked up. The rebuttal to the *local jobs* argument is there, too. I open my mouth, but before I can speak—

"As I said," the mayor emphasizes, "we are happy to provide a full written response. I see another hand on this issue, but I ask you to please be brief as we really do need to close. Mr. Finnigan."

I look over my shoulder. A well-dressed man in the third row has his hand raised. You don't see many tie clips in Lakewood. He stands and makes a point of looking at everyone before he speaks.

"As many of you know, my name is Brendan Finnigan, and I represent Puget Sound Energy," he says.

I've never heard of this guy.

"I'd like to start by saying that I commend Darius and the Lakewood High School Environmental Justice Club on their civic engagement." He gestures toward me companionably, then brings his hand to his chest.

"It's PSE's mission to assure the community that the pipeline will provide jobs and good, clean energy for a sustainable future. We are more than happy to follow up with our comprehensive environmental impact assessment, and I welcome any questions folks may have."

I stare, incredulous.

"Excellent," says Mayor Malone. "Thank you, Mr. Finnigan and Darius, for that lively debate. *If* there's nothing else, we'll bring this meeting to a close. Apologies again that we're so over time. We meet again in two weeks."

Before I can process or respond, he bangs his gavel.

The council meeting is over.

In the noise of the remaining participants stretching and chit-chatting, I sit back down. The council members shake hands. Mrs. Blanch folds up her laptop. My legs are stiff from hours of sitting tensely, waiting for . . . that.

"Son?"

I watch Mr. Finnigan make his way to the front of the room, where he claps hands with Mayor Malone. They do a full-on bro shake and start chatting about the Blazers game. I'm still holding my notecards.

"Son?"

Someone claps my shoulder from behind. I turn and have to look up to take in the owner's face. His hair is black and curly. And he's huge.

"Well done, son!" The man extends his hand.

I shake clumsily, slow to react.

"I'm Emanuele Brown," he says.

"Sorry, Mr. Brown?"

"That's right." The man's grin widens. "Isa's dad."

The familiarity registers, and there, obscured by his mass, Isa stands in her father's shadow. She was here, in the room, the whole time. She saw everything. And now she's looking at the floor. Despite how angry I am at her, I can still feel my heart rate speed up at the sight of her. How pathetic.

"Oh," I finally say. "I'm Darius."

"Well done, Darius." Mr. Brown thumps my back with surprising force. "It takes a brave soul to sit through that amount of bureaucracy."

"Uh. Thank you, sir," I manage.

"Are your parents here?" he asks, looking around. "I thought your mom was the legal brains behind this operation?"

"No. I mean, yes, she is the legal brains. But she's not here." Of course she's not. Of course she bailed out, too. "She had to work."

Mr. Brown looks between me and Isa, who moves to stand beside rather than behind her father. He suddenly laughs with the force of his back clap.

"You two look like you could use a stiff drink," he says. "But I suppose milkshakes will have to do. We're headed for the diner across the road. It's nearly nine, and I know you've missed your dinner, too, Darius. Come along with us."

I blink in surprise.

"He doesn't have to, Dad," Isa says in a small voice.

"Nonsense. We can't send him home without food. Look at him, Bo!"

"Dad!" Isa whines. I watch Mr. Brown throw an arm around her, which she unsuccessfully tries to shrug away. Without waiting for a response, Mr. Brown tucks me under his other warm shoulder. Then he spins us all toward the door.

🔥

A short walk later, I'm in a booth in the nearly empty diner. Mr. Brown orders a couple of veggie burgers and a "real" burger from the chatty waitress who greeted him and Isa by name. Her name tag says ALICE, and she wants to know more about their family background. She asks questions while noting down our additions of one chocolate peanut butter milkshake, one strawberry lemonade, and a Coke.

"I grew up in American Samoa, where I started on ships. I was a Marine Corps recruit in San Diego when I met Lena. She was working at this dingy restaurant that did the best chop suey in town. She was the most popular waitress, but she just couldn't resist this man in a uniform."

"She's gorgeous. You tell her that we miss her at the diner. She's working over at J's now?"

"That's right. Better hours and she's hoping to cook, which was always what she wanted."

I listen halfheartedly, my thoughts still down the street. I don't want to think about what happened. Or to look at Isa across the booth.

"How's her mom doing?"

Now that my adrenaline's subsiding, I register just how hungry I am. Starving, actually. I wonder how long they're going to talk.

"Oh, thanks. She's certainly known better days. That's why we moved up here, you know. To take care of her. It seems to have helped a bit."

"I bet she loves having you around, Isa." There's a pause. Isa isn't following the conversation, either.

"You're awfully quiet tonight," Alice goes on. "Guess that's due to your handsome friend here?"

Alice pauses, then very deliberately winks at me.

Thunderstruck, thy name is: Darius.

"Don't mind them, they've just had a run-in with the city council." Mr. Brown grins. "Grandma Queen certainly does like seeing more of Isa."

"How are the twins?" Isa asks.

I'll never see that burger.

"Oh, they're great—look!" The waitress pulls a phone out of the pocket of her uniform. "You'll have to babysit again soon. They're still singing that song you taught them. It's so adorable."

A man appears behind the counter, looking almost as impatient as I feel. He wipes his hands on a cloth, saying "One moment please" to the couple that have just come through the door.

"Oh, shoot. I'm gonna get yelled at for dawdling," Alice says. "And I'll bring you a basket of fries." She says this more loudly. Then she goes to seat the new customers.

I hope they're not hungry.

"We'll have to tell Mom that we saw Alice," Isa tells her dad. "And that Darrel's still the manager."

"Where's your family from, Darius?" Mr. Brown asks me.

"Uh." It takes an effort to bring myself into the conversation. "My parents grew up in New Orleans. Most of our family still lives in Louisiana."

"Ah, beautiful part of the world. I'm sure Isa's told you that her grandma's family is from Alabama, though her mom spent most of her childhood in Texas."

She hasn't, though I never thought to ask.

"We're one big American family." Mr. Brown squeezes Isa, who rolls her eyes in response. She pushes her curls back from her face, tucking them behind her ears. Mr. Brown continues, "We're spread all over. Do you get to visit much?"

"No, sir," I answer. "My grandparents died in Hurricane Katrina. It was before I was born, but I've seen pictures. Of the house. Of how things used to be. And of after . . ." I trail off.

I can't believe I said that. I've never told Isa, never told anyone, really, and I'm still talking, "I never met my grandparents, but I know my parents really miss them. They haven't been back south since."

"I'm sorry, son," Mr. Brown says. "That must have been really awful for your family."

Isa is watching me now, too.

"That explains it, though, why any kid would work so hard to solve such a big problem. Brave or reckless, both of you deserve our admiration."

I don't know what to say.

Mr. Brown turns his attention to the TV above the counter. The Blazers are playing the Clippers. They're up by three, with four minutes to go. This is probably the game Mayor Malone was so desperate to get home to. The one he and Mr. Finnigan were chatting about. I look back out the window at the darkened parking lot. Down the road and across the street, the front of city hall is the only thing left illuminated.

"It all happened so fast," I say aloud.

My comment brings Mr. Brown back to the table. "It certainly did," he chuckles. "Good on you though, Darius, for the attempt."

"The council was supposed to let us present."

I visualize the line on the city council's website that states *Each speaker will be allowed three minutes during the public comment portion of the agenda.* The last part, *unless revised by the mayor*, hadn't registered for me. Until now.

"In the meetings I watched online, the speakers all got to say something. The council even answered their questions. This wasn't how things were supposed to go. And who is Mr. Finnigan, and how did he even know to be there?"

"Looks like they had a lot of business tonight, or that they wanted to make it seem that way," Mr. Brown says. "Mayor's probably under pressure not to make a fuss. That Mr. Finnigan's been coming to town for months, meeting with the port authority and the long-shoremen's union."

His eyes are on the screen.

"Dad's big into the union," Isa says. She pokes him in the side, prompting him to say more.

"Puget Sound Energy is promising to rebuild most of the docks. Pave the roads. And they'll hire locals for the construction work, at least. They've got several bids out. With money flowing in, I'll bet the council's mind was made up long before you got to them. No matter your facts, there, son. I'm sure the mayor didn't want it on camera, either."

I suddenly feel about six years old. A child who believes a fairy leaves money for teeth, or that straw can be spun into gold. Everything we've been working toward for months, all that effort and all that hope, only for the council to dismiss me with a preplanned platitude of empty words.

We never stood a chance. And I had no idea. My hands ball into fists, which I press against the pleather booth. I'm dangerously close to punching something. Or crying. When the food finally arrives, I have to unclench my jaw in order to chew it.

I need to focus on something else. Anything else.

I can't imagine lively Mr. Brown at the port. The only person I know who works there is Haruto, whose face now seems to permanently wear a drained expression. I've been trying to talk to him when I see him at the Takahashis', but he never says much. He's the reason Marina couldn't come to the council meeting. She had to pick him up from his shift and drive him all the way to her aunt's.

Oh.

Marina took the pictures. That's why she was so weird and fidgety all day. I was so angry with Isa, I couldn't see it. Couldn't understand why the anonymous posting bugged me. It didn't make sense. Unless you didn't want people to know that you were at the port, too. And Marina isn't supposed to talk about her cousin. *Marina* posted those pictures.

And that is yet another thing I hadn't seen coming.

"Well, would you look at that?" Mr. Brown's exclamation almost makes me choke on my last bite of veggie burger.

The ten o'clock news is playing on the TV over the counter. A local anchor stands by tents on a riverbank. Native American flags are flying in the background. I recognize the different salmon symbols of the Nisqually, Puyallup, and Cowlitz tribes. The camera pans out to the bridge. Painted against the most prominent concrete leg, illuminated by the port's floodlights, is a giant climate change mural.

It's a collection of faces and animals that surround the outline of a Puyallup woman who's standing strong. To her right is the Pacific Northwest of the past. To her left is the future, assuming what happens now is that we do indeed stop the pipeline, depicted by the jagged line attempting to cross the present in front of her. The mural's profiles are haunting. The hope of the future vision is both beautiful and powerful at the same time. I can make out the largest of the painted words: WE ARE PUYALLUP.

"Seems like city council might have to respond after all."

I feel my eyes bulge as Mr. Brown pokes his daughter in the ribs. They bulge again when Isa answers him with an open grin before turning to stare intently at the TV.

"You know what they say," Mr. Brown huffs as he slides out of the booth. "It takes a village." He heads for the counter.

For the second time tonight, I feel like the wind's been knocked out of me.

"Did you . . . ?" I sound half drowned. I take a moment to swallow. I don't need to ask it as a question.

"You painted that mural."

It looks like Isa's trying not to laugh.

"Not by myself," she says slowly, "but, yes. I helped. We've been going down there for a while."

I stare at her like a fish out of water, meeting her eyes for the first time since this afternoon.

"The tribes have been protesting around the construction area for weeks, and we had no idea. All this outreach about the pipeline, and we didn't even know that they were there," Isa says, the story starting to tumble out of her now. "Their protest has gotten zero press. Nathan thought doing something together would help. They were the ones who got us the convenience store mural, remember?"

I have literally no idea what she's talking about.

"Oh, um. Before Christmas, Kat and I did a mural on the convenience store by the casino out on I-5. We met Nathan and Eliyah when we were asking for permission. They were the reason why Mr. Sue let us. The Puyallup tribe are some of his most loyal customers. You might have noticed the mural?"

I can't even blink yet.

"Anyway, after that, Nathan and Eliyah took Kat and me to meet the occupiers. The tribes eventually decided that they wanted to do a mural, too. But if they were going to do it, it had to make a statement, which of course would require trespassing."

Isa takes a deep breath and starts fiddling with the sleeve of her jacket.

"I'm sorry I didn't tell you. I wanted to, but . . . it was complicated, and I didn't think that you'd go for it, even as nonviolent civil disobedience. I didn't mean to get the club into trouble."

She raises her chin, like she's bracing for the words that will come next.

"I don't regret painting the mural," she says. "But I understand that not everybody can take the same risks. I don't want to, but if it's best for the club that I resign, I will."

I gape at her.

"I've settled the bill." Mr. Brown's voice startles me. I hadn't noticed him come back from the counter. He stands a few feet from the booth, behind Isa.

I automatically reach for my wallet.

Mr. Brown holds up a hand. "Your money's no good here, son. I'll be in the car when you're finished talking, Bo. Not too late. It was nice to meet you, Darius."

He turns and waves to Alice.

"Your dad calls you Bo?"

"Isa means 'rainbow' in Samoan. Both sides of my family shorten it to Bo, though they mean different things by it." I look at the iridescent blue streaked through her dark hair while she watches her dad walk out of the diner.

"Sorry," she says. "He can be pushy sometimes."

Of all the things to apologize for.

"Don't be. That was really nice of him," I say. "It was really nice of *you*."

I feel like my mind's losing a footrace. Like I can't catch up to the present. The anger I felt this afternoon seems a lifetime away.

"I shouldn't have yelled at you today."

Isa nods once in acknowledgment.

"I know why you did, though." After a second, her passion grabs the wheel, and she's regular chatty Isa again. "But seriously, I can't believe how badly tonight went."

I grimace.

"No!" she nearly shouts. "Not that you did anything wrong. You were way braver than I would have been. I wouldn't—I probably wouldn't have said anything."

"Lot of good it did us."

"At least you tried! You really tried. My dad wasn't kidding. We were both really impressed that you insisted on speaking. I just can't believe how badly we got shot down. After everything. All that time learning council procedures and preparing. Collecting all those signatures, filing all those forms. I really thought it would pay off."

"So did I," I confess. "I was so positive that they would reconsider. Sure, maybe not at first. But we had to at least talk about it. Get them to see why they shouldn't do it. And even if they blocked our motion, Halve by 2030 would refute them at the next meeting."

Hours ago, this seemed like such an achievable, well-thought-out plan.

"I didn't know that they'd already decided. That there was nothing we could say that would change their minds. I feel like the world's biggest loser."

Overhead, the ten o'clock news captions my pain. They're playing the mural clips again. STREET ART SPOTLIGHTS PIPELINE PROBLEMS and TRIBES FIGHT CLIMATE CRISIS scroll across the bottom of the screen.

Isa takes it in along with me. "At least you're not an anarchist." The side of her mouth pulls up. "Yet."

I guess I deserve that.

I laugh. At her joke. At myself. Six hours ago, my biggest concern was that Isa Brown would mess up my spotless student record. I really lost the forest for the trees today. Guess I've been losing the forest for the trees for a long time now.

"Your way's probably the right one," I concede. But I can't help adding, "I'm pissed that you didn't tell me. I would have listened."

She smirks.

"Okay, fine. I would have *tried* to listen." I exhale and look down at my hands, still clenched into fists at my side. "I guess after tonight, it's pretty clear that I don't have any idea what the hell I'm doing."

A lump is lodged in my throat.

"Neither do I." Isa's voice is soft. "None of us do."

I glance up. She's right. Solving the climate crisis isn't some school assignment. There is no clear solution to what we're up against. It's never been done before.

Isa's looking at my face in a way that makes me want to lean forward. Into what, I don't even know. The pull grows, until she blinks and looks away.

"I am sorry about the picture." She sighs. "I thought we were being so careful. I honestly don't know who took it, or how it got out."

I'm relieved to finally have an answer.

"I think I do. I'll take care of it."

Isa's forehead crinkles with confusion. I want to enlighten her, but there's someone else I have to talk to first. And I have more to say.

"I won't tell," I say quickly. Because that's what I'm most sorry about. "I never should have said that I would turn you in. I won't tell Principal Banner."

That whole conversation still feels so distant. Like it happened years ago. Back when things were simpler, the rules clearer. I don't even understand the game now. The thought of facing the club without Isa hits me like a sucker punch. Fast and hard, seemingly out of nowhere.

"Please don't resign," I practically beg her.

She exhales, standing up. Outside the window, Mr. Brown is waving from the Toyota Tacoma N150 he's pulled up to the curb. I wonder where they parked. My Volvo is down the block.

I stand up, too. Before we reach the door, Isa turns to look me in the eye again.

"Only if you promise the same."

CHAPTER 17
STANDOFF

Darius

I'M LATE FOR SCHOOL THE NEXT MORNING, WHICH HAS literally never happened before. I don't know if my alarm didn't go off or if I just managed to sleep through it. I do know that Jordan had to shake me conscious ten minutes after we were supposed to leave.

I walk in halfway through homeroom, and Marina isn't the only one who mouths "Are you okay?" as I sit down. After the bell rings, I have to convince Ms. Patten that everything's fine before she'll let me leave. Tardiness is essentially nonexistent among the AP crew. Unless someone has died, we're in our seats before the bell rings.

When Ms. Patten finally lets me go, I run down the hall to catch up with Marina. Her face is full of concern. "What's up? Did something happen? How did the city council meeting go?"

"Abysmally," I spit. "Isa was the only club member who stayed until the end." Last night, the club's Signal chat was full of people apologizing for having to leave. It ended with pictures of the climate change mural on the local news.

Marina slows down slightly, still heading for our next class. "What? Isa went?"

"Yup, she was there with her dad. He works at the port, remember?"

"Oh, yeah."

"You were there, too, right?" Marina looks up at me, confused. "Last night, when you were picking up Haruto. That's where you've been all week, right? That's where you were two nights ago, waiting for him. When you took the picture of Isa."

Marina is suddenly preoccupied with the floor. I stop walking and stop talking, and she still doesn't look at me. People have to move around us in the crowded hallway.

"What the actual fuck, Marina?" I'm still too out of it to yell. The anger in my voice is clear, though.

She doesn't say anything. She's still looking at the floor.

"Why didn't you tell me those were *your* pictures?"

The bell rings. I don't move.

I can't think of anything else to say except "I thought we were friends."

"Yeah," she says, finally looking up. Her eyes are narrowed, and her face is closed. "So did I."

"What's that supposed to mean?!"

"Oh, please!" Marina yells. "We have been best friends our entire lives. And suddenly you're ditching me for some girl who's ruined everything we planned. Like I'm some afterthought!"

When she speaks again, her tone is more level. "You basically live at my house, and you can't even bother to tell me what's going on. Acting like you just can't wait to spend time with her. I was doing you a favor."

"What?!"

"Come on, Darius. Like she's going anywhere. We haven't worked this hard for this long to blow everything in our junior year," Marina hisses.

I don't even know how to process that sentence.

"Who cares if the mural was why she cut that fence? She could have been arrested the other night. The next time, she probably will be. You're not going to get into Harvard with a record, Darius. Are you really going to ruin your entire life for *her*?"

I'm so angry that for a moment, I can't speak. The final bell rings, and Marina walks stiffly away, determined to reach Lit on time.

I stand there, fuming in the hallway.

It takes Mr. Smith calling "Darius, are you joining us?" to get me to move. I sit down and don't hear another thing he says. I'm raging, but there's something else. A hollow, nagging feeling that I don't want to own up to.

Two rows ahead of me, I glare at Marina's fingers furiously scribbling in her notebook. Like everyone else in the room, she's hanging on every word Mr. Smith is saying. Capturing it. The next test is in two weeks. The next essay is due in three.

At the beginning of the year, I would have been paying as close attention as everyone else in here. Back when my obsessions were solely focused on doing well in this institution so that I can do well in the next one. Every step categorized and planned for. Every moment occupied, color-coordinated in my meticulously kept schedule.

Six months ago, I would have said exactly what Marina just did. I hate realizing how I used to think exactly the same way.

Slowly, I take the notebook I use for Honors American Literature out of my backpack. I stare at it for a moment.

Then I write *There's more to life than school* as big as I can across its cover.

CHAPTER 18
LAB ROOM EPIPHANIES

Isa

FOR THE SECOND TIME THIS WEEK, I WALK AGAINST THE TIDE of students leaving the building as the last bell sounds. I haven't really been paying attention all day, just waiting. Waiting for this conversation. I'm fairly certain Darius and Marina aren't going to yell at me today. But that's about it. Here and at home, I don't really know what to do anymore.

When I make it to Mr. Mendoza's lab, I'm not surprised that Darius is here. I am surprised that he's the only one in the room, though. I walk over to the lab bench where he's still working. His laptop sits off to the side of a giant textbook.

"Hey. Where's Mr. Mendoza?" I ask.

He was the one who wanted to know how Wednesday's city council meeting went. The one who asked us to come here on a non-club-meeting Friday.

"He had to run to Principal Banner's," Darius explains. He pushes the empty stool next to him toward me. "He said he wouldn't be long."

I sit down beside him and lift my backpack onto the lab table. "So, what the hell are we going to do now?"

He laughs. "You're the one with all the ideas. I thought you were going to tell me."

Darius is smiling, joking.

"Why are you in such a good mood?"

He shrugs. "Because the entire AP crew spent the last two days asking me about the mural and what the club's next step is with city council. I say, fuck it. Let's do this. Keep going. Make the rally the biggest splash possible—even if it means shouting about how the city's still building the pipeline rather than celebrating how we stopped it."

I stare at him, stunned. "Really?"

The tables feel oddly turned. I was not expecting his enthusiasm.

"Yeah." He grins. "Why? What do you think we should do?" He closes his laptop and looks into my eyes.

"I honestly don't know." I blink, staring back. The past forty-eight hours have been a bit of a mess.

In his enthusiasm, he's leaned toward me. I study the line of his jaw, the definition of his arms under his long-sleeve T-shirt. My mind goes oddly blank, and I don't know what to say. We're still looking at each other. My hands are still on the lab bench where I dropped my bag, right next to his. Darius has a mole on the left side of his lower lip. I've never noticed it before.

I exhale a shaky breath and scramble to think of something.

"Um." My eyes dart around the room. "I've always wondered who the people in these posters are? I don't recognize any of them."

Darius blinks, turning his head away to the nearest one. "You don't know who Robert Bullard is?"

I look pointedly at him, then make a show of rolling my eyes. At least we know each other well enough now that I can just tell him when he's being an ass.

"Sorry," he laughs.

Then he stands up and with a sweeping gesture waves toward the man on the wall. "This is Robert Bullard, the father of the environmental justice movement."

I let out a laugh at the announcer tone he's put on. Happy to let him distract me by showing off.

"He's famous for conducting the first extensive study of eco-racism, which exposed illegal waste disposal practices that poisoned Black communities throughout the American South. The repercussions spurred action in places like Afton, North Carolina, and Anniston, Alabama."

What?! What did he say?

Darius makes another sweeping motion and steps toward the next poster. "This is Susana Almanza . . ." The announcer voice continues as he introduces the next person, but I'm no longer listening.

I stand up and walk over to Robert Bullard's poster. I try to read his quote and the description of his work under it for the first time. My mind refuses to take it in.

"Where?" I ask. "Where in Alabama did you say?"

Darius walks over to stand next to me. "Anniston, I think. We learned about it last year. Does it not say it there?"

If it does, I can't see it. My eyes are suddenly full of water. "My mom's from Anniston, Alabama. She left for Texas when she was young, but Grandma stayed. She lived in Anniston most of her life." I stop.

I don't think I've ever actually said this. Not out loud. Not to anyone.

"She has cancer."

And there it is. The memories I've been suppressing all day scream back through my mind. The fight from Wednesday afternoon, the things I've been refusing to acknowledge. That I yelled at Mom over. That Grandma keeps trying to talk to me about. How has the past week managed to be such a colossal shit show? How is there *another* thing I'm not emotionally equipped to deal with?

I turn my face up to Darius's and a tear leaks out. His eyes grow all wide, and I'm suddenly looking down at our fingers. The ones entwined in the space between us. When did we do that?

The door bangs open, and I jump away from Darius.

"Hi, guys," Mr. Mendoza says. "Sorry to keep you waiting, but when Mr. Banner calls . . ."

The tears are coming thick and fast now. There's no way I'm going to be able to talk about the city council meeting. I'll be lucky if I can make it out the door without having another full-blown meltdown. I grab my bag and race out of the lab.

How many times am I going to leave Mr. Mendoza's room upset? That's what kicked all of this off in the first place. With an awful sense of déjà vu, I barrel through the empty halls toward the atrium, thankful that everyone else has already left.

It's absolutely pouring outside the school. The sky is choked with a low, unbroken cloud of gray. I jog through it toward the bicycle hanger. My fingers slip against my lock. I cannot stop crying. Whatever. It doesn't matter. I'm soaked and can't see anyway.

I turn to free my bike from the rail and nearly run into him.

"Isa?" Darius is standing behind me in the rain. Did he follow me out here? How long has he been standing there? Before I can ask, he says, "Come on, I'll give you a ride."

Blankly, I watch as he takes my bike. I should argue with him. I don't want him to see me like this. But I really want to get into his car, and not just because cycling in this would absolutely suck.

He hustles toward a new Volvo, and I follow. Inside, the back seats are already down and covered with a tarp, as if prepared for a bicycle's arrival. I had forgotten that he drives to the skate park, but I guess it's farther away from his house than it is mine.

"It's open," he says.

When Darius gets in, he doesn't start the car. We sit submerged in the torrent for several minutes. Lost in the thudding of a drowning universe while I wipe my face with the wet sleeve of my sweatshirt. In the quiet, my mind circles back through everything I've been trying to avoid. It takes a while for me to get ahold of myself.

"Sorry," I finally choke out. "Thanks for giving me a ride. You can drive, if you want."

"Are you okay?"

"Not really, but I think this is going to go on for a while," I say. "You don't have to wait."

Darius clears his throat. "Well, um. Can you tell me where to go? I don't actually know where you live." His apologetic tone makes me smile.

"Oh, right." I forgot that he's never been to my house before. After I give him basic directions, he starts the car. The wipers have to move frantically across the windshield for us to see.

"I'm really sorry about your grandma."

"Me too." My voice breaks again, and I look down at my hands.

Darius adds, "You don't have to talk about it, if you don't want to."

"No, it's not that I don't want to talk about it." Well, that is part of the problem, but it's not what's making me bawl. "It's just. How did I not know that? How did I not know . . ." I struggle to explain.

"Know what?" he interrupts. "Know that about Anniston?"

"Yes!" I burst. "You knew! You just rattled it off."

"Hey, only AP geeks like me know that kind of thing. Don't beat yourself up." I know he's trying to make me feel better, but it's making me feel worse. "It's okay."

"No, it's not! I keep yelling at everyone to get their shit together. All year, I've been pushing people to do something, and I can't even bring myself to read a fucking poster?!"

"What are you talking about?"

I'm aware that I'm shouting at the wrong person and that I've started crying again. I also know that giving him all the information he needs to make sense of my mess is going to be a lot. But I don't seem to have the willpower to stop now.

"I got into a massive fight with my mom after you . . . before the council meeting," I amend. "I didn't want to go, and she told me to see it through and I just flipped out on her. I yelled at her."

"You *yelled* at your mom?"

"You never fight with your parents?"

"*With* my parents? Hell no." Darius sounds almost appalled by the thought. "The communication stream only goes the one way. They yell at me, not the other way around. Why were you yelling at your mom about the council meeting?"

"I wasn't yelling at her about the council meeting. It was about the seeing-things-through part," I clarify. "She never sees things through! She's complained about waitressing my whole life, but she never does anything about it. She's the best cook I know. And she just won't put herself forward for the job, and it's always over some flimsy excuse. I can't stand it anymore! And then she tells *me* to see things through?!"

My voice rips up an octave, just like it did Wednesday afternoon after I made it home.

"But then, why am I yelling at her? She's looked after me, essentially by herself, my entire life. She's the one person who has *always* been there for me, you know?" I choke. "And she was all, 'Well, we can't all be as brave as you are, Isa.' What's that supposed to mean?! I have no idea what I'm doing! I could have known this whole time why Grandma's sick. But I was too busy making excuses and pretending like everything's going to be fine. Like we'd always be together."

I've definitely entered full-blown meltdown mode. I don't even know if he can understand me at this point, I'm crying so hard. Snot is coming out of my nose, and I'm still talking.

"I just want us to be together, and now Mom won't even talk to me about it. And all Dad says is 'Give her some time.' *What?* And I cannot bring myself to think about how my grandma actually has cancer, and even *you* know why."

A box of Kleenex appears on my lap. I blow my nose and sob until the car stops moving. The ten-minute drive lost in a tsunami of emotion. Darius has pulled into my street and parked against the curb.

That was probably way more information than he wanted. But once this round of tears subsides, I do feel slightly better for getting it all out.

Darius must think that I'm absolutely nuts.

We're still submerged in water; the rain continues to drum against the roof. There's no other noise in his car. Across the street, the lights in our living room are on, and I wonder who's home. I don't want to move yet. I'm guessing he wishes I would get out, though.

"It sucks that you're fighting," Darius eventually says. "I can't really imagine what it's like to have a mom who's not constantly pushing for career gains."

God, he's right. I also can't picture anyone stupid enough to yell at Mrs. Freeman.

Then he asks, "Wait, so after you were up all night painting the mural, and I yelled at you, and you fought with your mom, you still came to the city council meeting?"

I look at him.

"Well, yeah." My voice sounds gross. I clear my throat. "Dad talked me into it. And I couldn't let everyone else in the club down. I knew not many of us were going to make it through the meeting. Kat fell asleep right after school. I had to, really."

While I'm talking, I pull down the visor above my seat to check my reflection, then wish I hadn't. I look about as good as I sound. At least there isn't snot on my face.

"You are brave, you know," Darius says.

Yuck. I really don't want him to try to make me feel better right now.

"I don't mean to take your mom's side or anything," he adds quickly. "But you are. You're braver than me."

I take a deep breath. "It really doesn't feel like that. Thanks anyway, though. For that, for the ride, and for listening."

Darius is still looking at my puffy face. I wish he wouldn't, but the urge to reach out and take his hand nearly overwhelms me. Another false move will make me cry again, and I really don't want to do that. Not before I can get inside.

Once I manage to get myself and my bike out of his car, I wave from the cover of the porch while he drives away. Inside, I can hear that Grandma's TV is on in the back. I can't face her yet. Instead, I march upstairs and run the hottest shower our pipes can manage, sitting on the closed toilet lid while it heats up. My phone vibrates in the bag at my feet.

I reach for it, eager for a distraction. Eager to think about anything else. There's an email alert from Doug with the subject: *Summer Internship*. I rush to open it without thinking.

Dear Isa,

Many thanks for your message and your interest in work-
ing with Halve by 2030 this summer. It's been wonderful
meeting you and the LHS Environmental Justice Club, and
we truly appreciate your work helping collect signatures for
the petition and bringing our community's concerns about
the pipeline to city council. We would love to have your help
over the summer, but at this time we can't offer you a paid
position. As you know, our internships are typically un-
funded. We're truly sorry that this may limit your ability to
participate, but we hope you'll still be able to join us.

Best wishes,
Doug

I don't even finish reading the message before I'm crying again.
The phone hits the bath mat with a dull thud, and I barely remember to strip before I get into the shower. I'm sobbing hard by the
time I'm standing under it, adrift in another deluge.

What just happened? I feel like I'm caught in the ocean. Like wave
after wave has beat all sense of direction out of me. It's only been
three days since we painted the mural, and I don't know which way
is up anymore. Absentmindedly, I start scrubbing at my scalp, and
the water turns blue. An ocean of blue. Then I realize, and in desperation I use squirt after squirt of shampoo to wash the streaks out
of my hair.

I watch, feeling very far away, as my brilliant colors run slowly
down the drain.

CHAPTER 19
WATERLOGGED

Isa

"ISA! ISA!" KAT CATCHES UP TO ME AS I SHUFFLE UNWILLINGLY toward Mr. Mendoza's lab. I'm dreading the club meeting. She's got her phone out, which she found right where she left it. Back in the before times. Back when the world made sense.

Everyone knows what happened with city council. Darius sent a write-up about it over the Signal chat and filled in Mr. Mendoza. He's been texting me all week, mostly about how it was Marina who posted the picture there in the first place, which has been deleted. I'm not surprised it was her. I'm just past caring, especially now that it's gone.

Besides, it wouldn't really matter that people from the club saw it. Everyone thinks the mural is brilliant, and most linked the posted images with it, no further explanation needed. People keep coming up to me, saying how awesome it is. How they want to protest the pipeline with the tribe. Asking what more we can do.

No one even seems that upset that the club got so utterly shut down at the city council meeting. All their families know about the pipeline now, thanks to the tribes and the news coverage. They're all full of renewed enthusiasm.

"Look! Eliyah just texted," Kat says giddily. "Mr. Kiona was interviewed by the *Seattle Times* today. They shot it in front of the mural!"

She scrolls through the article with her thumb. It's a long one, and it already has a bunch of comments at the end. "They're supposed to air his interview on national news tonight!" She beams.

"That's great, Kat," I say without enthusiasm.

I'm exhausted by having to pretend that I want to keep doing this. I can't stop thinking about Grandma and how I haven't worked up the courage to really talk to her yet. How Mom and I haven't said more than a few words to each other since our argument. How I overheard Dad and her fighting about who should take on more shifts now that his schedule is more up in the air. How there's no future in organizing. Not for someone like me, anyway. Everything seems worse than it was before I stuck my neck out with this co-president thing. Part of me wishes I never had.

"This is huge. Better than we thought it would be!"

One of the comments catches my eye. "What are they saying?"

"Huh?" Kat's already clicked through to the social media links. It doesn't matter. I can see the same things I noticed under the article.

"There." I point. Most of the comments are people talking about the pipeline or climate change or environmental protection, cheering them on. They're the same types of things Kat gets when she posts about our murals. But under Mr. Kiona's article, there are others, too.

"WTF?! So many climate deniers." She scrolls, flipping back and forth between social media platforms and where the article's posted.

I shake my head. "No, not those. Look." I point again. *Stop the blame game, you lost! Not your land. Real Americans first! Get back on your patch.* They're terrible.

"Racist assholes," Kat says. "There are always such creeps hiding behind the internet. You don't even have to give a username on this site."

We round the corner to C Hall.

She flicks over to her accounts. "I still can't get over how many people are liking the mural, though! I bet Mr. Kiona nailed the interview. He's a great speaker."

When I don't join in her excitement, she studies my face.

"What's with you lately? You've been all weird ever since that city council meeting. Who cares what they think."

She mock punches my shoulder. The gesture usually makes me smile. Now I just hug my binder closer to my chest and answer, "Right."

I haven't talked to Kat about stuff, either. I don't even know if she saw the trespassing picture on the club's Signal chat, though I heard Dad filling her in on the council meeting the other morning. I haven't told her about Darius—yelling Darius or holding hands Darius. Or about any of the stuff with Mom and Grandma. Or about Halve by 2030 rejecting me.

I'm just trying to get through the week.

When Kat and I arrive at Mr. Mendoza's lab, almost everyone else is already there. Darius waves at me from the front.

Kat laughs and whispers, "Someone's happy to see you."

"Cut it out," I snap before I can help it. Great. Now I'm fighting with everyone. "Sorry," I mumble. "I better go get things started."

At the front of the packed room, I attempt to return Darius's smile. I don't get very far. "Can you lead today?" I ask him. "I'll take notes."

Darius's brow scrunches, but he nods. "Okay."

He starts the meeting by giving the room a summary of what happened with city council. People boo and hiss when he details the mayor's lackluster response. "I've asked my mom's firm about what will happen now. At the end of the public comment period, if the council decides to move ahead with the pipeline, we can file an appeal," Darius explains.

"But that will take money, which we don't have. They recommend consulting with Halve by 2030 after they make their appearance at the next city council meeting. Given that they'll present the petition and the amount of attention the pipeline's generating, the council will likely need to give an indication of how they intend to proceed. They don't have to, though; they can simply put out a written statement sometime next month."

"Next month?!" Collin says.

"Yeah," Darius confirms.

"Well, that's shit! After all that, they can just do nothing?"

"Language," Mr. Mendoza chides. "I'm disappointed, too, but we're a school club. School rules still apply."

"I do think the club should follow up and see how Halve by 2030 does," Darius continues. "And I know the rally won't be the celebration we planned, but I think we should go ahead with that, too. We'll have to reframe it, but what the hell? We could use it to raise money for an appeal, if we want? At the very least, it would be a good way of updating the student body on where things stand."

"We should do some more art projects about the pipeline, too," Kat says.

"More?" Mr. Mendoza asks, eyebrows raised.

"I mean *some*," Kat amends quickly. I forget that not everyone knows she's one of the artists behind the mural. Apparently, so does she. Unlike the last time she pitched this in a club meeting, though, more kids have made the connection. "There are a couple spots in the town center that would make excellent canvases."

"I'm in!"

"Let's do it!"

Susie raises her hand. "I think using the rally to fundraise is a good call. And I've been thinking. In addition to the city council appeal, could we also raise money for Snoqualmie's recovery?"

"Oh, that's a wonderful idea, Susie!" Mr. Mendoza says. "We could establish a mutual aid fund for families in the school district."

Susie beams. "Thanks, Mr. M. I'd love it if the club could help the wildfire survivors. I know my cousins are only just getting their lives back. They want to be home, but there's so much to do to make things livable again. I really want to help them."

"We've already had several clubs say they're interested in the rally. We should go for it!" Darius says with an enthusiasm I can't wrap my brain around. "We can't give up now. And I agree with Susie. It's important to support communities recovering from climate crisis–fueled disasters."

Jazz hands and clapping fill the air. I duck my head over my scribbled notes, overwhelmed by how much my mood differs from the mood in the room. I wish I could disappear.

"OH!" Jake says. "Let's do some protest art for the rally!"

Someone laughs. "They won't be able to ignore us then."

"I love it." Kat grins.

"Me too," Darius says. I'm not the only one who raises their eyebrows at him.

"What?" It's a new voice, and my head swivels as I place it. Marina is staring at Darius. Almost glaring at him. I've literally never heard her speak in a meeting before. She wasn't expecting Darius to be up for protest art, either.

Darius thinks for a moment, and when he speaks, it's mostly to Marina.

"I mean, we've got nothing to lose, right? We played by their rules, and they ignored us. I guess making a difference is going to take doing something different, something that gets their attention. Or gets them the kind of attention they don't want."

He turns and looks at me. "What do you think, Isa?"

I blink at him and at all the people in the lab who've become my friends. "Sure," I answer. "Let's do it." I so wish that I meant it.

Before the bell rings, Darius has volunteers to follow the city council's progress, liaise with Halve by 2030, meet with the tribes, update the club's web page and social media with our plans, and reframe the rally's theme. Kat's leading the art team, which has several enthusiastic mural participants.

Mr. Mendoza beams. "Alright, that's the last club meeting before spring break. I just want to say how proud I remain of all of you! We'll see you back here in April."

Sure, I think.

"Come on, Isa. Who spends all of spring break in their room?" Kat demands over the phone. "What's going on with you?"

My chin raises a fraction. "I'm not in my room. I'm in the living room." I don't want to admit that up until last night, she would have been right. My voice still sounds rough.

"Well, you're biking with us today. No excuses," she threatens. "I'll see you in five minutes."

Exactly five minutes later, she and Isaac are at my door. Kat's got her backpack loaded and is wearing a miffed expression. I can't really blame her. I've been pretty MIA. We ride over to the skate park in uncharacteristic quiet, until Isaac asks if Eliyah's meeting us there. "Or is he too tired from sucking face all night?"

"What?!" I say.

"Shut up!" Kat yells. Isaac just laughs and pedals away.

"Sucking face all night? What happened, Kat?"

Kat's face is so torn that it's comical. After a few seconds, the part of her that's clearly dying to tell me defeats the part that's annoyed by my absence. "So," she says grinning. "Eliyah and I went out last night."

I laugh. "Obviously. What did you do?"

"Nothing," she says nonchalantly. "Just got some bubble tea. Went to a movie. And then made out in the driveway for a bit." Her face has become a twitterpated grin. "It would have been perfect, except of course that was the night that Liam decided to come home."

"No!" I put on a mask of mock horror. "He didn't see you, did he?"

"Yeah. It was over the top. He started banging on the hood of Eliyah's car. Scared the shit out of him. Liam thought it was hilarious. Eliyah nearly wet himself."

I can't control my laughter as I picture the scene. Liam's six feet tall and huge these days. "Poor Eliyah! Is he okay?"

"I think so. But Liam wouldn't apologize or anything. He acted like such an ass. It'll take me forever to convince Eliyah to come over again."

"OMG! So is Eliyah your boyfriend now??"

"If he's not completely freaked out, then yeah. He is."

"Aww, you really like him!"

"Stop it!" She laughs, all shy with new love. It's fun seeing her this way. We round the last corner to the skate park. "We're supposed to meet him here. Don't say anything! Oh, and I think Nathan's coming today, too. He wants to ask you something." She winks.

"Ask me what?"

"Well, don't be mad, okay? For some reason, Eliyah really wants to go to prom."

That's not where I thought this was going. "Prom? Our prom?"

"They don't do one at their school, so he's curious. He probably just wants to make fun of how us white people dance all night."

I laugh. "Or bone after, but go on." I'm still not sure what this has to do with me.

She scowls at my comment, but then her face turns apologetic. "Well, he doesn't want to go alone, so . . ."

"So?"

"Nathan's probably going to ask you to prom," she says quickly. "That's okay, right? You're not going with Robert? I couldn't remember if he was going to his own prom."

I don't even know where to start. "How'd—? What did—? *What?!*"

"Just say yes, Isa. Please! Nathan's cute, and we'll all dance together. It'll be fun! Your mom can do our hair before and everything!" She's dying of excitement.

This is not the prom that I had in mind, but what am I supposed to say? *Sorry, I can't go with Nathan because I'm going with my imaginary boyfriend. You might know him as Darius, the guy you think I hate and whose messages I haven't been returning.* 'Cause that's not ridiculous.

"PLEASE!!" Kat's still begging as we pull up to the park.

"Fine," I tell her. I remind myself that prom is in less than two weeks, and it's not like Darius asked me to go with him.

We paint for a while. When Eliyah and Nathan show up, I do my best not to stare at Kat's flirting. It's pretty easy. Nathan wants to talk about the tribe's protest, and he hasn't heard about how things at the city council meeting went down. He does, slightly awkwardly, ask me about prom, and I say I'll go with him. "Mostly to keep an eye on those two." I point.

He laughs. Eliyah has an arm around Kat's shoulder and is playing with a strand of her hair. It's both precious and gag inducing at the same time.

Eventually, the guys have to leave for their shifts at the casino. Isaac heads to the mall with the friends he's been boarding with. Eliyah offers us a ride back, but I let him and Kat go together. I want to cycle anyway. I really haven't been out of the house much the last several days.

Besides, I need some time to think.

I push off on my bike, heading toward the trail that leads to American Lake, the one that gets closest to home. Patches of late afternoon sun have finally broken through the spring clouds, and I can hear the birds rejoicing in it, smell it warm the rain-soaked earth on either side of the trail. My legs kick slowly, moving me forward, the cool air on my face. I ride mindlessly for a while, until I can't help thinking again.

At home, the ice was officially broken yesterday morning. I walked downstairs to find Mom and Grandma at the table. Not eating. Not talking. Not even looking at each other. There were some hospital forms lying open between them.

I was crying before I even got my arms around her.

"Bo! What's wrong? What happened?"

"It's not me!" I slumped down into a chair. "Grandma, how are *you*?!" It's not as though I never ask her this. I just could never bring myself to hear her answers for what they were.

"I'll be alright, Bo . . ."

"Mom!" Mom snapped, cutting her off. "You promised. We can't keep doing this. Tell it to her straight."

And before Grandma could say anything else, I was crying again. "Mom, I'm so sorry! I shouldn't have yelled at you. I've just been such an idiot, such a mess."

"Stop it, Bo!" Grandma said. Was she crying, too?

"What are you two doing?" Mom choked out. Great, I made everyone cry. The three of us sat there, sobbing for a minute. I didn't look up until I felt Grandma's hand take mine. She reached over to take Mom's, too, and eventually, Mom let her. She squeezed it once and then let go. But I kept Grandma's hand in mine, holding on.

"I think we all have some talking to do," Mom said. To my surprise, she looked at Grandma, not me. "Mom."

Grandma exhaled, then started. "Things aren't so good, Bo."

And that's as far as my thinking gets before I have to pull over. It's a good thing the trail is mostly deserted. Eyes welling, I get off my bike and lean it against the closest tree. Then I trudge blindly through the ferns, seeking the cover of the forest. I only stop when a moss-covered log painfully hits my knees. I turn and sit on it, my feet hanging above the ground, thinking about what Grandma said. What we talked about. The way our hands stretched across the table, holding on.

I've cried so much recently that my tear ducts may actually fail from overuse. I feel like I'll never stop. I have absolutely no idea what to do. How anything will ever make this better. How desperately I wanted the four of us to live here together, always. To never be apart.

I knew it was impossible, but after a lifetime of never being close, they are all I really want.

The last of the sun's light filters through the trees, and I take deep breaths until I can hear the noise the leaves make in the wind. Until the moisture stops leaking from my eyes.

"Isa?" I look up, dumbfounded. Darius Freeman is standing on the trail next to my bike, holding his and looking around. How does he keep finding me like this?

"Isa?!" he calls. Louder this time.

He hasn't seen me yet. I'm about thirty yards away, hidden by the trees and the undergrowth. I wipe my face with the sleeve of my jacket. This can't be happening again. I bet I look terrible. Maybe he'll believe that I've been attacked by a swarm of bees or a bear. Anything to get out of admitting that I'm sobbing—again.

"Hey, Darius." Ick. I sound worse than I did that day in his car.

His head turns in my direction, and his eyes widen as soon as he spots me.

"Are you okay?"

"Yeah," I croak. "No worries, I'm fine."

I wave, unsuccessfully trying to convey that he should feel free to cycle on and leave me here, falling to pieces. Like it's totally normal to sob alone in the woods. But, of course, he's already walking toward me through the trees so he can sit beside me on the moss-covered log.

"So," I ask. "Having a good spring break?"

"Not as good as yours."

Despite my misery, his joke makes me bark a laugh. "Sorry that I haven't responded to your texts. I've been . . . kind of out of it."

He looks me in the eyes. "Dude, what's wrong?"

"I finally talked to my mom. And my grandma." I take a deep breath. Just stick to the facts, that should keep the crying to a minimum. "You were right. Grandma lived most of her life a few miles from the Anniston Monsanto plant. She's always had health problems, but she's known for a while that something was really wrong. She has uterine cancer, and her doctors just started her on another medication. They don't know how effective it will be."

Darius swears under his breath. "I'm so sorry, Isa."

We sit there, watching the shadows get longer. The canopy under the trees grows dark, and the temperature drops. Despite the warm winter, spring has been cold so far. The sound of the wind fades in the stillness of the coming night. Darius doesn't seem in a hurry to leave. I'm not, either.

"At least you talked to them about it?" Darius asks after a while.

I nod. "Yeah, I'm glad we did." Because that's the one truth of this terrible tale. That I'm glad to have finally asked. To finally know. If I hadn't, I wouldn't know the one thing that I want now.

"I think I'm going to take some time off school and help out with things. If Grandma will let me, anyway."

"Oh, right," Darius says. "I hope she . . . I hope you get to spend some time together."

My response catches in my throat and my eyes well up, again. So instead of attempting an answer, I lean over and rest my head against his shoulder, silently praying that he's right.

CHAPTER 20
DANCE WITH ME

Darius

"I'M SORRY, ALRIGHT?" MARINA FINALLY SAYS. WE'RE SITTING on the Takahashis' front stairs, somewhere no one will hear us.

We've mostly avoided each other since I confronted her. Almost a month of only cursory texts. Our one attempt to talk ended in a shouting match and several rounds of clarifying messages about what *is* and what *is not* acceptable behavior.

Via passive-aggressive text, Marina admitted to understanding my logic that if nothing yet has solved the climate crisis, solutions must lie outside of the box. Apparently, though, she's not interested in stepping outside the box until after college. Which, I suppose, is her decision to make.

Now that school has started again, avoiding each other isn't practical. I'm at the Takahashis' to pick up Jordan, and not hanging out just seems stupid.

"I shouldn't have posted the picture without talking to you about it. But then," she counters, "you haven't been talking to me, either."

My eyebrows shoot up. "What's that supposed to mean? We talk like every day."

"I mean," Marina clarifies, her eyes swiveling to mine, "what's going on with you and Isa?"

Oh, that.

What *is* going on with me and Isa? *Between* me and Isa? My shoulders slump as I let out a frustrated sigh.

Marina's eyes narrow in impatience.

"Look, if you like her, just tell me. I'm tired of being ditched, and I'm not interested in living with more secrets. Jordan says you weren't really 'training for STP' all spring break." Marina's fingers twitch in air quotes. "You were really biking around looking for the 'hot girl with fun hair.' That's Isa, right?"

Shit.

"Just tell me!" Marina yells.

"I honestly don't know," I begin. Then, before Marina can get her objection out, I holler, "Where to start!"

Our sudden increase in volume makes us both turn and look apprehensively at the front door. We wait; nothing happens. I take a deep breath.

The squirmy, nagging feeling builds in my chest while I rub my face, thinking.

"I'm embarrassed," I finally say. "I feel so differently about Isa than I did when we first met. I didn't even give her a chance. I wish I'd listened to her. She's brilliant, and I wish I'd seen that sooner."

Marina hugs her knees into her chest and looks out beyond the eaves of the covered porch.

I guess that wasn't what she was expecting to hear. It is one of the things I've been thinking about. Caught up in all the time I spend thinking about Isa are the regrets I have about Isa. All the things I wish I had done differently are attached to all the hopes I have for things we *will* do—together.

"And then, I don't know, stuff happened, and I didn't know how to tell you."

Marina raises an eyebrow in my direction. My lips turn down in a frown as the squirmy feeling resurfaces. I kick the right toe of my sneaker against my left. "But I should have," I say in a rush. "I'm sorry."

As soon as the words are out, I realize what I'm feeling, and that I owe her better than this. I put my glasses back on so that when I meet her eyes, I can seem them clearly.

"I really am, Marina. I'm sorry."

Marina's chin lowers to meet the tops of her knees. She hugs herself, and we sit in silence for a while.

"I've missed you," she says with a sigh. "You're my best friend. One of the few people I find it easy to be around. A kindred nerd spirit."

This pulls the side of my mouth up into a grin.

She takes a breath. "For me, doing well in school isn't just the expected next step. It's my ticket away. Far enough away that I can be someone else."

My forehead crinkles while I take this in. Then I nod.

I feel the ease that always existed between us settle in again. Marina was one of the first people I found it easy to be around, too. For so long, I didn't think we needed to say anything to know what the other was thinking. Maybe now, though, we'll need to do things differently.

"Hey, best friend?" I ask her.

Marina tucks her hair behind her left ear, so I can see her grin back. "Yeah?"

"I like this girl Isa, she's co-president of the Environmental Justice

Club." Just saying this out loud makes me feel a million times lighter. So giddy that I smile a wide, goofy smile.

Marina spends a solid five seconds rolling her eyes at me.

"I know," she says. "And I guess, if you like her, then so do I."

I'm glad things with Marina are starting to feel normal again. In spirit, anyway. Tonight is going to be a bit of a production. Even though I told my parents and Marina told hers that we're going to prom together as friends and with a group of friends, they're still insisting on taking pictures.

My dad and her mom are beaming from behind their phones while Marina and I stand, smiling awkwardly in the Takahashis' downstairs living room.

I think Mrs. Takahashi might die of happiness at the sight of Marina all dolled up with her hair done, wearing a floor-length gown. She keeps rushing up to tuck strands of hair into place, get Marina to apply more lipstick, turn slightly. Marina seems excruciatingly aware that all her cousins are making faces at us from behind the row of camera-wielding adults.

After five minutes, my cheeks feel like they're going to fall off, and Marina loudly declares, "Alright, we're leaving!"

We get dinner with the AP crew and roll up to Lakewood High School for prom with Collin, Hai, and Abigail. We're the first car in the processional of our group. It does feel a bit like nerd squad on parade, but it's definitely less awkward than I thought it would be.

I park and the AP crew heads in together. The pep squad has transformed the cafeteria dining area into a dance hall. Lights are strung across the ceiling, and the wall of double doors that lead out to the back fields are propped open, more lights shining from the trees outside. The tables around the dance floor are covered in table-cloths and flowers, and a band is playing on the small stage set up near the doors.

If I didn't know I was at school, I'd think I was at a wedding. Even the people look different in formal wear.

Our group claims a table at the far side of the room. We dance a few fast songs together, and Levi, who's been especially obnoxious this evening, shocks everyone by pop-and-locking over to this bulky senior wrestler. "How is Levi challenging *him* to a dance-off?!" I ask Marina.

She laughs. "Not a dance-off. A date!"

My mouth falls open in surprise. How did I not know?! When the senior grabs Levi's hand so their arms can form a connected worm, I clap along with everyone else.

"Go, Levi!" Marina cheers.

The music changes, and people start pairing off for the first slow song.

I hold out my hand in offering, even though I know Marina's not much of a dancer outside of *DDR*. After a bewildered look at the couples on the floor, she shakes her head. "That's okay. Why don't we go get our picture taken?"

"Good idea. Let's get some punch, too."

I spot some people from the track team in the line. One of the senior captains, a high jumper with amazing braids who I never thought noticed me, asks me to dance. Her date is too busy trying to photobomb his teammate's prom pictures to pay her any attention. We dance until the band takes a break and a DJ starts up. She says she's happy to keep going, but I thank her anyway.

"I'm looking for someone," I say.

Because, really, I've been looking for Isa since we got here. And the longer the night goes on, the more anxious I get that she didn't come. The songs are more slow than fast now, so the AP crew isn't on the floor as often. I start milling around, searching. I don't see Kat anywhere, either, and she was the one I'd overheard pestering Isa about prom last week. I assumed they would be here.

Just as I reach for my phone to text, I see her. Or at least I think I do. Across the hall there's a girl wearing a gold dress, sitting at a table in the far corner. She has her back to the dance floor, and there aren't the easily recognizable streaks of color through her hair. This girl's dark curls are twisted into an elegant knot at her neck. Susie and Josh are sitting at the same table, talking with each other. It must be Isa.

Why isn't she dancing?

The band's taking the stage again, warming up for another slow song. Before the pairing starts, I quickly cross the room toward them.

"Hey, Darius." Susie waves. "You're looking sharp!"

"Thanks." I smile, grateful that her compliment makes Isa turn.

"You look nice, too," I say. But I'm only looking at Isa. "Would you like to dance?"

Isa smiles smally. "Sure."

She takes my outstretched hand. Hers is soft and warm. I really hope my palms don't start sweating. We walk to the center of the room together, where she turns to face me. It feels so natural when she puts her left hand on my shoulder. When I put my right hand on her waist. We step and turn to the beat, our other hands held out slightly. Her smile grows, and I pray she can't hear my heart hammering. My mouth's gone dry.

"I didn't think you danced," she says.

I laugh once, then—to demonstrate—raise my left hand and spin her under my arm. She giggles, and the sound makes me feel almost homesick. It's been too long since I've heard it.

"Impressive."

I grin. "I might not be from the South, but my parents are. I know how to dance."

"I believe you." Her smile starts to fade. "Thanks for asking me."

"How are you?" Because that's what I've been dying to ask her since spring break. Since I found her crying by the trail and escorted her home through the fading light. The last time we were alone together. I've seen her at school this week, but just in passing. She wasn't at the last club meeting, and we haven't had the chance to talk.

"Oh, I'm great," she scoffs. "Never better."

I swallow. Isa looks me in the eyes.

"I'm sorry," she says. "I'm okay, thanks. Nothing's really changed. I haven't even missed all that much school. Just dance classes, really. How about you?"

"I'm fine," I tell her. "I've been enjoying some quality time with Kat."

Kat saw me bring Isa home that night. I don't know why Kat was in a parked car down the street, and she told me not to ask. She's been surprisingly communicative ever since. This week, she tracked me down at lunch to tell me about the mural that went up on the side of a local bookstore. She looked less than thrilled to be standing in the library. After she sneered, "Don't worry, we have permission," she didn't leave. Instead, she asked me how Isa was, like I would somehow know things that she didn't. Kat and I mostly talk about club stuff, but really I think we're talking because we're both worried about Isa.

The Kat comment makes Isa laugh again. "I heard about that. It's good that the club's still working. That everyone still wants to be involved."

The club's doing more than working. I've never seen anything like it. Everyone is buzzing to keep the rally afloat in the face of the city council defeat. We've got the theme reframed and have messaged everyone we can think of: school clubs, community groups, the college. Kat's even in touch with a local news crew.

I don't miss that it doesn't sound like *Isa* wants to be involved, and the words "Do you?" pop out before I can stop them.

Isa looks away. She starts to slowly shake her head. "I'm sorry. I still don't know. What have we actually achieved? After all of this effort."

"Everyone's talking about the new mural," I start.

Isa cuts me off. "So what? She's dying, and they're still building the fucking pipeline, and all we've managed to do is awaken the haters on social media." Her voice breaks twice. "Have you seen the garbage they're writing about the tribes? About us? My feed is just blocked comments now."

My arm tightens around her, pulling her closer. Once the national interview aired, everyone who's liked the tribes' mural on social media has had their profiles covered in abuse. It only took about a week before the trolls connected the mural to the club and our profiles. Mr. Mendoza had to spend ten minutes of the last club meeting talking about online safety.

Isa lets out a shaky breath. I can feel it against my shoulder.

"I thought we could actually do something about this—change things for the better. Protect the people we care about. But the more we do, the more I realize how much is wrong and how we don't have a hope in hell of changing anything."

She looks utterly devastated, so unlike herself. My eyes get all wet.

"I'm sorry!" she says quickly.

Why is she always apologizing to me?

"I know you've lost people, too. It's all just so much, you know?"

She takes another shaky breath, then ducks her head into the hollow of my neck, her face turned into my chest. She doesn't say anything else. We sway, turning in a slow circle. It feels like that moment in Mr. Mendoza's lab again. When everything seems suddenly lost, we're holding on to each other.

I rest my chin lightly on the top of her head and wrap both arms around her waist. She's the perfect height for this. Isa moves her right hand to my chest. I don't think that I've ever felt closer to anyone than I do to this girl, who at the beginning of the year I genuinely thought was ruining my life.

The song ends, and she doesn't let go. I don't move away. We keep turning in a slow circle.

A guy's crossing the dance floor toward us. I'm guessing it's Nathan, the guy from the Puyallup tribe that Kat was pestering Isa about coming to prom with. He looks like he wants to ask her to dance. But she hasn't moved. She hasn't even turned her head.

I don't know exactly what expression is on my face, but as soon as my eyes meet Nathan's, he stops walking. I hold his gaze. Another slow song starts, and I gently change the tempo of our sway to match the beat, our slow circle continuing unbroken.

As much as I don't want this to end, there are things I need to tell her, and I have a feeling this is our last song.

I clear my throat. My lips are basically at her ear, so I say softly, "I don't know exactly how you feel, but I do know what losing people to this is like."

She pulls away slightly, her eyes searching until they meet mine.

"I didn't really realize until I met you why I wanted to lead the club. Why I cared. And now that I do, I know why I'm not going to stop. Why the club is about so much more than my college applications. It's the most important thing I do."

Her eyes get all misty again.

"I wanted to tell you—thank you. If there's anything I can do to help you and your grandma, I'm happy to. I don't know what she'll want or need, but I'm great at using Google. And I have access to legal advice."

She pushes her full lips together until they form a thin line. It looks like she's trying really hard not to cry. "Thank you, Darius. I mean it."

I nod. I told myself not to do this, but I can't help it. "We're in this together, right? We promised not to quit," I remind her.

This almost makes her laugh. "That's not exactly how I remember it," she says. "But yeah, I guess we did."

I beam. The club isn't the same without her.

She studies my face for a moment. "You look amazing, by the way."

My palms start sweating almost instantly. I may not be here with a date, but I'm determined to play it cool. I *have* danced with an older woman tonight.

"Enjoy me while you can," I say, lifting my chin. "Before your date notices."

She laughs this time, then looks around. "And yours?"

I spin her slightly so she has a clear view of the AP crew's table, where Marina is talking to Abigail. "Ah, well. I'm here with a group, actually. What can I say?" I laugh. "Everyone wants a piece."

She giggles and moves closer. It feels like too soon when I have to let her go.

CHAPTER 21
HANDOVER

Darius

"HOW IS IT MAY NEXT WEEK?!" I HEAR FROM THE HALL OUTSIDE homeroom. It's zero hour on Monday morning, and unlike the jocks who have come in early for weightlifting, nearly the entire AP crew is already assembled in Ms. Patten's. Getting an extra hour of studying in.

"Next week!" Levi's spiraling.

He's not the only one freaking out. Most of us will pay to take the Advanced Placement exams for US History, Calculus, and Biology. That's up to thirty college credits to play for, and the exams start next week.

"Shut up!" Abigail yells from the back row. "We're trying to work here."

I claim my seat and take out my laptop just as Ms. Patten comes in, a large Starbucks cup in hand. Every morning at 6:45 a.m. she unlocks the door to her classroom, makes a coffee run, and then returns. We can ask her questions if we want to, but really this is just collective study hall. We're that into it.

I've got essays to write and Honors Chemistry homework to do.

I'm feeling pretty good about the AP exams, though US History will probably be my weakest. Mostly because I can't keep myself from writing about parallels with my current research interest: understanding the fallout over what happened in Anniston, Alabama.

I focused my last essay on contemporary litigation. I wrote about Johnnie Cochran's procurement of the largest class-action settlement ever won in the United States for Anniston victims. Fine. I went on to discuss legislation's role in the regulation of PCBs and other toxic chemicals, which were dumped in the majority Black town for over seventy years by Monsanto, its subsidiary Solutia, Pfizer, and the US Army. Great.

My ending, though, may have taken things a bit too far. I compared Confederate States negotiating the date of emancipation with fossil fuel companies negotiating dates for reaching net-zero emissions. It doesn't take a genius to work out that any date they agree to is never going to arrive. And that litigation cannot regulate those more powerful than the law itself. I don't know if the metaphor is the most accurate. But the underlying conclusion is certainly where my mind's been recently.

Though she gave me an A+ and wrote *Bitchin'! Exceptional critical thinking, Darius* across the top of my essay, which I took as the ultimate compliment, Ms. Patten did warn me that the AP graders may well score things differently. Environmental justice isn't exactly a core theme of the AP US History curriculum.

"Darius, are you working on Calculus stuff?" Collin asks me.

"Ah, no. I'm on Chemistry." I close my browser windows and dig for my Honors Chemistry textbook in my pack. If I'm going to be here, I guess I should at least give schoolwork a try.

"Why are you working on Chemistry? Didn't you see the leader board?"

I shrug.

I haven't, actually. I mean, I did walk past it yesterday in Mr. Davis's, and everyone told me I had returned to number one. As expected, replacing Spanish III with Honors Chemistry and Honors American Literature with Honors Speech and Debate this trimester has pushed me ahead. It's just, obsessing about finishing junior year at the top of the top one percent seems a bit ridiculous now. Nearly everyone in this room will graduate with a perfect 4.0. Clearly, adding the additional stress of worrying about class rankings is super helpful.

The same feeling has taken over my approach to the SAT. My March results were good, so why add another exam to my May schedule? Arriving in homeroom an hour early and still being on track to valedictorian status might not look like I now know that *there's more to life than school*, but I can see the changes in myself. Putting things into perspective is more of a journey than I realized.

My phone buzzes, and I smile. Isa's up.

Her text is pretty businesslike: She's asking if I can respond to the Model UN crew about the rally. We invited so many groups that we've set up an email address for the club. It was getting way too messy to have people contacting club members individually. And no one seemed as enthused about logging everything in a shared spreadsheet as I was.

Having one email address seemed the best solution, and having the co-presidents cover it together was Mr. Mendoza's suggestion. I don't think either of us anticipated how much work would go into managing that in the rally's run-up. Isa now texts me more than anyone else I know.

But really, the messages picked up after prom. I woke up the following morning to see Isa's name at the top of my notifications.

> *Thanks for the dance. Maybe the next time I see you, I won't cry*

> 🙂 *Don't make me any promises*

> 😆 😆 *Fine. Bring Kleenex.*

> 😂 😂

I smile at the phone, remembering. We've been texting ever since. Her messages are breaking down all the inhibitions I felt over the last few weeks, when she wasn't returning my texts. We're talking again. The things I've wanted to ask her, I just . . . should. With this resolve, I type:

> *I've been meaning to ask you if you've heard from 2030? About the internship?*

> *Yeah, no dice. They like me, but they can't pay me.*

> *Unacceptable. I'm taking back their invite to the rally!*

> 😔 😔 *It was a long shot anyway.*

> *Really sorry. It's their loss. You should tell them so.*

> *Please!*

> *Seriously, did you write them back?*

> *What?! No.*

> *I would. "Thanks for your response. I really hope you'll reconsider. I would love to work for you and let me tell you again all the skills I can contribute to your organization . . ."*

I watch the typing bubbles drum across the screen while she thinks in text. No message materializes, so I add:

> *Don't give up!*

> *You're so bossy! I should probably respond though I guess. But I'm not promising to be as pushy as you.*

> *Well, we can't all be champions.*

> *Gah! Fine! You're the worst.*

>  *You're welcome*

So, the messaging's not all about club stuff. I wish we could hang out more. Spring trimester has us back to sharing the same lunch hour, but chatting in the cafeteria where we'd be strange brokers between our existing friend groups isn't what I had in mind.

I miss biking around together. Track practice means cycling after school isn't an option for me. Marina keeps telling me to just ask Isa out, but I haven't had the guts to do that yet, either. Though I do think about what we'd do. Ride out to Puget Sound and go tide pooling or whale watching. Go see those dance troupes in Seattle that Isa's talked about. Try that new bubble tea place.

With the rally coming, there's genuinely so much to do that we keep having to find new ways to see each other. I forgot about our plans for this afternoon. Which is why after AP Biology ends, I'm sprinting off toward the track rather than following the other members of the club. Keeping an immaculate calendar's another thing that's slid off the list of priorities these days.

I round the hall to the athletics complex just in time. "Coach Kerry?" I call. I've caught him just as he's leaving his office.

"Darius! Star of the eight hundred meters!" Good. I was hoping my win at this past weekend's meet would make him happy enough to do me a favor.

"Hey, Coach." I come to a stop next to him. "Sorry, but I'm not going to be able to make practice today."

His brow furrows, and his fists go to his hips. He exhales disappointment in the most coach-like fashion. "That's the second time this month, Darius, and I'm already giving you special treatment for every other Friday."

"I know, Coach, and I really appreciate it. It's just, the club's got a lot of organizing to do for this end-of-the-year rally," I explain. "I can do laps on Saturday?"

"You're already lapping on Saturday to make up for Friday."

"Oh, right." The bell rings overhead, and Coach Kerry looks annoyed that I'm already turning away from him—back into the school and not out toward the field or locker room. I'm just hoping he's not so annoyed that he'll kick me off the team. I'm missing practice whether he likes it or not.

I put an apologetic look on my face, slowly completing the turn on my heel. His fists stay on his hips, but he doesn't say anything to stop me.

"Thanks, Coach!" I yell behind me as I start jogging away. I'm late, and I don't know exactly where I'm going.

"I'm not happy about this, Darius!" follows me back down the hall.

I make my way to the far end of A Hall, to Mrs. Vethanayagam's art studio. I've never been down here before. Nerve-racking flashbacks to the last time art was required start running through my mind. My attempts at drawing were a dangerous threat to my GPA. It's the only time in my academic career that I seriously considered cheating. I was six.

The door bangs, and I'm the last one here.

It takes me a minute to orient myself. This doesn't look like a classroom at all. The ceiling's twice as high, and the walls are covered in color. There aren't desks, just large tables spread around the room. Mrs. Vethanayagam's in an adjoining office, and I spot a door labeled KILNS. Through it I can see some kind of storage area—there are garage doors on its far side. Wild.

Jake seems to have already started the protest art brainstorm. He and Mr. Mendoza are at the front of a huddle of club members standing in the center of the room. That's why everyone interested is meeting in here, rather than Mr. Mendoza's lab. You're not meant to paint things with what he keeps in his storeroom.

"If we're trying to shame the mayor, why don't we just draw him?" Harper asks.

"How are we going to show a drawing at a rally?"

"Like, do a poster?" Jake says.

"We could make an effigy," I suggest, crossing the room toward them.

Isa smiles and waves. Kat asks, "A what?"

"An effigy. A likeness. Like the Europeans do at protests," I explain. "We could make a giant papier-mâché version of the mayor."

"Oh!" Jake says. "We should do that Puget Sound Energy rep, too—the one they've been interviewing on the news."

Mr. Finnigan's been doing an exceptional amount of PR recently. He went from someone I'd never seen to someone I can't *stop* seeing. And *his* articles and posts aren't littered with racist comments like ours have been.

"Who?" Kat asks.

"Mr. Finnigan, the guy who was at the city council meeting. Red hair, tie clip." My eyes roll involuntarily. "I've done a bit of digging on him now, too, and he could definitely use some public criticism."

"Yes!" Brian exclaims. He takes the sketchbook he's been frantically drawing in and moves toward a clean whiteboard.

I bend down, digging in my bag for the profiles of the city council members that I've been toting around for months.

"Brian!" Mr. Mendoza shouts.

I jump, my head snapping up. I've never heard Mr. Mendoza yell like that. Several people laugh as he rushes toward the whiteboard. I only get a glimpse of what Brian's drawn before Mr. Mendoza's arm wipes it clean.

I can't help laughing with everyone else. Next to me, Kat says to Isa, "It's the gooey duck all over again." And they both laugh even harder.

"What?" Brian's saying in an innocent tone. "I was just illustrating the relationship between money and politics, sir."

Mr. Mendoza grabs the sketchbook Brian's holding. His eyes bug.

"No!" he shouts, tearing off the top page.

Then his eyes get even wider. "Noooooo!"

Rip.

"Nope."

Tear.

"NO!" Crumpled pieces of sketch paper go flying. Brian's choking with laughter, and he's not the only one. Mrs. Vethanayagam's head appears at her office door.

"To be clear," Mr. Mendoza says in the raised voice of authority, though he looks like he's holding back laughter himself. "Any depiction of public figures will be kept respectful and strictly PG. I *will* give detentions for any sketches that depict them otherwise. Brian, put those in the recycling bin."

He points to the balls of crumpled paper on the floor.

My sides hurt from laughing. I can only imagine how Brian has depicted Mr. Finnigan "interacting" with Mayor Malone. A sound from the hall drifts over the remaining giggles.

"Mr. Mendoza? Is that you in there?"

All traces of humor vanish from Mr. Mendoza's face as Principal Banner walks into the room. He's the only person I know who wears a suit at school. I've never spoken to him. Members of the AP crew tend to only interact with the principal at end-of-the-year assemblies, when he hands out prizes for top marks.

"Working on some kind of art-science crossover?" Mr. Banner asks curiously.

"No, sir," Mr. Mendoza responds. "The Environmental Justice Club is just borrowing the creative space to start preparing for the end-of-the-year rally."

"Ah, that's right," Principal Banner says. "A collaboration with the pep squad."

"And several other clubs, yes." Mr. Mendoza nods.

"All geared toward school spirit and celebrating another year at Lakewood High."

The room goes very quiet. Mr. Mendoza looks lost for words.

Isa clears her throat. "Well, it is a coming together, sir." She smiles. "To showcase all the ways LHS clubs engage with environmental justice."

Mr. Banner looks between her and Mr. Mendoza. Isa pokes me in the ribs.

"That's right," I say. "The pep squad has screen-printed some secondhand shirts to sell. The Future Foresters club and the fire department are doing a talk about how to prepare for wildfire season."

"The FFA are selling drought-resistant seeds," Isa adds.

"And the diversity club is raising awareness about environmental racism," I say.

"Environmental racism." Principal Banner's eyes have taken on a disapproving stare. "We've certainly seen an uptick of social media comments that bring this to mind. It's a shame the school's profiles have been generating so much negative attention. And the clubs are selling things to raise money for . . . the school?"

"Well." I hesitate and look at Mr. Mendoza. He's got a hand pressed to his temple, but he nods once. I guess there's no point in trying to hide things. "Actually, we're raising money for a mutual aid fund for wildfire victims. And to appeal city council's ruling to continue with the natural gas pipeline."

Principal Banner's eyebrows raise. "You want to hold an environmental justice rally now, to raise money for a political campaign?"

"Lakewood City Council is a nonpartisan body, sir," Mr. Mendoza says. "Petitioning them is a civic act, not a political one, as I explained in my most recent email."

"I doubt it will be seen that way. I would hate to attract even more negative attention to the school," Principal Banner says. "Mr. Mendoza, a moment of your time in my office, please."

He turns without another word and walks into the hall.

Mr. Mendoza sighs. "Carry on, folks. If I'm not back by the extracurricular bell, be out of Mrs. Vethanayagam's studio when the hour's over." Then he stops, points straight at Brian, and says sternly, "PG-rated ideas only."

A couple of people giggle, but I have an ominous feeling. Mr. Mendoza looks like Jordan does whenever he breaks one of Dad's golf clubs. I look at Isa.

"Shit," she mouths. She walks over to stand beside me. "I thought Mr. Mendoza said we had permission. We've been announcing the rally for weeks. Talking to other clubs about it for months. It was hardly a secret."

"I know," I tell her. "That was weird."

"Ideas, people," Kat says to the room.

"Let's keep it simple," Jake suggests. "Why don't we just put Mayor Malone in the gas company rep's pocket?"

"That's good! Give me the marker, Brian," Kat says, moving toward the whiteboard. On it, she draws what looks like a large bust of a suited man. In his chest pocket is the figure of another suited man.

"What does the mayor look like?"

I grin, triumphant.

"This!" I say, slapping my profiles of the city council members down on a table at the front. I knew that they would come in handy.

CHAPTER 22
RALLY

Isa

"AM I DOING THIS RIGHT?" DARIUS ASKS. I LOOK AROUND THE giant piece of shoulder until I can see him clearly.

"Yeah," I say indulgently. "You should be finished in about four years."

I'm flabbergasted by how bad Darius's art skills are. Like, they're truly shocking. I guess the gifted kids skip coloring. Who needs art when you have spreadsheets? Kat's still struggling to accept Darius's presence in Mrs. Vethanayagam's studio. Today she marched deliberately to the other side of the room as soon as he picked up a brush. I think he's in on the joke. He must be.

At this point, though, we're essentially the only ones left in here. Kat and a couple of the more artistically inclined club members are spread out among the giant papier-mâché body parts. Most of them have their earbuds in and are dead to the world. Pocket Mayor, as he's come to be known, has taken a solid month to construct. His final coat of paint needs to go on tonight before we can assemble him at the rally.

"You know that most people hold paintbrushes like they hold pencils, right?"

"This isn't how you're supposed to hold it?" Darius asks, tone thick with mock innocence.

He has to be joking, egging me on. Yesterday, I had to make the conscious decision to stop making fun of him. I'm about a second away from not being able to hold it in any longer.

"Why brush," I say, adding a few more strokes of navy blue to what will be Mr. Finnigan's suit jacket, "when stabbing's just as good?"

"Exactly." Darius smiles. "Like this, right?" The brush he's holding like a dagger stabs me in the upper arm. I can feel the cold blob of the paint. My mouth pops open in mock horror.

We're wearing the terrible brown zip-up smocks that live in Mrs. Vethanayagam's studio over our clothes, but I still act outrageously offended. In retribution, I slash a thick band of navy blue across his chest.

"Noooooo! Mortal wound!" he cries, laughing.

His arm moves to get me back, but I dash around Mr. Finnigan's enormous head. "You'll never take me alive!" I shout while we chase each other around the art studio.

Darius catches up to me in the back corner of the cavernous storage room. In desperation, I grab one of the mascots the pep squad uses to base their paintings on. The stuffed toy otter is resting on his back. There are two Lakewood High–colored pom-poms in his front paws. He's adorable.

"Come any closer and the otter gets it," I warn.

I wrap my hand around the paintbrush that I'm still holding and raise it in a mimic of Darius's knife-fighting style. "I'm not messing around with this thing!"

"You wouldn't," Darius challenges. "Not Ottey! Not the fighting otter!"

He inches toward me.

"Not another step!" I laugh.

"Would you guys just make out already so you can get back to work?" Brian asks in a dull voice. He's been in this room the whole time. Up a ladder, painting Mayor Malone's face.

I burst out laughing, and Darius follows suit. Things have been like this between us for weeks. We've spent a lot of time together finalizing stuff for the rally. We even grabbed dinner one night, just the two of us.

That's when Kat finally got the "I'm crushing" conversation she's always wanted. I rushed over to her house straight after and admitted through a series of embarrassed giggles that I cannot stop thinking about Darius. How much he makes me laugh, how easy it is now to spend time together. How I wonder when I'll see him next. What I think kissing him will feel like. Kat lost it, and then gave me way too much information about what kissing Eliyah is like.

I've finally admitted my feelings, but I haven't worked up the nerve to make a move. I do really like that Darius and I are . . . whatever it is we are now. And I really don't want to mess that up.

We do eventually get second coats on all the segments of Mayor Malone and Mr. Finnigan. Kat does the final flourish of painting the Puget Sound Energy logo onto Mr. Finnigan's lapel pin before reminding the art squad that we'll assemble Pocket Mayor on Friday morning, when we've got special permission from Mrs. Vethanayagam to get things for the rally set up in the stadium.

I've been on the phone with community groups for the past several weeks, fielding their last-minute questions. The fire department wants to know how to get a truck into the stadium. Pastor Scott wants to say a few words about the Black church's role in organizing before the choir performs. Yoga club is running a donations-only class and leading an eco-anxiety meditation. They want us to have their mats moved out from the gym.

In a shocking turn of events, Marina's family is helping the Japanese club with the food they're going to sell. Halve by 2030's booth is dedicated to briefing people about the pipeline. The Lakewood High choir is doing some environmental covers, whatever that means. The school's resident punk band is playing, too. Darius invited the Model UN kids, and Dad invited everyone from the Asia Pacific Cultural Center, so most of my dance troupe is coming. The rally is going to turn out even better than I hoped.

I'm not surprised when I get a message that Mr. Mendoza would like to see me after school. There are so many things going on that even between both of us, Darius and I can't keep track of them all. We had to add our phone numbers to the club's web page because the email account wasn't enough to handle all the questions. I bet Mr. Mendoza's feeling a bit out of the loop.

After the final bell rings, I make my way toward his lab. It's weird to think that this is probably the last time I'll do this as a junior. Everyone in the halls has their summer swag going. Graduation is this weekend, and the last day of school is less than a week away. The atrium's all decorated with the names of seniors. Someone dressed the Ottey statue in sunglasses and a Hawaiian shirt in celebration of our upcoming vacation.

I'm smiling by the time I get to the end of C Hall and arrive at the lab. I walk over and stand next to Darius at the front, only then registering Mr. Mendoza's expression. I'm not sure what's happening, but this doesn't seem to be what I thought it was.

"Hi, Isa. Thank you both for staying after. I have some news."
Mr. Mendoza takes a deep breath.

This is going to be bad.

"Mr. Banner has rescinded his permission for the rally."

It's quiet for nearly a minute. This has to be some kind of joke.
He doesn't say anything else, and after an indeterminable amount of
time, I break the silence.

"I'm sorry, what?"

Before Mr. Mendoza can respond, Darius does. "That's insane!
The rally is TOMORROW."

Mr. Mendoza takes a deep breath.

"Trust me, Darius, I'm very aware of the inconvenience of the timing of Principal Banner's decision," he says. "As you know, I spoke
with him months ago about the rally and attained his permission.
After the theme was changed, I followed up in writing, several
times—emails which he apparently did not read. Ever since his visit
to Mrs. Vethanayagam's studio, I've been attempting to persuade
him to let the rally continue."

"What?!" I choke out.

"Unfortunately," Mr. Mendoza goes on, "I have not been suc-
cessful."

How is this happening? Again?! After months of effort, the club
is getting shot down.

"He says that we have to cancel the rally?" Darius asks in an
incredulous tone.

"He says that a fundraising rally is no longer a befitting function
for our school. In light of recent online comments, he's concerned
that the eco-justice focus will attract the 'wrong kind' of attention,
and—even though I have explained to him many times that the city

council is a nonpartisan body—he says he will suspend anyone using a school function for 'political purposes.'"

The quotation marks I can hear in Mr. Mendoza's tone barely register. I feel like all the air's being sucked out of the room. It's like the city council meeting all over again. I'm freaking out, and all I can think to do is look at Darius.

I don't understand the expression on his face.

Darius's tone changes. "So, just to be clear," he says slowly, "Principal Banner is more concerned about attracting racist attention than he is about promoting environmental justice, which is the aim of this school-sanctioned club? And he chose to wait until today to tell you that the rally should be canceled?"

"That is correct."

"And you chose to wait until after school to tell us?"

"That is also correct," Mr. Mendoza says. Why are they talking like this?

"And, for the record, what do you think about this sequence of events?" Darius asks.

The part of me that's not drowning in disappointment is confused. Now that I'm thinking about it, I don't even know if we'll be able to tell everyone that the rally's been canceled before tomorrow morning.

"I think that it's my duty to relay Principal Banner's message to the two of you, as co-presidents of the Environmental Justice Club, in as timely a manner as was befitting the request."

Well, that's a mouthful. I suddenly have a flashback to holding the laminated piece of paper we used when we were sworn in as co-presidents of the Environmental Justice Club. The words they're using are weird, but I understand their meaning: That's it. The rally's over, and literally nothing I thought the club would do this year will happen.

Mr. Mendoza goes on, "It would be remiss of me not to say that the work you two have done together is some of the most impactful I have ever seen. The rally would be the perfect way to finish the year."

Why is Darius smiling?

"Thank you, Mr. Mendoza," he says. Darius's eyes dart to the wall clock, and he's suddenly in a great hurry. He reaches for my hand and leads me out of the classroom. My heart pounds in my chest so loud that I can hear it in my eardrums. I'm devastated, but I'm not dead.

"What's happening?" I ask. We're hustling through the halls toward the atrium, fingers laced together.

Darius pulls me slightly closer and whispers, "I think we should keep this information to ourselves, and let the rally happen."

"What?!" He's lost his mind. "It's not like Banner's going to forget. I don't mind getting suspended, but I bet you would. And what about everyone else? We have to tell them."

"I don't think we do." He tilts his head, thinking. "Not yet."

We've reached the atrium. The double doors leading to the parking lot are propped open to let in the June breeze. He stops just after we pass through them, and we stand recklessly close in the afternoon sunlight, our hands still linked together. I hope he thinks it's the running that has me breathless.

"Do you trust me?" he asks.

I can't think of a reason not to; school is way more important to him than it is to me. I can't think of where his confidence or reasoning is coming from, but as I look into his eyes, I'm sure of my answer. "Yes."

He gives my fingers a squeeze and jogs away from me. "I'll call you later" floats behind him. I watch his Volvo basically peel out as he leaves the parking lot.

I don't know why he's in such a hurry. Or where he's finding this reason to hope that our efforts haven't spectacularly failed—again. I do know that he would never risk a suspension. Even so, if I don't hear from him soon, I'll have to at least email everyone. And what? Hope that they see it before lunchtime tomorrow?

This is so shit.

Dazed, I cycle home through what is otherwise a beautiful afternoon. The trails are rich with the smell of pine and cedar, and I catch glimpses of Mount Rainier sparkling in the distance. The air cool and clear. Grandma's in the kitchen when I step through the door.

"Hey, Bo. How was school?" She's sitting at the table snapping green beans, so I wash my hands and take a handful.

"Not great." I start popping the pieces into the appropriate bowls alongside her. "I think tomorrow's rally is in trouble."

"What? Kat's grandma was over here today. She's going to take me over tomorrow and get us camp chairs set up to watch. We'll all be there, Bo. Only don't let Pastor Scott go on for too long before he makes our church's donation. You know how he gets."

"The principal wants us to cancel it. Says we're being political and that we'll attract the 'wrong kind' of attention."

Grandma does a drawn-out um-hum. "He said this today? Doesn't sound like he's serious. You've come too far to not put it on now. And those—what do you call them again? Those internet monsters, ogres?"

I laugh. "Trolls, Grandma. They're called trolls."

"Right. He should be canceling the trolls, not you. Letting them have their way just emboldens them more."

She's right, but I'm dangerously close to being overwhelmed.

When I finally decided not to give up on being co-president, I promised myself that I wouldn't cry over the club anymore. I haven't so far, and I don't want to break.

"It's great to see you getting out there, using that voice of yours to work with people," Grandma goes on. "Organizing is hard and thankless, but I don't know how else to make this world a kinder place. I know the summer job didn't work out, but there are other ways to make money. I'm proud of you, Isa. You and Mrs. Freeman's boy. I'm still reading all that stuff they sent over."

A fat envelope of resources for Anniston survivors was delivered several weeks ago. Inside were glossy pamphlets and numbers to call for medical and legal assistance. On top was a handwritten note thanking Grandma for the best pecan pie Mrs. Freeman has ever had. The note is still hanging on the fridge.

"That was so kind of them," Grandma says.

"I know." I reach over and hug her gently. I can't believe how much has changed this year. How far I've come. She's right about organizing, too. It is what I want to do. It's been staring me in the face this whole time. All the places, outside of home, that I love the most— the Asia Pacific Community Center, church choir, the murals and the occupation, the Environmental Justice Club—they're where I feel connected, alive. Part of something bigger than myself.

Even if I don't know yet what organizing means or how to make a career of it, at least I know it's what I want for myself. I also know that we'll do it together. Of course Grandma will be at the rally tomorrow. Tama and Mom will be, too. Changing things, or at least attempting to change things, to create a safer future brought us closer than just living together did.

I love them all so much.

Grandma gives my shoulder a squeeze and I let go, sitting

back down. I wipe my eye with the back of my sleeve. So much for not crying. "How was your day?" I ask her. "How are you feeling?"

"Oh, just alright. This medication's taking its toll, but I want to give it a shot. Your mom and dad are both working tonight, so it's you and me for dinner."

"I'll cook," I tell her. "We can have pasta and beans."

She doesn't try to object. Not anymore. At the end of spring break, when I told her what I wanted, Grandma was adamant. "Spending time together will not cost you your future." And she's stuck to it. The only school she'll allow me to miss is when Mom and Tama are working and she needs someone to drive her to appointments. So instead I'm helping more around the house. My cooking and baking skills have already massively improved.

"Sounds good." She smiles. "There's garlic bread in the freezer."

We snap through the rest of the beans, and Grandma goes to lie down, shuffling forward in weak steps. It's painful to see her deterioration for what it is. I'm so glad that we're talking about it, though. That I'm not hiding from the truth anymore. That I'm not acting like the twelve-year-old I was when we moved here. I shouldn't be.

Besides, finally airing the truth about Grandma's illness also meant learning the truth about Mom. How she felt that pushing herself to cook while trying to take care of Grandma was too much. Learning this made Grandma's chin crease in deep frown lines. She had harsher words for Mom than me, but their message was the same. Her illness wouldn't cost Mom her future, either. Grandma threatened to dial Jay herself if Mom didn't. He's coming to the rally, too, and Mom is set to cook for him next week. Finally taking the chance we've all wanted her to for so long.

It takes me much longer to get dinner ready than it would have taken either of them. I do eventually manage to dish up plates of spaghetti and red sauce, green beans, and garlic bread, and I even do it without having to ask Grandma too many questions. She's got her plate ready and the TV on before *American Idol* starts.

When I come back to the kitchen, I notice my phone buzzing. "Darius?"

"Hey, Isa. I'm just leaving my mom's law firm."

"You went to her office?"

"Yeah," he answers. "I thought we could use some legal advice. My mom thinks that we should hold off on telling everyone that the rally's been canceled, too. She's agreed to speak to Principal Banner about it herself tomorrow morning."

"What? Are you sure?"

"I'm sure that my mom will go. I've never talked to her quite like that before. She promised that she'll come to school with me tomorrow and talk to him."

"Oh God, you didn't yell at her, did you?" I'm terrified on his behalf.

He laughs. "I'm not stupid. No, I um. I told her that I needed her, and I told her why I care."

"Really?" I smile. "Why?"

"I'll give you one guess." I can hear the smile in his voice. "My reason just put turquoise streaks back in her hair."

I die. "What?" I laugh.

"Yeah," Darius says. "Hey, I'm pretty sure this is going to work tomorrow. I really don't think Principal Banner has anything on my mom. But if it doesn't, you should pretend that I said I'd tell everyone and it's my fault that I didn't—"

"No way," I interrupt. "If we're going down, we're going down together. Besides, you've never been suspended before. You're going to need someone to show you the ropes."

"Bo, you coming back in? Should I start the show?" Grandma calls.

"Oh," Darius says. "I'll let you go."

"Hey, Darius?"

"Yeah?"

"You're one of the reasons I care, too," I tell him through an embarrassingly wide smile (that I'm glad he can't see). "I'll see you tomorrow."

I end the call and basically skip through to Grandma's room. My plate of spaghetti bounces around in front of me. I have to keep myself from drawing *I ♥ D* in my red sauce with my fork.

So what if we get suspended tomorrow? At least we'll be together.

I sleep surprisingly well. I do wake up to emails and text messages about the rally, though. I hesitate, wondering if I'm really doing the right thing, not warning people about Principal Banner.

My phone rings as I'm getting ready. "Hello?"

"Hi, Isa? It's Channel twelve news," a voice says. "We're on our way to the rally. Could you let us know where's best for us to park?"

Oops. I kind of forgot that we invited a local news crew. They will definitely be zooming in on Pocket Mayor. Not that we didn't invite city council to come, too.

This could go very badly.

My stomach's in knots as we drive to school. Kat has roped Tama into helping assemble Pocket Mayor, and I'm part of the art squad contingent that has permission to spend the morning setting up. Well, at least, we *had* permission.

No one says anything when I arrive over an hour before the first bell and make my way to Mrs. Vethanayagam's studio. From her office, I hear the electric kettle pop. She emerges, stirring her wonderful-smelling tea. "Morning, Isa," she yawns. "Everyone's in the storage room."

I blink. Really?

I try to wipe the bewildered expression off my face.

They're all there, loading pieces of Pocket Mayor and the other supplies that clubs have dropped off for their booths onto the large trolleys we use to move things. Kat's all business this morning, moving purposefully.

"Let's open up the loading doors," she calls. "Time to get things started!"

She presses the correct buttons on the wall, and I hear the panels groan in the early morning light. Dad has backed the truck up and stands on the other side of the doors, ready and waiting. It will take most of the morning to move all the stuff out through the athletic complex and onto the football field. The maintenance crew already has the stage set up for graduation, and the requested number of booths went up yesterday afternoon.

Kat enters full-blown director mode with the art squad. She oversees Pocket Mayor's assembly at the far end of the stage. Mr. Finnigan's a massive bust. The Mayor Malone sticking out of his chest pocket is essentially life-size. No wonder figuring out how to construct the sculpture took a month. He looks amazing.

As soon as I step onto the field, I'm surrounded by people asking questions. The Spanish club, the Japanese club, and the culinary arts club—selling an all-vegan menu—need their booths connected to a power supply so they can get food prep going. Yoga club wants to know where to set up their mats.

More adults start calling to ask for directions. The room where the pep squad stored the screen-printed T-shirts is locked, and someone needs to go get Mrs. Vethanayagam for the key. The art squad has the booths all decorated and signposted, but no one can find the banner Halve by 2030 dropped off. "Please can you call them to ask if they have another one?"

I dial Debbie, who I've been in touch with quite a bit since I followed up about the internship. Their petition was shot down by city council just as roundly as ours was. But they're being vocal about their appeal and have staged several marches protesting for more renewable energy projects. Doug and Debbie thought the rally was a great idea, and they'll be running 2030's booth today. I'm glad that community groups are still working hard against the pipeline, even if my joining them isn't in the cards—yet.

"Oh, Isa," Debbie trills after the second ring. "I'm so glad you called."

She continues to be a whirlwind, and now that I'm more over my disappointment, it's easy to smile while I wait for an opening and remember how much I like her.

"I was just getting our new pamphlets together, ready to load up, when the email came through to Doug from 2030's headquarters. We finally got it, Isa! We got funding for your internship!"

My phone slips, falling flat on the AstroTurf. I get bits of the black plastic dirt under my nails in my scramble to get it back to my ear.

I interrupt Debbie's unbroken stream with "What?! You've been asking for funding?"

"Of course we have! Ever since you first wrote to us," she carries on. "All the work you've done with the club and the petition and now this rally. I knew we had to get you over for the summer if we could. We just had to. I'm so glad we can make this happen! It's only just above minimum wage, but it's full-time, and I hope it's enough. I'll email you the details now and we can talk about it today. I'm so happy, Isa. It would be great to have you on board! Oh, and we've got to pick up the placard-making stuff on our way to the high school. I'll need to remind Doug. Doug! Leave some room in the back seat. We'll see you soon, Isa."

It isn't until after she's hung up that I realize that I didn't ask her whether they have another Halve by 2030 Banner. I didn't even get the chance to thank her. Is this really happening? *Do I have a job for the summer, doing this? Really?*

I lose track of time completely, my mind only half on the questions and tasks before me. My phone's constantly buzzing, and after I help Mom hang the APCC's banner—she's made the food they'll sell there, dishes of her own fusion design—I see a bunch of new messages from Darius.

Oh no. This is it. The warning that Principal Banner is on his way, stack of suspension slips in hand. I click on the notifications to open them. Yikes! He's texted a lot. How did I miss these? It might be too late to tell the students already on the field to clear off, quick. I frantically scan the text messages.

Trial commencing. Defendants ready.

Plaintiff Banner is off to a clumsy start. Intransigent and inflexible.

There are voice notes! I click on the first one and hold the end of the phone to my ear. I think it's Mrs. Freeman speaking; her voice sounds authoritative but controlled. Darius must be recording her talking to Principal Banner. I strain to hear over the school choir that's warming up onstage.

"Come, Mrs. Freeman, you must understand my position," Principal Banner says. "We're living in such a polarized environment that any hint of politics will only hinder the school's ability to create a welcoming environment for all students. We can't be seen to favor certain politics over others."

"As we have discussed," I hear Mrs. Freeman say, "the club is not engaging in politics. They are not raising money or support for the election of any particular person or party. Nor are they protesting a city council decision that is set to appear on an upcoming ballot. You have no grounds to say that they are favoring certain political positions over others . . ."

The voice note ends, cutting off. Darius's next message reads:

Points for the defense. Plaintiff Banner is on the back foot now, but not giving up.

Another voice note. I press the phone to my ear again. Mrs. Freeman is speaking. "Am I correct in thinking that the Environmental Justice Club notified you of their intentions for the rally, in writing, within the time frame stipulated by the LHS Student Handbook?"

Mr. Banner's voice replies quietly, "Yes, they did."

"Am I also correct in thinking that the club received your permission for the rally months ago, via the club's advisor?"

"Well, yes, they did at that time."

"Principal Banner, do I need to remind you of my son's right to freedom of expression? I would hope very much that a man such as yourself would stand as an ally to the cause of justice in what you've called 'these polarized times.' I'm certain that people like my son and me can count on your support."

The voice note cuts off.

Noooo! What did he say?! How is that the last message? I raise my thumbs to type a response, but Darius beats me to it.

The defense has it! We're good! We're all good!

I spin on my heel, looking out toward the stadium's entrance. From here, I can just make out the entrance to the school, where on the right Banner's office sits behind reception next to the counseling center. My eyes strain, as if I could somehow see through to Darius and Mrs. Freeman sitting there right now. What I do see are the students who have first lunch already trickling out of the building, done for the day.

All the booths are assembled, volunteers present. Delicious food smells waft across the field as the stalls open for business. The sun, such a rare presence in the Pacific Northwest, shines down on us, warming my skin. The yoga club clangs a massive gong, and onstage, the Lakewood High choir falls to a hush, waiting for the vibrations to finish so they can start their set.

Students enter the field, milling around the booths. Some head toward the stage to watch their friends perform. Others are drawn straight to the lunch options. A group of boys is running toward the lit-up fire truck. The rally's started. It's already started!

As I'm realizing this, I see Darius walking purposefully toward me from across the field. Behind him, Mrs. Freeman and Principal Banner are deep in conversation. Darius is beaming and giving me two thumbs up.

Overwhelmed, my nose crinkles up with delight. He's done it.

We've done it!

The school choir begins their first number, "All the Good Girls Go to Hell," and I'm running. Laughing and running, right at Darius. He's laughing now, too, probably because I look ridiculous, but this just breaks down the last of my inhibitions.

I jump at him.

Throw my arms clear around his neck, and, before my thoughts have the chance to catch up, I kiss him. Full on the lips, pressing myself against his chest. It only lasts a second before I realize and pull my face back. "OMG!" I look into his eyes. "I'm so sorry!"

He's still holding me off the ground, and his expression changes from shock to something else. He smiles so wide that I can see all his teeth and sets me on my feet. But the arms wrapped around my waist don't let go.

"You always apologize for the wrong thing," he laughs. Then he lowers his face to mine and kisses me back.

I close my eyes and ignore the expressions I imagine on the faces surrounding us. Kat, whose laughter I can hear. Mr. Mendoza, Mrs. Freeman, and Principal Banner. Everyone else in the Environmental Justice Club. The booths of parents, teachers, and students. My church choir, come to perform, my grandma and Kat's in their chairs in front of the stage. The local news crew. Halve by 2030 and the other community groups. Mom and Tama with the APCC crowd.

Everyone is here.

We're headed into another summer of record-breaking temperatures and what will probably be an even worse wildfire season. The city is still permitting the construction of a new natural gas pipeline—for now. But we're here. Showing up to do something about the real-life impacts of the climate crisis and environmental injustice. Together, for what will be the start of my summer as a community organizer. For the first time, I feel like I know what we're up against and the tools we have to change things.

And as I pull back so that I can look into Darius's eyes, I also know why I've never cared more.